The Book of Atrix Wolfe

Ace Books by Patricia A. McKillip

THE FORGOTTEN BEASTS OF ELD
THE SORCERESS AND THE CYGNET
THE CYGNET AND THE FIREBIRD
THE BOOK OF ATRIX WOLFE

The Book of
Atrix Wolfe

PATRICIA A. MCKILLIP

ACE BOOKS, NEW YORK

THE BOOK OF ATRIX WOLFE

An Ace Book
Published by The Berkley Publishing Group
200 Madison Avenue, New York, NY 10016

Book design by Irving Perkins Associates

First Edition: July 1995

Library of Congress Cataloging-in-Publication Data

McKillip, Patricia A.
    The book of Atrix Wolfe / Patricia A. McKillip. — 1st ed.
        p.   cm.
    ISBN 0-441-00211-0 (hardcover) : $18.95
    I. Title.
    PS3563.C38B66   1995   94-33999
813′.54 — dc20   CIP

Printed in the United States of America

10   9   8   7   6   5   4   3   2   1

Prologue

The White Wolf followed the ravens down the crags of Chaumenard to the wintry fields of Pelucir.

In wolf shape, among the wolves, he had scented danger sweeping toward the mountains he loved. His dreams turned dark with the coming of winter, chaotic, disturbed by fire, blood, the sharp, hoarse cries of ravens calling to one another, the cries of humans. Darkness rode a dark horse into the heart of Pelucir, wielding a sword of fire and bone that pierced the Wolf's dreams. He would wake suddenly in human shape, in a close tangle of fur and smells, trying to see beyond stone, beyond night, into the fire that burned toward Chaumenard. Finally, harrowed by dreams and unable to rest content in wolf shape, he ran to meet the dark rider in Pelucir. He would stop it there, somehow, in the broad fields and gentle hills of the kingdom bordering Chaumenard, before the rider cast its blank, hungry eye into the land of mages and scholars and farmers who raised goats in the high peaks, and plowed a furrow from light into shadow down their sharply sloping sides.

The mage was old, and lingered, every year, longer and longer in the mountains among the wolves. That year, he had forgotten it was winter and that he was human. Pulled so abruptly back into the world, he had not stopped to tell anyone where he was going. Nor did he know who fought in Pelucir. He ran, in wolf shape, faster than any wolf; he was a shimmer of icy wind blowing down the mountain's flank, the white shadow of his own legend, barely perceptible, moving swiftly, silently, under the staring winter moon, toward the eye of the terrible storm: the castle of the Kings of Pelucir.

He had seen Pelucir in fairer days, when the massive, bulky castle stood surrounded by flowering fields, the slow river running under its bridge reflecting such green that drinking it would be drinking summer itself. The ancient keep, a dark, square tower beginning to drop a stone here and there, like old teeth, faced lush fields and meadows that rolled to a rounded hill where an endless wood of oak and birch began. Now the trees stood stark and silvery with moonlight, and on the fields a hundred fires burned in the burning cold, ringed around the castle.

The mage, still little more than a glitter of windblown snow, paused under the moon shadow of a parapet wall. Tents billowed and sagged in the wind; sentries shivered at the fires, watching the castle, listening. Wings rustled in deep shadow; a sentry threw a stone suddenly, breathing a curse, and a ragged tumble of black leaves swirled up in the wind, then dropped again. Another sentry spoke sharply to him; they were both silent, watching, listening.

The mage drifted past them, searching; dreams and random nightmares blew against him and clung. Within the castle, children wrapped in ancient tapestries wept in their sleep; someone screamed incessantly and would not be comforted; young sentries whispered of fowl browning on a spit, of hot game pie; old men trembling in the ramparts longed for the fires below, the sturdy oak on the hill. On the field, men feverish with wounds dreamed of feet made of ice instead of flesh and bone, of the sharp end of bone where a hand should be, of a mass of black feathers shifting, softly rustling in the shadows, waiting. The mage saw finally what he searched for: a flame held in a mailed fist on a purple field, the banner of the ruling house of Kardeth.

He had known rulers of Kardeth in his long life: fierce and brilliant warrior-princes who grew restless easily and found the choice between acquiring knowledge and acquiring someone else's land an arbitrary one. Scholars, they spoke with equal passion of the ancient books and arts of Chaumenard, and of its rich valleys and wild, harsh peaks. This ruler, whose name escaped the mage, must have regarded Pelucir as a minor obstruction between Kardeth and Chaumenard. But while his army ringed the castle, laying a bitter winter siege, winter had laid siege to him. He had the wood on the hill for game and firewood; he had only to sit and wait, starving the castle into surrender. But there was nothing yielding about the massive gates, the great keep with its single upper window red with fire, the torchlit battlements spilling light and the shadows of armed warriors onto the snow. In the wood, the game would be growing scarce, and what remained of it, thin and desperate in the harsh season.

So the chilled, hungry, exhausted dreamers around the mage told him in their dreams. He took his own shape slowly in front of the prince's tent: a tall man with hair as white as fish bone and a face weathered and hard as the crags he loved. He wore next to nothing and carried nothing. Still the guards clamored around him awhile, shouting of sorcery and warding invisible things away with their arrows. The prince pushed apart the hangings and walked barefoot into the snow, a sword in one hand.

The mage, noting how the prince resembled his red-haired grandfather, finally remembered his name. The prince blinked, his grim, weary face loosening slightly in wonder. Around him the guard quieted.

"Let him go," Riven of Kardeth said. "He is a mage of Chaumenard." He opened the tent hangings. "Come in." He nodded at a pallet where a man, white and dizzy with fever, struggled with his boots. "My uncle Marnye. He was wounded last night." He took the boots out of his uncle's hands and pushed him gently down. His mouth tightened again. "They come out at night — the warriors of Pelucir. I don't know how. They have a secret passageway. Gates open noiselessly for them. Or they slip under walls, through stone. At dawn I find sentries frozen in the snow, dark birds picking at them. My uncle heard something and was struck down as he raised an alarm. We could find no one. That's why my sentries are so wary of sorcery."

"There is no magic in that house," the mage said. "Only hunger. And rage."

He knelt by the pallet, slid his hand beneath Marnye's head and looked into his blurred, glittering eyes. For an instant, his own head throbbed, his lips dried, his body ached with fever. "Sleep," he breathed, and drew the word into a gentle, formless darkness easing through the restless, shivering body. Marnye's eyes closed. "Sleep," he murmured, and the mage's eyes grew heavy, closed. Sleep bound them like a spell. Then the mage opened his eyes and rose, stepping away from the pallet. He said, his voice changing, no louder, but taut and intense with passion, "This must stop."

The prince, feeling the whip of power behind the words, watched the mage silently a moment. He said finally, carefully, "Thank you for helping my uncle. The ancient mages of Chaumenard do not involve themselves with war."

"You are threatening Chaumenard itself. I know Kardeth. You will crack Pelucir like a nut, take what you want. But you will not stop here. You will not stop until you have laid claim to every mountain pass and goatherder's hut in Chaumenard."

"And every rich valley and every ancient book." Still Riven watched the mage; he spoke courteously, but inflexibly. "Chaumenard is ungoverned. It is full of isolated farmers and wealthy schools where rulers send their children, and villagers who carry their villages around on their backs in the high plateaus."

"They will fight you."

"That will be as they choose."

"If you survive this place."

The prince's eyes flickered. He drew breath noiselessly and moved, letting the weariness show in his face, in his sagging shoulders. He unfolded a leather stool for the mage, and sat down himself. He said, surprising the mage, "Atrix Wolfe."

"Yes. How —"

"I saw you, when my grandfather ruled Kardeth. I was very young. But I never forgot you. The White Wolf of Chaumenard, my grandfather called you, and told us tales of your power when you had gone. He said you were — are — the greatest living mage."

"I am nearly the oldest," Atrix murmured, feeling it as he sat.

"I questioned him, for such power seemed invaluable to Kardeth."

"As a weapon."

The prince shrugged slightly. "I am what I am. He said that such power among the greatest mages has its clearly formulated restrictions."

"Experience teaches us restrictions," the mage reminded him. "They are not dreamed up in some peaceful tower on a mountaintop. If we involved ourselves with war, we would end up fighting each other, and create far more disaster than even you could imagine. Power is not peaceful. But we try to be. The rulers of Pelucir are not peaceful, either," he added, sliding away from the dream he saw glittering in the prince's eyes. "This one will turn himself and his household into ghosts before he will surrender to you. I know the Kings of Pelucir. Go home."

"And you know the warriors of Kardeth." There was an edge to the prince's voice. "We do not retreat."

"Your warriors are battling inhuman things. Pain. Hunger. Madness. Winter itself. Things without faces and without mercy."

"So is Pelucir."

"I know."

"They loosed their hunting hounds two days ago. The hounds howled with hunger all night long within the walls. So." His hands closed, tightened. "Now they roam at night in my camp; they scavenge with the carrion crows. Among my dead. I will outwait winter itself to outwait the King of Pelucir. And then, in spring, I will march through the greening mountains of Chaumenard."

"Spring," Atrix warned, "is another time, another world. In this world, you are trapped in the iron heart of winter, as surely as you have trapped the King of Pelucir, and unless you want to turn into an army of wraiths haunting this field, you must go back to Kardeth. There is no honor for you here. And therefore no dishonor in retreat."

"I will see spring in Chaumenard." The prince seemed to see it then: the green world lying in memory, in wait, just beyond eyesight. His eyes focused again on Atrix Wolfe, the fierce and desperate dream still in them. "And the King of Pelucir will live to see it here. And so will his wife, and his heir and his unborn child. If."

"If."

"If you help me."

In the green wood on the hill, within the endless dream of spring, the Queen of the Wood's daughter paused to look across worlds, hearing the thin, wolf-whine of bitter winds, scraps of human words in a darkness she found both perplexing and tantalizing. There was a drop of human blood in her, and in her father, the Queen's consort; it brought both of them visions at times, living dreams of the world beyond the wood. Her father had learned to ignore them, for they meant nothing to him. She, still learning words for her own world, did not make such distinctions: Everything was new, everything spoke to her and had a name; she had not yet learned that something could mean nothing.

Her mother, disconcerted by their visions, reined beside her. They sat, three riders on three white horses, two watching a distant world, the third watching their faces. "What is it?" her child heard her murmur. "What do you see, Saro? Ilyos, what does she see?"

They did not answer immediately, lost in the peculiar vision of a white-streaked dark, trees as barren as bone under moonlight, fires blossoming everywhere on the white field. They were alike, the Queen's consort and her daughter: both with pale, gleaming, pearly hair and eyes as dusty gold as acorns. The child spoke first.

"Ravens." Her small body, supple and restless, tautened like a scenting animal. She shook her head a little, bewildered, and produced a human word. "Sorrow."

The Queen looked at her consort. Her long hair held all the reds and bright golds and yellows of autumn leaves; her eyes were dark and gold, owl's eyes. Even in her wood, they could be troubled. "You taught her that word," she said. "I didn't. Ilyos."

"I am teaching her the language of power," he said absently. Her voice, sharpened, drew him back into the wood.

"Sorrow is a word that means nothing until it means everything."

"That," he said softly, "is what makes it powerful." He

looked at her then, and touched her slender, jewelled hand. "Don't be afraid. Humans learn many words they never learn to use."

"But what is it?" Saro asked, hearing voices now, more clearly, glimpsing dreams and nightmares, images that appeared and drifted apart like windblown clouds. She turned her head and saw the word in her father's eyes. So did the Queen; she turned her mount abruptly. "You explain it," she said, and rode away from them to a silver stream into which Oak, during one of the wood's arbitrary seasons, had dropped gold leaves to lie like coins at the bottom of the clear water. Downstream, a white deer lifted its head, jewels of water falling from its muzzle, and looked at her fearlessly.

Saro's eyes followed her mother, watched her thoughtlessly a moment: how her long hair flowed like a fiery mantle down the deep green silk she wore; how the white deer and the white horse mirrored one another, their heads dropped to the silvery water to drink; how the oak beside her mother lowered a leafy hand to touch her hair.

"Death," said her father, and she turned her head, looked at him out of his own eyes.

"What is death?"

He could not seem to say; he tried, and then smiled a little, brushing her cheek gently with his fingers. "Come," he said. "We are troubling your mother." But the dark dream caught at her again, mysterious and urgent as it was. Her father did not move, either. She felt his mind, which flowed between them more easily than language, absorb itself in her curiosity, sensing what compelled her attention in the grim and dangerous human chaos.

The Queen rode back to them, a disturbance of fretful thought. "Why must she watch?" she asked. "Why do you let her? What fascinates you so?"

"It is my heritage," Ilyos said apologetically. "There is a

force at work here; terrible as it is, it will do her no harm to recognize it now, so that she will not be troubled by it later."

"I hear hounds," Saro said suddenly. Hounds, she knew: her mother's were gold as sun, red as fire, white as bone. "And I hear someone crying. Or dreaming about crying." She listened, picked out the snow's voice, rustling dryly across the field, a raven's voice, a muttering that turned into a sudden shout, then subsided into muttering again, whispers, more weeping, some talking. She picked out a word. "A wolf. A wolf is talking."

"Wolves don't talk," her father said.

"Yes —"

"Not in that world."

"Listen."

He listened. "Saro, come," the Queen said, putting a hand on her daughter's reins; the tiny silver bells sang. But Saro, immersed in the strange, unpredictable place, tried to see more clearly, pouncing, like a wild thing, on scents, movements, sounds. The sweet spring air grew misty; a wind tumbled over them, carrying hints of smoke, snow, into the Queen's wood. "Saro," the Queen repeated, alarmed. "Ilyos." But her consort only watched, as entranced as his daughter, while, with her powerful, focused attention, she drew the dark world closer to them.

"A mage," she said suddenly, and looked at her father without seeing him. "Like you. A mage is talking."

"I hear," he said. The Queen twitched her reins restively; sapphires sparked along the leather. Around them oak, flurried in the strange wind, moaned. The birds had already fled. But she could not leave them; she watched them worriedly. Both their faces, child and father, wore the same spellbound expression.

"And now someone is answering the mage."

"Hush," her father breathed. "Listen."

* * *

The Wolf was on his feet, pacing back and forth in the prince's tent, agitated but unable to leave. The prince watched him.

"I cannot help you."

"Then we will all die here," the prince answered, "eating our pride and stubbornness at the end, when we have nothing else to eat."

"You know I cannot use sorcery for Kardeth against Pelucir."

"Not if it will save our lives?"

The Wolf turned, his shadow splayed, looming across the tent walls. "You don't need my help to stop this. Put down your arms. Pack your tents and go. I will help you with the wounded."

"I will not stop." The prince's eyes followed the prowling mage; his face remained impassive. "The warriors of Kardeth die before they retreat. Even from winter."

"This is between Kardeth and Pelucir —"

"And will be between Kardeth and Chaumenard, when Pelucir falls."

"And still you expect me to help you!"

"I will exercise so much restraint in Chaumenard, you will hardly recognize the army of Kardeth. I swear this." He held up a hand as the mage whirled. "I swear it," he repeated softly. "You will save lives here and in Chaumenard."

"No."

"Then the King of Pelucir and his heir and his unborn child will die here, and I will show even less mercy to the goatherders and wanderers of Chaumenard."

The mage stood still, his eyes, the color of tarnished silver, suddenly expressionless, holding the prince's gaze.

Around them, shadows cast by nothing visible trembled in the air. "I could force you to leave," the mage said.

"You would have to kill me."

"Don't tempt me." The mage was shaking, he realized, with a fury the wolf might have felt, caught in the iron teeth of a trap. The prince was very still, as if he feared a movement, an eyeblink, might spark the charged shadows around them.

He said, again softly, very carefully, "This is as close as I can come to begging. Please. Help me put an end to this. I cannot."

The mage walked out into the snow.

He moved blindly through the field, appalled by the landscape of war: the hunger and the nightmares, the bloody snow, the unburied, frozen dead, the terror, the pain, the howling, maddened hounds. The formless fury took shape in his mind then, into a vision more terrible than war or winter: something that both armies would end their war to flee from.

He fashioned his making out of the black, endless winter night, the fire from burning arrows, the last words of the dying, the cries of dreamers, the images in their nightmares. He made it out of the bloody claw-print of a raven in the snow, out of the reflection in the eye of a warrior staring into the raven's eye, out of the hunger and cold and hopeless fury of those trapped within the castle walls, the cries of children wearing themselves to sleep, their dreams when they finally slept.

He made it out of the wood on the hill.

He found fearful memories there, among the lean, exhausted animals, of gaunt hunters stalking them. Green, or a wish for green, colored the winter trees in their minds, or in his scenting mind. He scarcely noticed it, in his great anger and despair. Nor did he notice any faces that were not memories, or cries that were not quite human, nor recognize any power not his own. His power snagged a hunter out of a dream, turned his acorn eyes as black as ravens' eyes, crowned him with an immense tangle of horn. Among the horns the mage set the moon that warriors most feared: the black moon that cast no shadows, under which anything might move. He took the fierce, starving hounds out of the field, turned them huge and black as night. He did not notice, as he took the memory of a white horse and turned it black, and set sparks of flame between its teeth, the reflection of green in its eyes. He made a warrior with no allegiance but to death, and when his own passion had exhausted itself, he saw it at the edge of the wood: the dark rider he had come to Pelucir to stop.

He bade it come.

In the Queen's wood, seasons fought: Snow swirled across the torn boundaries of the worlds, clung to grass, oak boughs, the Queen's bright hair. Saro, wraith-pale in the snow, watched streaks of light change the color of her father's hair, change his shape, the expression in his eyes. He fought it until he could no longer move, until the strange power held him motionless. "Saro!" she heard the Queen cry, somewhere beyond the raging storm of snow and magic. "Saro!" Terror and wonder shaped and reshaped Saro's face; the cold winds of power snatched away her voice, changed the position of her bones. She seemed to grow small in the chill world, hunched and helpless, like the animals she glimpsed in that frozen wood. Her mother's voice seemed very far away. Her father had vanished. A rider with the black moon rising among his burning horns looked at her without recognition. She tried to scream; no sound came. He turned away from her, rode out of the timeless wood into the human world.

Opening gates spilled torchlight across the snow as the King of Pelucir led his warriors among the sleeping army of Kardeth for one final, desperate battle to end the siege.

The dark rider met him on the field.

One

"The great mage moves," the mage Danicet said twenty years later at the mages' school in Chaumenard, "from moment to moment, from shape to shape, to meet the constant, ever-changing needs of life. From stone, to eagle, to healer, when stillness, flight, life are required, Those mages of greatest power must involve themselves in a continuing flow of power, for power unused, power neglected or refused, will find its own shape, its own destructive path in the world. So the greatest of mages, such as Atrix Wolfe, have written, out of their own vast and varied experiences. Each moment must concern itself with life, for the renegade mage who chooses to deal in death, will wear the face of death, and, in the end, become the motionless, powerless shape of death."

She paused, searching the dozen faces in front of her for questions. Her calm eyes, Talis Pelucir noted, were the exact shade of blue framed by the broad window behind her. A question moved in his mind, and, somehow, into his face. She said, "Talis?"

All the faces turned toward the prince of Pelucir, who had been born in the midst of a curious and deadly whim of a renegade mage. But his eyes, behind lenses reflecting the brilliant light above the mountain peaks, were opaque; his question was mild.

"What of Atrix Wolfe among the wolves?" he asked,

fascinated with the legendary mage. "Is he neglecting his powers?"

"The White Wolf is very old," Danicet said. Her face had changed, assuming the gentle, wondering expression the mage's name evoked; the tone of her voice had softened. "I believe that he is choosing his final shape among the wolves. Wind, stone — Who knows, on the mountain he loves, what he will become in the end?"

"I think," Riven of Kardeth's youngest daughter, Lares, said abruptly, causing all the faces to swing toward her, "that since war is part of life, that mages should concern themselves with that. Then the forces of the last battle between Pelucir and Kardeth would have been equal."

The faces swung again, not toward Danicet, but toward Talis, who still studied the color of the sky. He and Lares had been at the mages' school for two years, but the siege that Lares had laid to bitter memory seemed endless. He sat silently, unmoved, listening to Danicet's answer.

"Mages do concern themselves with war," Danicet said simply, "as was evidenced in Pelucir. I am only explaining the conclusions the greatest and most experienced mages have reached. You, of course, will make your own choices. Now. To continue practicing your shapechanging abilities, I want you each to hide somewhere within this part of the school. Lares will search for you."

Lares, Talis thought wearily, watching her stiff shoulders beneath the fall of her heavy hair; as if she sensed him, her shoulders drew even straighter. He rose, left the chamber with the other students to fan through the corridors. A closet beckoned immediately; Lares would never look for him among mops.

A clutter on a shelf caught his eye as he opened the door. Closing it, he smelled a mingling of beeswax, lamp oil, dusty cloths, old leather. While his eyes adjusted to a mage's vision in the dark, he let his mind roam among the shapes on the shelf. He felt supple leather, fine parchment. Curious, he let his mind linger, and, following his curiosity, turned himself into a page within the book.

Some time later he emerged, blinking in the dark, with a sense of having dreamed some very odd dreams. He pulled the book off the shelf and opened the door. The line of windows along the stone corridor arched across a view of the highest peak in Chaumenard, where the trees fell away and the thrust of barren rock began. The windows were black now; the hanging lamps lit. He noted it absently, still chasing an image in his head, or perhaps a word, left by a dream. It eluded him. He leaned against the stone wall and opened the book.

The spells in it seemed very clear, precise, fundamental, as if written by some great mage for beginning students. Their simplicity masked a broad experience and a powerful sense of order. Intrigued, he searched: There was no name anywhere in the book. He continued reading. The feeling grew stronger in him of some mystery, some ambiguity in the book, or perhaps in the writing of it, or perhaps that it was not a book at all, but something entirely different. So he felt, and turned pages, still caught in the odd sense of timelessness he had carried out of the closet, as if part of him still dreamed within the book.

Talis Pelucir.

In the distance, someone called someone. He pushed one hand beneath the circular lenses and rubbed his eyes. Then, still spellbound, he continued reading. He had his father's height and raven's wing hair, his mother's cheekbones and her smile. This his older brother, Burne, among others, had told him; both their parents had died the night he was born.

Talis.

His attention wandered suddenly up the mountainside; he glanced up. But the windows were black; night hid whatever he had sought: a puzzle-piece of dream, perhaps an eagle's swift flight up the granite face of the mountain, so swift that stones and trees blurred . . . *Talis* . . . He closed his eyes, trying to remember the strange, elusive dreams that seemed like someone else's memories. . . .

"Talis!"

Something loomed at him. Startled, he vanished and moved, then reappeared as quickly to catch the book before it hit the floor, ducking at the same time to avoid a darkness streaking through the air. He settled the lenses on his nose and eyed Lares warily, wondering what else she had in mind.

She smiled tightly, with little pleasure and less humor; her eyes were chilly. "Very nice."

"Thank you," he said politely.

"I've been searching for you for hours."

"I've been here."

"Why didn't you answer when I called?"

"I didn't hear you."

Her eyes darkened. He took a firmer grip on the book, prepared to jump into it again, flea-like, if she lost her temper. She had a precarious hold on it at best; just the sight of Talis caused it to flare sometimes in unexpected ways. She had been raised, as he had, listening to tales of Hunter's Field, the only field which the entire army of Kardeth had ever fled. She bore her father's shame, and blamed Pelucir for the sorcery, despite the fact, as Talis reminded her, that the sorcery had killed the King of Pelucir. Bitterness only fed her temper; courtesy and alacrity seemed the best defense against it.

She said, "You hid from me."

"We were instructed —"

"I mean deliberately. After I gave up searching for you. You must have heard me call."

"I didn't — " He stopped abruptly, his brows puckered, hearing the echo of a name in his head. "I did hear you call," he said slowly, his gaze directed into some nebulous realm of memory between them. "It was as if I didn't recognize my name."

She was silent, torn between temper and curiosity. Curiosity took precedence, briefly. "Where were you hiding? I found everyone but you."

"In here."

"In a book?" Her mouth tightened again; she said with irritation, "The mages were beginning to worry. No one could find you. It's past supper, I'm starving, and we were starting to think you must have climbed the mountain to hide among the wolves."

He shook his head. "I was among the mops. I'm sorry," he added for safety's sake, seeing her eyes narrow, as if the idea of mops was a personal affront. He said irrepressibly, weary of continuing a battle that had ended twenty years before, "It's just as well your father failed to take Pelucir; the princes of Pelucir have so little dignity."

"And less honor," she snapped.

Her words struck; his head went back a little. He felt his habitual patience founder suddenly against all the tales of horror and despair that had been his legacy.

"Why," he breathed incredulously, "must we refight that battle every time we meet? I have told you and told you: Pelucir had nothing to do with the sorcery on Hunter's Field. Your father ran from it, yes, but at least you have a father."

"Who would have died himself rather than ask a mage to fight his battles for him."

"And mine, of course, would have hired some sorcerer inept enough to kill him."

"And shrewd enough to run when he realized what he had done."

"Is that what they believe in Kardeth?" he demanded, amazed. "That some fly-by-night sorcerer worked such a deadly and terrible magic that has kept even a prince of Kardeth afraid to fight since then?"

"My father is not afraid!" she retorted furiously. "His dreams were broken. In Pelucir. By the King of Pelucir, who was losing his land, and should have lost it honorably."

"He lost his life instead," Talis said bleakly, thinking of his brother, Burne, younger than Talis at the time, watching their father die. "Your father lies to you," he added, reckless and depressed with the argument. "He summoned the mage to the battlefield himself. That's the shame he bears."

He saw the blood flame in her face beneath her flaming hair. What she might have done, he never knew. The mage Hedrix stood with them suddenly, a small man with golden eyes and an owl's tufted brows, his ancient, fragile voice making soothing noises, his hands patting the air around them, as if to calm the tension in it.

"No one knows what happened on the last night of the winter siege of Pelucir," he said gently. "You could argue about it until the crags of Chaumenard crumble into the ground. No mage or sorcerer has ever claimed the sorcery; the sorcery itself vanished with the dawn." Lares opened her mouth; he patted her wrist, still talking, and she subsided. "All we know is this: The Kings of Pelucir have been through the centuries so oblivious of the magic around them that it is hard to believe they could summon up even the name of a mage, let alone summon a mage."

"So —" Lares began furiously. Hedrix shook his head, his frail fingers closing on her wrist.

"No. It makes no sense that your father would have been frightened off the field by something he asked for.

Rulers of Kardeth are far too intelligent and experienced with various kinds of power."

"Then who —"

"No one knows," he said simply. "No one knows." He released her wrist. "But you must stop blaming Talis, who was, after all, not an hour old when the battle ended."

"I cannot help it," she said, not looking at Talis. "It's all I have heard since the day I was born. The tales of the winter siege. The betrayal and dishonor of the King of Pelucir."

"That's what I heard," Talis said softly. "The only tales I was told as a child were of the horrors of Hunter's Field, by those who survived it and could not forget. It's why Burne sent me here."

Lares looked doubtful, but at least she was looking at him. "Because of the siege?"

He smiled a little, tightly. "To have some sorcery in the house, in case the King of Pelucir finds the rider with his hounds and burning horns and the moon that is no moon at his doorstep again. Burne thinks I could fight it." He leaned back against the wall, watching the expression change on her face. "I know. Hedrix is right: The Kings of Pelucir have only the vaguest notions of magic."

She was silent, her eyes hidden again, uncertain, he sensed, but, being of Kardeth, unwilling to yield a battle-field. The mage touched her lightly.

"You did well today; you found all the hidden magics, even Talis."

"He wasn't exactly hidden," she said tartly, but without her usual bite. "He was standing here reading a book."

The mage looked at Talis, then at the book in Talis' hands. His eyes seemed to grow paler, filmy with thought. "And we could not find you . . ." He took the book, opened it; Lares looked over his shoulder.

"It's nothing," she said surprisedly. "Just a beginner's spellbook. Am I finished, Hedrix? Are there any more lost things you want me to find?"

"Only your temper," he said mildly. She smiled. Talis watched her face change again, and thought ruefully, She would smile like that for me if . . . His eyes followed her down the hall, her long, lithe stride, her hair, straight and thick and of a red darker than fire, with mysterious shadows in it. Hedrix made a noise.

"What is it?" Talis asked.

"I don't know whose work it is. Atrix Wolfe wrote something here years ago, when he came down from the mountain to teach a while."

"When?" The name, Talis thought, was like a spell, something enchanted.

"Years ago. Not long after you were born, it would be . . . But he didn't stay long, and I don't believe he finished his writings, for he never showed them to anyone. I doubt he would have been writing anything this elementary. Perhaps a student wrote it." He handed the book back to Talis. "Take it to the library when you are finished with it. You chose an awkward time to vanish," he added, his tufted brows ascending, descending again. Talis settled his lenses with one finger.

"I didn't mean to."

"Messengers came from Pelucir this afternoon. They were already uneasy at being among mages, and became very alarmed when we couldn't find you. They seemed afraid — "

Talis nodded. "Yes," he said softly. "I know those fears. What does my brother want?"

"The King wants you to return home." He touched Talis' shoulder; Talis looked at him silently, guessing. "He says he needs you now in Pelucir, since he has no other heir."

Talis drew breath noiselessly, loosed it, his eyes hidden behind the lenses. He pushed himself away from the wall. "Another legacy of Hunter's Field," he said briefly. "He was badly scarred by his wounds." He stared at the mountains, saw only night beyond the stones. His eyes dropped, found leather, parchment, a book without a name. "May I take this with me?" he asked impulsively.

"Only," Hedrix said, "if you explain to me some day why it fascinates you so."

"I will," Talis promised. "When I know."

He made one last journey up the mountain at dawn. A brief one, he promised the uneasy messengers. But something drew him, more than love of the sun-struck peaks, where light poured from stone to stone like water, and the wind roaring up the mountain smelled of wildflowers and pitch turning to amber and the plowed earth in the fields far below. He forgot time. As he climbed up the bare face of the mountain, he saw the mages' school, blocks of stone built on stone, looking small and fragile above the vast green forest that spilled away from it. Sometimes mist obscured the mountain's face: The Shadow of the Wolf, the students called the mist. They climbed the mountain to look for the White Wolf, impelled by legends of him, tales the mages told. Perhaps he is there among the wolves, the mages said, perhaps he is dead: He has not been seen for many years.

Look for the white wolf who casts a white shadow.
He leaves no footprints in the snow.
He vanishes like mist when you chance upon him.

His name followed Talis like his misty shadow, for no

reason that Talis could discern, except that the mountain seemed to belong to the mage. The winds sang with wolves' voices; the higher he climbed, the stronger they grew, until he felt surrounded by invisible wolves. He stopped before he reached the top. The crown of crags, massive upthrusts of stone through which the sun flashed, looked airy and magical at a distance; closer, they became impossible. He had already gone higher than he had ever climbed. He turned, breathless, sweating; the world below reeled with him. He sat for a moment, watching hawks below, chips of gold fixed in the air an instant before they plummeted toward the shadowy green. His lenses were steaming with his sweat. He took them off, cleaned them on his shirt. Then he pulled himself up against the dizzying angle of stone, and turned again toward the mountaintop.

It pulled at him, the stark edge of the world, beyond which he could step into pure light. He knew he should turn back; he had climbed for hours. But he had left the world behind, it seemed; he had shrugged it off like the stones that climbed toward the nothingness above the trees. Still he climbed, trembling with weariness, driven by nothing, the white light, the mist of light around the stones. He fell once, slid down a small avalanche of stone; he pushed the lenses back up his nose and climbed again. The winds pulled at him, wailed at him, pushed past him; they seemed to strip him of magic, their voices too loud; he could no longer hear himself think.

He stopped again, vaguely aware that above him the stones had begun to separate one from another, jutting out in cliffs and overhangs at impossible angles. Light and shadow streaked through them, working illusions among the stones. He swallowed, bone-dry, and took off his lenses again to clear the mists away. There was blood on his shirt, he noticed, from his scraped hands. He lifted his lenses again. His hand shook; the lenses slipped from his fingers, dropped.

The stones blurred; light and stone and shadow became indistinct, flowing into one another. He swayed, pushed by the wind, then heard his own breath, raw and exhausted, in his throat. He could not take his eyes off the stark white line of light beyond the mountain. But he could not move; his body refused to take one more step away from the world. Nor could he turn, spellbound by the mountain's magic. He stood motionless, feeling scarcely human, understanding why a mage, drawn to such high places above the human world, would relinquish his own form.

He took one more step upward, even while every muscle and every threadbare shred of sense protested. Something was wrong; he had forgotten one small detail. A white mist crossed the stones above him, and, falling suddenly back into himself, he remembered his lenses.

He blinked. The mist had stopped: a blur of white against the crumbled granite. He could not see it clearly. *Do you cast a white shadow?* he wanted to say. *Do you leave no path to follow?*

He said, "Atrix Wolfe?"

His lenses sparked suddenly, a star of white fire near his feet. He bent, reached for them. He put them on and saw the wolf.

It watched him from the edge of the overhanging stones, ready to melt into their shadows: the White Wolf of Chaumenard. He looked for its shadow.

"It's true," he whispered, trembling with weariness and wonder. The wolf became a streak of white in the air, and then a memory.

Go home, the mountain said. He nodded.

"Yes," he told it. "Now I can return to Pelucir."

Two

❧

Saro dumped a bucket of steaming water into a cauldron, plunged chapped, cracked hands into it, and began to scrub. Scorched strips of onion and potato peelings floated to the surface. She flicked them out onto the flagstones, where a wizened old man hunched over a gnarled broom swept them up in his ceaseless path around the kitchen. She washed pots in a corner, near the drains. A line of them, copper and cast iron, waited. She never looked or counted; pots appeared and disappeared, reappeared according to the great tidal forces of consumption that ruled the castle kitchen. She dealt with the pot or the leftover scraps or the cry of her name, whatever was under her nose, in her hands, in her ears, at the moment, never looking ahead or back, for both past and future were an unbroken, unending string of pots, distinguishable only by the present, when under her busy hands a dirty pot became a clean one.

Someone cried, "Saro!"

She jerked herself out of the cauldron, wiped her hands on the skirt of her coarse woolen dress, which was too long and too big, a castoff from one of the plate-washers. The plate-washer had pulled it up impulsively one day, and now was too big herself to wear it.

"You must never make that mistake," she'd said to Saro. Her eyes were big, her belly was big; the bones beneath her skin were sharp. She touched Saro's cheek with one finger, as Saro gazed at her. "You don't understand, do you? Then it's just as well you are so plain. Never let them touch you and you'll be safe. Poor child," she murmured, looking down at herself. Saro never saw her again.

Saro was, one of the spit-boys said one day, as she emerged unexpectedly from the depths of a cauldron splashed with water, fish bones and grease, hardly human. Pale as candle wax, with a face as unremarkable as the underside of a saucepan. She was dependable, like fire; if she was fed, she worked. She never cried, she rarely smiled. She never spoke. "Sorrow's child," they said, when they found her crouched naked and trembling beside the wood-pile. No other name occurred to anyone. She slept and fed with the kitchen cats until she was strong enough to work, a knobby, spindly girl who grew taller through the years, but still retained a curious blankness in her features. There seemed nothing to snag the eye, nothing for the memory to preserve, as if her face induced forgetfulness, and only her name and her constantly busy hands were remembered.

"Saro!"

She followed the thread of her name through the vast, crowded kitchen. She remembered voices, perhaps because she had no voice. This cry belonged to one of the apprentice cooks. She ducked through a squall of goose feathers the pluckers sent flying through the air, rounded a table full of bread dough being kneaded and pulled apart and shaped into loaves, doves, rings, through clouds of smells: onions spattering in butter over fires, spices and brandy from huge bowls of minced meat, seared flesh from rabbits and game hens roasting on spits slowly turned by sweating spit-boys.

She dodged a stray dog and the elbow of the head cook as he flung a wooden spoon at one of the undercooks stirring a sauce. "Lumpy!" he growled. "Unthinkable! Impossible." He was a lean, fiery, pepper-haired man who looked as if he would be happier riding a horse across dangerous lands to deliver a fateful message, than inventing fifty different ways to cook venison. Saro found the apprentice cook dumping a pot of stew in a wooden bowl for the dogs.

"Scorched," he muttered. Saro smelled it in the steaming mess. The bottom of the pot was black inside and out, from smoke and charred food. He kicked it over to her. She wrapped her fingers in her skirt against the hot pot handle and heaved it up. On her way back to the soap and bristles and cauldron, she found herself overrun by a proud flock of liveried servants come to bear trays of cold beef, whole poached salmon, loaves of braided bread, salad, fruit dipped in chocolate, cakes of cream and walnuts chopped as fine as flour for the midday gathering in the hall. She eased through them carefully, knowing that a smudge from the pot on their fine purple and grey plumage would set them hissing and trumpeting like swans. Preening with gossip, feathers rustling, they gave her no more notice than their shadows.

"Prince Talis is due back within the day. A messenger was sent ahead, last night, to tell the King."

"He rode all night, the messenger, I heard."

"And was rewarded. A fine gold chain, I heard."

"I heard a dagger with a haft of gold."

"No, it was a gold — "

"Gold is what we all heard, then. The King is that relieved, that the prince is safely home from Chaumenard, and away from all that sorcery."

"It was the King who sent the prince to learn sorcery."

"He learned what he learned, and now the King wants him to marry."

"He won't need sorcery for that, with what came to show themselves to him: young ladies as fine and stately as he could wish for in his dreams."

Saro shifted the pot away from a scalloped hem, and found a clearing between four tables where one cook laid raspberries as carefully as jewels on an enormous cake festooned with cream; another overlapped thinly sliced carrots and parsnips like fish scales on a school of pâté fish; a third turned radish, celery and parsley into rose trees, and the fourth sculpted a flock of swans out of meringue. Saro crept past them cautiously; they were all of nervous temperament, and inclined to hysteria if their tables were jogged.

Another ember of gossip flared as she hauled the pot safely past the delicate tables. The head hall-servant was speaking to the tray-mistress, who inspected everything that left the kitchen, and everyone who carried it.

"I've heard the King favors Lady Maralaine of Terine. Some years younger than the prince, and not overly talkative, but a flower, a wild swan — "

"Maralaine of Terine," the tray-mistress mused, straightening a border of parsley sprigs on a platter of beef. She was a massive, obstinate woman who wore her black hair in a topknot so rigid it seemed carved, and who could keep even the spit-boys subdued. "She's of a large family, isn't she? Every year, it seems, brings another Terine lady or lordling to court for a betrothal feast. Maybe the King hopes it will be hereditary."

"What will?"

"All those heirs." She polished a corner of a silver tray with her apron, frowning. "It's been a grim house, without the prince. Sorcery or no, it's time he came home to enchant some heirs out of somebody."

Saro edged between a wood-boy filling the woodbin, and an undercook pulling a tray of bread out of the stone oven. She got the pot back to the huge cauldron standing over the drains. She poured hot water from a kettle simmering over a flame into the wash-cauldron, immersed the

dirty pot and, leaning deep into the cauldron, began to
scrub.

"Saro!"

She straightened, trailing soapy water and charred
food, and made the journey again, this time for a frying pan,
hot off the fire and full of grease and broken sausage. She
had to crawl under a table to avoid the hall-servants, who
were moving quickly by then, hefting heavy trays and
speeding toward the hall before the food cooled. Back at the
drains, she set the pan down to cool while she finished the
stewpot. The sweeper paused to nibble the broken bits of
meat out of the pan.

"Saro!"

For a while, dirty pots grew everywhere; she collected
and washed, crawled and pulled and carried from every
corner of the kitchen and washed, while a tower of gleaming
copper and iron grew high beside the wash-cauldron. Then
the kitchen grew almost calm. The small mincers and
peelers napped under tables with scavenged bits of beef and
bread in their fists; cooks and undercooks discussed supper;
the tray-mistress counted napkins and gossiped with the
head hall-servant; the plate-washers sat beside their vast
sinks near Saro's cauldron, eyed the restless spit-boys and
whispered.

Supper was a prolonged drama of great pies of hare
and venison with hunting scenes baked in dough on their
crusts, vegetables sculpted into gardens, huge platters layered with roast geese, woodcocks and pigeons, and
crowned with tiny hummingbirds made of egg white and
sugar. The liveried servants came and went, imparting
breathless scraps of gossip. Musicians played fanfares for
each sculpture that appeared for consumption; between
fanfares they wandered in and out of the kitchen, cooling
their throats with wine. One of them, hearing distant music

even through the kitchen din, said urgently, "Listen! Someone's at the gate." The musicians quieted, picking out the trumpets' flowing voices amid the chatter, the clash of undercooks fuming over sauces, and the underlying mutter of pots.

"It's the fanfare for Prince Talis," they announced, their haughty faces loosening. "He's safely home." The head cook grunted and produced a bottle of cherry brandy. The tray-mistress, pouncing on an idling spit-boy, lost the cutting edge in her voice, and neglected to use the wooden spatula in her hand.

Saro, wet from head to heel, paused to eat burnt potatoes out of the bottom of a pan, and then a heel of bread tossed aside when the loaf was cut. Trays began to come back down then; everyone picked at the leftovers. Saro immersed herself in water again, building her tower of pots.

Finally the kitchen quieted. Cooks and undercooks and apprentices left. The tray-mistress counted trays, napkins and rings for the morning. The sweeper made his last rounds. The plate and cutlery washers wiped delicate porcelain and silver with handles and tines of gold with linen softer than their fingers. They finished and left. Fires were dying down. The peelers and mincers and pluckers found their places under tables, among the kitchen dogs. The wood-boys and spit-boys drifted out into the night, their faces tight, intent, like hunting animals. The cats, too, began to prowl. Saro finished one last pot and set it down on the stones to dry. Then she heaved the cauldron until it rolled off-balance, and splashed its dirty water down the drains. Pulling it upright again, she began to fill it with cold water.

She did this slowly, carrying bucket after bucket from the stone cistern in the corner. The tray-mistress left, yawning hugely, showing massive, marble teeth. Nothing moved in the kitchen but the cats and the fires settling down into their coals. Saro filled the cauldron partway, leaving room for hot water in the morning. She hung the bucket back over the cistern, then leaned against the cauldron on her knees, her arms folded along the rim, her face resting on her arms. She watched the water.

It stopped shivering finally, grew still, so still she could see her breath tremble across it. She watched it, eyes drooping wearily, but not closed, for what happened in the cauldron at night gave her the only pleasure she had. She never questioned it, any more than she questioned the hearth fires, or the tray-mistress's topknot, or the head cook's temper. The cauldron washed pots by day and dreamed at nights. Saro never dreamed, and so she watched the cauldron's dreams, coloring the surface of the water, speaking to her in its secret language. She did not understand, but the dreams made no demands. They flowed silently across the water, and she watched, for they soothed her, led her into sleep.

The dark water turned gold. Golden leaves hung everywhere on slender white trees, on massive, towering trees that had grown a graceful, arching filigree of branches. White hounds ran on a path of gold beneath the trees; now and then a leaf would fall, glittering, through the still air. Riders on white horses followed the hounds; leaves scattering in their wake spun whirlwinds of gold in the air, then fell again. The faces of the riders were sometimes human, sometimes of green leaf or of smooth brown twig. Above them, the trees drew up their branches, or sometimes bent a bough to touch the riders with a leafy hand.

A castle stood in a meadow. Its lower walls were fashioned of thick, entwined vines of ivy and rose; roses bloomed here and there among the leaves. Its upper walls were white as the marble cutting boards; its towers, round and crowned with peaked caps of gold, seemed as delicate as what the cooks fashioned from meringue. Rooms flowed through the dreaming cauldron, rooms where roses pushed through the inner walls to bloom, where fountains flung arcs of diamond into deep pools, where groves of pale trees grew beside colored windows jewelled with light.

The cauldron's random dreams shifted, showed Saro a room within a tower. Candlelight from a tier of deer horn and gold flowed across a dark, polished table. A book lay open on the table, its pages tidier than the cooks' stained, torn pages, and as incomprehensible.

The dreams always ended just as she knew she could no longer kneel upright; she had to seek out the warm place along the oven wall. Just before her eyes closed, a face formed in the water. She never saw it clearly. She caught a ribbon of pearls tangled in leaf-gold hair, a prong of deer horn and gold in the crown above the face, a glimpse of skin paler than the slender trees. She closed her eyes on that vision, hardly seeing it, but always keeping it in memory a moment, the last thing she saw before sleep, black and changeless as the bottom of the empty cauldron, transformed her into nothing.

Three

The White Wolf dreamed.

He stood surrounded by leaves touching his face, his hair, his eyes, as if he were somehow part of a tree. Then he detached himself from the tree and began to walk through a wood flushed with the first, vivid, light-filled green of spring. He wore a long, simple robe of rough-spun wool, ample enough to span his long stride. He carried nothing, not even, he knew in the way that dreamers know, in its deep pockets. He moved noiselessly through light and shadow, through the tangle of oak and birch, white and gold and tender green, and patches of impenetrable shadow. In the way of dreams, he knew and did not know that he had crossed some boundary between worlds. He knew and did not know that the dead leaves lying beneath the oak might also have been flakes of gold, that in the spider webs strung across his path each drop of dew reflected his face, that he left no disturbed ground behind him, and no shadow.

As he walked in the lovely, soundless wood, three deer as white as snow, with eyes of gold and shadows of gold, ran through a sunlit clearing in front of him.

Light streaked across his eyes and he woke.

"Healer!" Someone's grubby brat had opened his door, and was pounding on it; the voice was high, at once desperate and fearful. "Healer! You must come and see about our cow!"

He grunted, and rolled up from his pallet.

Scents followed him up: honeysuckle and lavender, and mint, mixed with the pine needles in the pallet. He ran his fingers through his fishbone hair, dislodging a pine needle, and ducked easily through the drying herbs and wildflowers hanging from the low beams of his cottage. It was more cave than cottage: wood built against an overhang of granite. Two walls were solid stone; he could not stand straight in parts of it. The child clinging to the door observed his movement and was off, like a startled rabbit, through the trees. The Healer's voice, deep and hale for an old man, hauled her to a stop.

"Whose cow?" A pale face turned; he glimpsed yellow hair and wide grey eyes among the ferns, and grunted again in recognition. "What's wrong with her?"

"She's all bloated and she's drooling!"

The Healer turned back into his cottage, put a mixture of mallow, meadowsweet, mistletoe and rue boiled in water and wine, into a pouch. The child was gone when he came out again, but he followed her path easily through the broken ferns.

The sun had barely risen; through the dark trees he saw the cold, jagged peaks high above, and the bright, cold light above them. Even in spring, the forest took its time warming, but still he walked barefoot through it, wearing an old, frayed tunic without sleeves; he had torn them out long ago to make bandages. It was his habits of sleeping within stone, wearing little, and appearing unexpectedly up a tree or on a high crag looking for plants, that gave him his reputation. "Healer," they called him to his face; behind his back, he was "the Wild Man." He answered to either, and gave them no other name. He healed their animals — he had a magic way with plants, they said — but he refused to extend his healing to humans.

He found the child and the cow in a tidy barn on the edge of a plowed field that sloped, as all fields that high did, down the mountain. The farmer and his wife and their cowherd looked at him anxiously.

"You see," the farmer said, indicating the cow.

"She ate something," the cowherd offered. The Healer said nothing, went to work, with his wet mixture of herbs and his hands. He patted the cow and prodded her, looked into her eyes, smelled her breath, then fed her. She bellowed, after a few moments, and they all stepped back.

"She'll be all right," the Healer said briefly, studying the reeking mass she had produced. "She'll feed now. She found some trevilbane in the pasture — that's the purple."

She was already picking at hay. The farmer and the child followed the Healer out. He did not stop for payment; the farmer's raised voice pursued him,

"I'll send the child back to you with something. . . ."

The Wild Man, loping among the ferns, remembered his dream then, and did not answer.

Three white deer with eyes of gold and shadows of gold . . .

Fierce, sweet wind leaped at him down the mountain; he smelled wolves, hare, wild strawberry, stone. Wind and longing threatened to pull him out of human shape; he clung grimly to his humanity, refusing to remember the few brief moments, days or weeks before, when after twenty years he had taken the White Wolf's shape. Someone from the school had climbed far too high alone, looking for a legend. He had watched students and young mages many times, as they sought a glimpse of the elusive White Wolf. Always before, winds and loneliness and the relentless stone turned them back before they wandered into danger. This one had fought the wind and would not be convinced by the emptiness ahead of him. So the man became the mage again, and then the Wolf. It was that, he thought, or watch another life in peril because of him. From the pinnacle, the Wolf watched the young man stop, wind-shaken, exhausted, stunned by the immensity of stone, his lenses sliding from his grasp, dropping among the rocks. The mage found his lenses for him, and then gave him what he had so stubbornly sought, so that he would finally turn and go back down the mountain.

It was the first magic the mage had worked in twenty years. The ease with which he had slipped out of human shape amazed him. Since then, winds lured him, stone, running water, wild things running, hawks in flight: His body yearned to melt into whatever shape his eyes touched. Wind, touching his bare skin, gave him the boundaries of his human shape; with it came memory, stark and terrible, which had bound him in that shape since he had walked through winter from Hunter's Field to Chaumenard.

He pushed memory away, and searched under ferns as he ran, and at the roots of trees, for the shade-loving violets and shepherd's moss. His hands were full of fern buds and wild garlic by the time he reached the cottage.

Someone was waiting for him: the stabler from the inn down the road a few turns in the deep forest. He went past the stabler without a word, to put the plants down, then came back out. The stabler, a muscular young man with dung on his boots, blinked at the Healer, as if he had just realized all the peculiar tales of him were true.

He lives in a cave.

He runs barefoot, summer and winter, like an animal.

He barely speaks, but he knows the name of everything that grows.

"The innkeeper down the road sent me. There's a lady going up to visit her daughter at the school. But her horse won't budge from the stable; he's down and won't get up, though none of us can find why."

The Healer stood thinking a moment, still as stone, his eyes, streaked and cloudy, like tarnished silver, remote and unblinking on the stabler's face, until the young man shifted uneasily, glancing down at himself as if he felt invisible. Then the Healer nodded briefly and disappeared back into his cave.

Returning with pouches of varying sizes slung over his shoulders, he followed the young man to the inn.

He came back late, having left the horse on its feet and looking vaguely surprised. He found a sack of new potatoes and some purple foxglove beside his door: payment for the cow. The woman at the inn had given him silver, which he tossed into a cracked crockery pot on the window ledge. He built a fire and steeped herbs in water, and hung others to dry. After a time, he found himself pacing through wood smoke and shadows, listening to the winds, listening for wolves singing in the winds to the moon rising above the mountaintop.

Three white hounds with eyes and shadows as red as fire ran through his dreams that night, pursuing the white deer. They made no noise. Their grim silence alarmed the mage in the wood. He wanted to find his way out of the trees then, but in the way of dreams he seemed fixed, earthbound as a tree. He had no choice but to see what followed the hounds.

Nothing followed that night. He woke, disturbed and restless, wondering what message in the language of dreams his mind was sending him. *Hunting*, the dream said. *Hunter*. But that dark rider had ridden into legend twenty years before, never to be seen again except in memory. The mage needed no dream to remind him: The Hunter, the final shape of his magic, rode through all his waking hours.

The culmination of all he had ever learned . . .

He spent the day high on the mountain, searching for a tiny wildflower that lived, it seemed, on stone and air; it made a soothing poultice for torn flesh. Stoneflower, the goatherds called it, and showed him places they had seen it. They kept watch for it; sometimes their goats ate too much of it and became intoxicated. The Healer climbed beyond the goats, trying to outclimb his dreams, the odd shadow over his thoughts, as if a black moon had risen out of nowhere and cast its black light across his heart.

Near dusk, he slipped off a ledge, reaching too high for one last plant. He fell in a rattling cascade of shards, astonished by pain, and resisting all his impulses to melt into stone, or soar from stone into air. For a moment, he wondered at the fragile shape he had taken, and how recklessly he had used it through the years; it would be a great relief, he felt, to leave it finally. Then he slid to a stop among a litter of stones, on the edge of a high meadow. He lifted his face out of grass and wildflowers and looked into a goat's yellow, slitted eye.

The goatherd helped him sit; she was a slender, tiny woman as agile as her goats, with a face so weathered she might have been born with the mountains.

"Never go where the goats don't," she advised him. "Where do you think you can jump that they can't, even as wild as you are?"

She boiled stoneflowers and made him a tea, which he had never tried before. It numbed his bruises and brought the stars far closer than he had ever seen them. He fell asleep on the meadow and heard, just before he dreamed, the bell from the school far below, warning the students and mages of the night.

Three white horses with eyes of bone and shadows of hoarfrost galloped after the hounds. Their invisible riders cast pale, glittering shadows of ribbons and mantles and windblown hair. Unlike deer and hound, they saw the mage. They turned their great mounts toward him and stopped. He woke just before they became visible.

The goatherd and her goats were gone; he could hear her voice bouncing here and there among the stones, calling one of the goats out of a ravine. She had left him some dark bread and cold lentils; he ate them, sitting on the meadow, his eyes on the tiny stone buildings at the edge of the forest. All that he had learned as mage seemed as remote and incongruous, something the mountain or the forest would engulf and render meaningless.

Then, just before he rose, he saw himself from a distance, out of a hawk's eye, or the eye of the moon: neither human nor inhuman, belonging nowhere, the powerless mage, the man trapped in time, haunted by the memory of power. Sorrow shot a barbed point into his heart, for that brief moment, tore it open to reveal all that he had lost.

He stood up, with mountain winds and the winds of memory pushing at him, coaxing him out of shape. He walked stubbornly, painfully, down the mountain, his eyes fixed firmly on the path he chose, his hands remaining empty, until he reached his cottage, and, in its silent shadows, he could finally rest.

In his dreams, the invisible riders became visible.

Three riders with no faces sat staring at the mage in the wood. He cried out in terror, then, but in the way of dreams, he knew he had made no sound. One rider was a man with pale bright hair; the second a child with his pearly hair, flowing long and unbound on the wind. The third rider had hair the colors of autumn leaves, with ribbons and strands of pearls braided into it. She wore a crown of deer horn and gold. There was a black oval where her face should have been. Behind them rode hunters with faces of leaves, of twisted willow boughs, or smooth white birch bark. As the mage's eyes slid across them in wonder and bewilderment, finding eyes within leaves, a mouth shaped of bark, the crowned rider fixed an arrow into her bow.

Sorrow, a voice cried, as she loosed the arrow, and he knew, in the way of dreams, that the voice, wild and sweet as running water, belonged to the dark, empty oval of the face beneath the crown. The air shattered into hoarfrost and light in front of the mage, white, glittering, cold as death. She cried again, *Sorrow*, and the arrow struck him.

He woke, astonished.

Four

In the King's castle in Pelucir, Talis, trying to Extinguish a Candle Flame by Will, shattered every mirror around him.

It was barely dawn. Awakening early, out of habit, he had forgotten for a moment where he was. He saw, from the window of his chambers, not the bare, harsh peaks of Chaumenard, but the misty green wood on the hill, the sky colored pearl around it. The habits of sorcery stirred restively in him, pulled him out of bed; he remembered, with relief, the book he had taken from the school. He opened it, began a spell at random. The only sounds, until the moment he spoke the final word of the spell, came from the kitchens and the kennels: wood chopped, hounds barking to be fed. Then the round, heavy mirror hanging above his clothes chest splintered as neatly as if he had thrown a stone into it, and spilled its pieces out of the carved oak frame all over the floor. He stared at the shards, puzzled. Then he heard the pounding on his door, and other doors opening, and the cries, astonished, fearful and furious, of sorcery.

He opened his door quickly, and found a dozen guards and the King, naked under a mantle, his hair awry, his mistress, Genia, behind him, blinking sleepily, her pale brows lifted in wonder.

"I'm sorry," Talis said quickly, assuming responsibility

for having gotten them out of bed, but hazy yet, about exactly what had happened. "What did I do?"

"I woke up picking pieces of Genia's mirror out of my beard," his brother Burne said incredulously. "Did you do that?"

"I was trying to extinguish a candle."

Burne stared at him. He was a burly, energetic man with golden hair and a greying beard; a fleck of mirror glinted in it, Talis saw with horror. When Burne was younger than Talis, he had ridden onto Hunter's Field and watched their father die; he had buried both their parents and raised Talis like the son he would never have. Talis, familiar with the mingling of loathing and fascination which sorcery inspired in Pelucir, heard his brother's voice tighten. "You broke mirrors all over the house trying to blow out a candle? What did they spend two years teaching you in that place?"

"I think," Talis said, perplexed, "it must be the spellbook."

"Then find another book," Burne said irritably. "Or go out in the woods to practice. You're supposed to learn to defend the castle, not demolish it. Our great-uncle is probably armed and mounted and out the gate by now, trying to fight ravens with a broadsword." He turned, left a bloody footprint behind him, and cursed pithily.

"I'm sorry," Talis said again, to his back. He wandered into his chambers again, where servants were sweeping up the glass. He stood at the window, musing at the wood, watching the sun rise behind the trees, spilling gold and shadow across Hunter's Field.

A corner of the massive keep, thrusting a dark angle of stone into his vision, caught his attention. Its roof sagged open in places; one beam was charred from a flaming arrow that had eaten through the roof slats before the warriors

within had put the fire out. The keep was said to be haunted
by all the maimed, hungry, bitter ghosts of warriors who
had died during the siege. It was possessed, household
legend ran, of a dark magic woven of the blood and fire,
anger and fear, that had filled it during the siege. No one
went into it.

"You want to what?" Burne asked, during breakfast in
the hall. Talis, ruthlessly breaking mirrors so early, had
deprived himself of the sight of younger, fairer guests, as if,
he thought ruefully, they had vanished along with their
reflections.

"I want to use the keep. I won't disturb anyone there,
except the ghosts."

"It's not a laughing matter," Burne said testily.

"I'm not laughing," Talis said gently. "But I'm not
afraid of ghosts. I grew up with them. They have haunted
this house all my life."

Burne was silent. He chose a salmon bone from his
plate, and leaned back, sighing. "I know. And they have
haunted you. No. It's grim in there. I won't have you lost
among that keep's memories."

I already am, Talis thought, putting the currant eyes out
of bread shaped like a swan. He broke its neck and said
patiently, "The book I brought back with me is unusual.
Words don't seem to mean themselves." Burne, picking his
teeth with the salmon bone, was looking askance at him.
"They don't mean what they should. Mean. What we expect
them to."

"What —"

"That's why I caused trouble this morning. The spells
seem very simple, elementary. Extinguishing a flame, like
this — " He concentrated, letting the flame of a single candle
from the branch in front of them burn in the dark of his
mind, then fade as he drew the darkness over it. The candle

went out. Burne blinked. " — is not difficult. That's all I was trying to do this morning."

"Then why did you break all those mirrors?"

"Because the spell in the book dealt with mirrors, not candles. But it said candles. And fire. So I was confused."

"So am I."

"I suspect all the spells are like that. They are in some unknown mage's private language. I must understand the language to work the spells."

Burne grunted. "I suppose you can't just forget about the book."

"No."

"All this sounds far more dangerous than it's worth."

"You sent me to Chaumenard," Talis reminded him. "How much is sorcery worth to Pelucir?"

"Not your life."

Talis shook his head quickly. "There's no question of that." He touched his lenses, evading Burne's skeptical gaze. "Mages don't kill each other with books. I'll be careful."

"No."

"Burne, I won't stop trying to use this book. It's too tantalizing. I'll go back to Chaumenard if you want — "

"No." Burne shifted, and changed tactics. "Anyway, the keep must be a rotten husk by now. You'll break your neck in there. It's probably full of bats and rats along with ghosts and bitter memories."

"That's another curious thing. If the keep did generate its own strange magic during the siege, I want to explore it. It may be a source of power that could be used to defend the castle. Sorcery not connected to any mage, but to the heart and life-blood of Pelucir."

Burne's brows knit. "I don't understand."

"I will. If you let me try."

The King was silent, frowning at the salmon bone. He made a decision; disapproving of it, he became abrupt. "You will at all times be guarded." Talis, surprised, did not argue. "If you come to harm, between that benighted book and the bewitched keep, I'll never forgive you. But at least, if you're guarded, I'll know what became of you."

"Nothing will happen to me," Talis promised.

He took two guards and the spellbook to the keep after breakfast. The guards, too young to be veterans of Hunter's Field, followed him grimly, tense and pale, as if they expected to find both the sorcerer and the sorcery from the legendary battlefield at the top of the keep. The thick door, closed but unlatched, opened easily; children, Talis guessed, looking for ghosts. Not being so adept at making fire as putting it out, he carried a torch. Light pushed at the filmy darkness within, but did not fully penetrate it. The narrow windows, even those facing the sun, were oddly opaque.

Something pale glided silently along the edge of the light. "Ghosts," he heard a guard whisper. The chipped flagstones were stained with blood. "The warriors came here," the other said softly, staring at the floor, "to get away from It." Their swords were drawn. Talis looked up, saw in a gentle crosshatch of faint, dusty light, high above, more white ghosts stirring along the rafters and rotted planks of the ruined middle floor. They questioned him distantly: *Who?* "Owls," he said to the guards, who looked at him doubtfully; they did not believe in owls. Ghosts, Talis thought, would have smelled less rank. He pushed into the darkness, found steps finally, worn stone shadowed with the footprints of wounded warriors fleeing Hunter's Field. The steps seemed to build themselves, one after another, under his descending foot; they angled endlessly upward along the walls. Even passing through the dim light in the middle floor, Talis could not see what lay beyond it. The steps darkened again; he heard a muttered word behind him. Finally he saw an end: a rectangle of black floating within four streaks of pale light. The door leaped suddenly quite close, in another step or two; his torch fire nearly singed it. He dropped the torch into a sconce on the wall and found a face in the door opening its eyes to gaze at him.

It was little more than knotholes, cracks and bubbles of pitch that the door had assembled into a rather dour sentinel, but one guard nearly lost his balance and tumbled back down the steps. "Sorcery," he spat like a curse, and the face looked mildly affronted.

"It's only wood," Talis said absently. Behind the door, he sensed, lay the dark heart of the keep's sorcery: its memories and its power. He touched the latch. "Stay here."

"My lord Talis, the King — "

"It's worse inside," Talis said, touching his lenses. They swam with sudden fire. He smiled. The guards sat down heavily on the stairs. "If you need me," he added, "I'll hear you."

He closed the door quickly behind him, seeing moving shadows on the walls. The room looked larger than it should have been. The stone walls were sealed against the weather by straw and clay and whitewash dimmed by smoke. Light from the torn roof and the single large window drew the shadows clear: He watched, transfixed, as an armed man drew back an arrow, then dropped both arrow and crossbow as a sword falling out of nowhere cut off his hand. The air seemed suddenly heavy to breathe, as if it had filled with smoke and too much heat from the thick, cold hearth. Another shadow roamed restlessly across the walls, stopped to look out the window, and ducked back; Talis saw a bolt of fire hurtling toward the window out of the placid empty field. The window moved.

He blinked. So had the window, dodging the ghostly fire. It looked over the herb gardens now, in the back of the kitchen. He turned, trembling slightly; the silence within the room seemed strained, as if at any moment the scream of the man who had lost his hand would break through the boundaries of memory and become real. He felt the sweat on his face; he took off his lenses, rubbed his eyes with his wrist. He looked for some place to set the book. Table, he thought, uprighting an overturned stool. A bucket to catch rain. A mirror, unbroken. Candles. He stopped thinking then, overwhelmed by the sudden, terrible despair and fury that seemed to flow into him from the stones under his feet, the walls around him. *Look*, the keep said to him. *See. This happened*.

"Yes," he whispered, "yes," and sorrow shook him, an ache such as he had never felt in his life for the death of a king he never knew. He stumbled to the door, leaned against it until his breathing calmed and nothing in his expression would alarm the guards.

He had various implements, pieces of furniture, and whatever might be useful brought up as far as the door. He would permit no one to enter the room. The window shifted randomly during the day, as if it fled a bombardment of stones, or glimpsed a stealthy, moonlit movement. Perhaps sensing his own calm among its memories, the keep seemed to grow more peaceful. Fewer shadows wandered across the walls; the tension of silent cries within the air lessened.

He tried no more spells that day, fearing Burne's wrath if something else went awry. But he stayed so long reading the book, trying to find a link between mirror and fire, what words might mean what, that twilight stole into the wood the window framed, and the guards, hearing the evening fanfares, thumped nervously on the door.

"My lord Talis, the King commands your presence in the hall."

Burne got his presence, but Talis was so absent-minded, scarcely seeing the faces around him, that the King said explosively, "If it's that disturbing, that bat-ridden tomb, I'll have it sealed shut. You look like a ghost."

Talis drew his thoughts out of the keep hastily, and applied himself to being as sociable as possible, causing, before the evening's end, at least three different rumors of impending marriage. Burne seemed pleased. But his mistress, a kindly and discerning woman, saw Talis' effort and said gently to him as they retired to their chambers, "Don't let the King worry you. Love takes time; it will recognize itself. Burne knows that. He is trying to put the past behind him, but he can't do that using your future. Be patient."

Talis returned to the keep before sunrise. The face in the door opened an eye as he opened the door, then went back to sleep. Most of the castle still slept. Only the kennels and stables were rousing, and the kitchen, for guests would be gathering that morning to hunt with the King. Talis, far more interested in the mysteries in the spellbook than in running down animals and slaying them, hoped his brother would not notice his absence. The window gave him a view of the field and the distant wood, a mist of green and shadow, where night still lingered beneath the golden oak and the birch whiter than bone. The sun and the hunters would waken it, sending great flocks of startled birds wheeling out of the trees. Now the wood dreamed. So did the castle. Talis opened the book.

The sun rose without catching his eye, for the window had shifted to overlook the formal gardens and fountains. Talis had risen also, tantalized by a spell. It seemed effortless: To Open a Latched Door Across a Room. Talis eyed the door and then the book. The spell, he knew, would have nothing to do with a door. More likely, it had to do with boots or wind. But, he reasoned, if he found what the spell in reality did, he could match the reality with the words, and prove that in this particular mage's teasing code door meant wind.

Implements, the book said. One gold cup. A large bowl of water. A candle lit in a holder made of gold.

He had brought them all into the keep: They were familiar requirements. He poured water from a bucket into a porcelain washbasin, and lit the candle. Beeswax scented the air; he had a sudden, wistful memory of spring in the high meadows on the mountains. He cleared his mind, concentrated.

Hold the cup upside-down above the water, the book instructed, so that gold reflects water and water reflects gold, reflection reflecting reflection. Stand the candle in water between them, so that fire, gold, water, lie within the hollow of the cup.

Repeat these words thrice. Backward.

Talis, holding the cup steady above fire, gold, water, hit a blank: The spell ended there. What words? he wondered, and was illuminated.

"Drawkcab," he said without much hope. "Ecirht. Sdrow. Eseht. Taeper."

He felt a stirring in the air around him, as if the keep, alarmed at the strange sorcery, watched him. "Drawkcab," he repeated, and thought he heard an echo, an unfamiliar voice, urgent, intense. "Ecirht. Sdrow. Eseht. Taeper. Drawkcab," he began a third time. "Ecirht. Sdrow. Eseht." He heard a scream then, faint and distant, a memory tearing into time, and his face tightened. "Taeper," he finished grimly, and light exploded out of the water.

The cup spun out of his hands, flew across the room and flattened itself against the far wall. The light, humming dangerously, left a white streak across Talis' vision, hit the ceiling at an angle, then arced out the window, which had moved again, attracted perhaps by the trumpets calling the hunt to order below.

Talis heard a tortured squeal from the trumpet, and the thunk of metal against stone. The noise of the dogs drowned human voices, but he could make out, in the second before he located his bones and could move, an isolated shout here and there among the frenzied howling. "Burne," he breathed, horrified, and flung himself at the window, clinging to it before it could move again. He leaned precariously over the edge, catching his lenses and then his balance as he looked down.

Burne was staring at a bolt of white fire burrowing mole-like into the ground in front of his horse. The horse, a favorite hunter, trembled in every muscle, but did not throw its rider. The trumpeter, sitting dazed among the hounds, had not fared so well. Servants bearing trays of spiced wine and hot brandy had flung them into the air, splashing themselves; goblets rolled among the hounds. The hounds whimpered and bayed at the light, horses fought to bolt; everyone else seemed frozen — hunters, musicians, kennel-masters, servants, dog-boys and the King — all staring at the light as, with a kind of mindless frenzy, it buried the last of itself underground.

The faces lifted then, to stare at Talis.

He saw only one: his brother's. It was a furious, glowing thing, a little, Talis thought, like the light he had created. He could not hear Burne well, above the racket the hounds made, but he caught the drift: What had he learned in two years at Chaumenard, and why had Burne bothered to send him there, and why had Burne even bothered to survive the winter siege, only to live to be killed by his own brother? Then he added something that caused Talis to hang even more perilously out the window, trying to hear. The hounds, having frightened away the light, began to quiet; the King's voice came clear.

" — out of that keep. It's a nightmare of foul memories and I want you down among people instead of ghosts, before you get as crazed as it is — "

"It's not the keep," Talis shouted back. "Burne, it's just the book — "

"Then throw it down! I want the book burned and the keep walled shut — "

"Burne, listen to me — "

"You nearly killed me!"

"It was an accident!"

"You accidently missed me?"

"No!"

"Then what were you trying to do?"

"Open a door!"

"With a lightning bolt?"

"Burne, please listen! Wait — I'm coming with you — "

The King refused to discuss the matter. Talis, mounted, and armed to kill anything that moved, caught up with Burne halfway to the wood. Everyone else seemed eager to ask him about the incident, to tease, to tell him what they were doing and saying the moment lightning leaped out of the keep and nearly hit the King. But lightning wasn't the word for it — it was more like something living, a strange being made of light with an urge to bury itself alive. And the odd noise it made. The hum. Like some vast, vibrating string. Thrum.

"Burne," Talis pleaded, but the King only showed him a tight-jawed profile.

"No."

The hounds, loosed, streaked toward the wood. The King urged his hunter into a canter. Talis, hesitating, looked back at the keep. Riders fanned around him; trumpets and horns called a warning to deer and hare, boar and bird. The single eye at the top of the keep looked back at Talis, opaque with memory or light. He had a sudden, crazed image of himself barring the doors from within and letting Burne lay siege against him. But Burne would never forgive him, and there was nothing he could do in the keep that couldn't be done elsewhere. Yet it drew at him, massive and ancient, dark with the ash of siege fires, as full of memories as the heads of warriors who had survived the night. It was a mystery, like the spellbook, which, Talis reminded himself, he should go back and rescue. He glanced at the riders disappearing into the trees and decided to try once more to persuade Burne.

He galloped after the hunt.

He heard the trumpets cry of a deer in two different places, it seemed. He followed one, saw the flicker of gold and scarlet and royal purple among the leaves; the riders were farther away than seemed possible. The trumpets sounded again, and then the gentle, silvery horns called of hare. Hounds belled everywhere, from every direction, though he saw none of them. He rode quickly, recklessly, to catch up, listening for the trumpets, for Burne would pursue the hart before the hare. A lacework of birch leaves brushed across his eyes; he ducked down, riding low beneath the outstretched boughs of oak, and far too quickly. But as fast as he rode, the hunt seemed to recede even more quickly away from him.

He heard the horn again, distant, teasing, and then suddenly close, and from another direction. The hunters had apparently scattered throughout the wood. He turned first toward one fanfare, then the other; he could see nothing but trees, the moving shadows of windblown leaves. He galloped through the shadows, bewildered and careless, and then across a shallow stream, its water slow and heavy with moss-capped stones. He felt his horse stumble, catch itself, and he straightened a little, pulling on the reins. The long limb of an oak stretched across the far bank caught him in the chest, lifted him out of the saddle, and threw him into the stream.

The world went black. Then he dragged his eyes open, unable to breathe, not knowing if he lay in air or water. He found air finally, pulled it in, trying to blink away the strange mist of green that had enveloped him. Leaves, he realized slowly: He had lost his lenses, and the world had blurred. Little explosions of pain flared in his knee, his ribs, one shoulder, the back of his head. He lay on his back in water and frog-spawn and long, slimy ribbons of moss. He groaned, and groped for his lenses, raising himself piece-meal among the stones, finding everything battered, but nothing unworkable. He fished his lenses out of the moss and put them on. One lens was shattered.

He cleaned the other, and found his boar spear, a few broken arrows and the sheath at his belt full of nothing but water. He groped again, found his hunting knife. He pushed himself to his feet with the spear and hobbled out of the water. His horse had vanished, which surprised him, since it was of stolid temperament and disinclined to startle. He stood on the bank, balanced against the spear to take the weight off his knee, and listened for the hunt.

The wood was soundless.

He heard no trumpets, no barking hounds, no hooves, no voices, not even disturbed birds complaining above the trees. Not even the leaves moved; they might have been carved of stone in the still air, though on the ground, his bemused eyes told him, their shadows moved.

A horn sounded, a single, sweet note.

Three deer as white as snow with eyes of gold and shadows of gold ran through the trees in front of him.

He heard himself make a sound; the hair pricked on the back of his neck. He tried to move; he could only grip the spear more tightly to keep from falling. The deer flickered noiselessly away into the trees, shadows flowing like sunlight across everything they touched.

Three hounds as white as bone, with eyes and shadows as red as blood, ran soundlessly through the trees in pursuit of the deer.

He tried to turn himself invisible; the only thing he managed, in that upside-down world, was to erase his shadow. His hands slick on the boar-spear, he turned desperately to stumble away, hide himself from what would come. But he could not move quickly, in or out of the vision, and what came next came fast.

Three white horses with eyes of bone and shadows of hoarfrost galloped after the hounds. Behind them rode three roan, and behind them three black, and behind them a great gathering of hunters that seemed to have fashioned themselves out of roots, tree bark and leaves, as if the wood itself were hunting. Through the empty frame of his lenses Talis saw a moving blur of green, trees riding a hard wind. Through the unbroken lens he saw the faces of leaf and tree-bole, the slender woven branches of willow, of pale, papery birch bark. Only the riders turning their white mounts toward him had no faces.

He swayed, caught his balance against the spear, watching the one with slender, jewelled hands ride forward, a bright white swirl of long skirt and mantle, flowing ribbons of silk and pearl, and crowned with gold and bone above long hair streaked with autumn fire and a dark oval that was no face. Frozen, Talis watched her notch the arrow in her hand, lift her bow. Just before she shot, he whispered, "At least, before you kill me, let me see your face. And then tell me why."

He saw her face.

He swayed again, trembling, wordless. Her eyes were gold and dark, troubled, in a face at once imperious and vulnerable and so beautiful there seemed no word, in human language, for what he saw.

She lowered her bow. She said, her voice like the horn he had heard, pure, regal, haunting, "I am the mother of sorrow."

"Oh," he breathed, his voice gone, the world gone, except for what existed in the circle of his unbroken lens. "How can I help you?"

"You can see me. You have crossed into my world. You are not dreaming."

"No."

"Tell me your name."

He drew a long, shaking breath to give her that and his bones and anything else she might want of him. "My name is —"

Someone shouted it behind him and the world within the lens shattered.

He turned, bewildered, stunned by the frenzied barking of hounds, not remembering where he had been, what world he had walked out of to see her. Hunters rode out of the trees, shouting; trumpets sounded; dogs swarmed into the stream, belling and harrying a boar that in its maddened panic was charging straight across the water at Talis.

He did not remember moving. He remembered blood on the boar's tusk after it tore open a hound with the toss of its head, and its rank smell as it came close, and then its small, furious and terrified eye. And then the spear shuddered in his hands, tried to wrench itself free. Something splashed across his eyes. He saw the world through a bloody haze.

Talis, he heard then, from another world, a secret within the wood.

And then he heard the King's voice. "Talis!"

He knelt on the ground holding a spear with a dead boar impaled on it that had pushed itself in its dying frenzy all the way up to the cross-guard. That much he could see through his broken lens. The hounds were swarming around him, barking with wild excitement in his face, trying to tell him what he had done. He opened his hands finally, let the spear fall. He stumbled, rising. Burne caught him, dragged him away from the hounds.

The King pounded him, saying something, his face still patchy with fear. Talis winced, aching suddenly in every bone. He pulled his lenses off, cleaned the blood from the unbroken glass, his hands trembling. His hearing seemed to return with his sight; as he put the lenses back on, his brother's voice penetrated.

"I thought you were dead. I thought you were dead, when it came at your back and you just stood there not listening, not turning, with enough racket behind you to make the trees jump. And then you turned, and brought the spear down and the boar ran up it as cleanly as if it were spitting itself for supper. One stroke, straight through the heart." He pounded Talis between the shoulder blades again, then took a closer look at him. "You're all wet. You have slime in your hair."

"I fell in the stream," Talis said dazedly. "Riding too fast after you. I broke a lens and maybe a rib. I was using the spear as a crutch. That's why I had it in my hands at all."

Burne eyed him wordlessly a moment, his face taut again. "Why didn't you use some magic or something? You could have been killed!"

"I don't know. I wasn't thinking clearly."

"You must have stunned yourself. That's why you didn't hear us."

"Yes." He touched his lenses and saw a face within the light and windblown leaves. "I was stunned. Burne, I'm sorry I nearly killed you this morning."

"Never mind." Burne sighed. "It's been tried before."

"About the keep —"

"Never mind about the keep. Keep it. You'd only find another place to have your accidents in, anyway."

"It's not —" Talis stopped himself. "Thank you."

"Well. Anyway, it makes a good story. Almost as good as you falling off your horse, breaking a lens, and killing a charging boar while you hobbled around using your boar-spear as a crutch." He slapped Talis' back again, loosing a grunt of amazed laughter. "You can tell it when we feast on your kill."

It seemed to Talis, as he stood dripping water and blood, seeing blurred green wood through one eye, and dogs scrapping over offal through the other, a peculiar exchange for magic.

He found his horse, which had gone nowhere but had simply declined to follow him into a dream, and rode home accompanied by various fanfares, with the gutted boar hanging upside-down on the spear behind him. The physician bandaged his ribs and his knee, forbade him to climb the keep stairs and gave him a tonic which, he thought, could have melted drawbridge chain, and which stunned him until evening the next day. It seemed mildly hallucinatory: As he sat through the long boar feast trying to keep his fraying thoughts together, he kept glimpsing the face of the woodland Queen among the guests. It was, he decided, a trick of his broken lenses, making him see double. Now a young girl wore the Queen's expression of power and vulnerability; now a fall of hair the color of autumn leaves made him catch his breath. Now he saw her face, just before it turned away from him to speak. It was a face full of opposites, he decided: delicate and regal, young and ageless, wild and controlled, fierce and sweet. . . .

Trumpets greeted the boar as it entered on a tray of silver and gold. Talis saw himself on the tray suddenly, blind and still. If he had not turned, if the spear had broken in his fall, if he had lost it in the water . . . He swallowed dryly, adjusted his lenses, and the odd vision vanished, along with his appetite. Later, the horns bade farewell to the bones and the picked meat and the tusks that lay like quarter moons on the bloody tray. Talis, wandering badly, forced himself to listen to his great-uncle relate a complex incident that had happened last autumn, or the one ten years before, or some autumn before Talis was born. There was One Great Hunt, he decided, that went on perpetually in some never-ending autumn. That was the Hunt out of which all stories came. Even his boar would come charging out of spring into autumn one day, during some drunken feast, when he would remember the leaves being all the colors of her hair . . . The story involved a broken stirrup, a hedge with a gypsy's laundry drying on it, and a pig. Talis' eyes strayed. There she was again, at the far end of the table, holding a hazelnut in her long white fingers, each finger ringed with gold. She laughed suddenly at the hunting story; her face changed, became human. The King said softly to Talis:

"You're not eating. Are you in pain?"

Talis shook his head. "I doubt that I'd feel pain if you dropped a table on my head. I just keep wandering out of the world."

Burne grunted. "Go to bed before you fall in your plate." Servants brought in wet linens scented with rosewater, and tiny, icy bowls of minced fruit. Talis wiped his hands and rose unsteadily; Burne added, "And stay out of the keep. You're dangerous enough up there when your head is clear."

"I will," Talis said absently. Shadows followed him, spun out of the flickering torchlight. Voices, laughter, music, seemed to follow him also, even through the dark night, as if he walked through some invisible hall where the gathering within celebrated yet another hunt. He climbed the keep steps slowly. There seemed far more of them than usual. He had reached the top and opened the door before he remembered, with some surprise, that he had been on his way to bed.

The room was lighted, he realized slowly, though he had found his way up in the dark. The light seemed not fire but sun, ancient, golden, still, like the wood on a soundless summer afternoon. He made a sound, seeing two worlds again: the bleak, shadow-ridden keep, the light trembling in it as if, in the otherworld, midnight did not exist.

In that light, not even past existed. All the tormented shadows had vanished on the walls. He saw only one shadow: tall, slender, crowned with what looked like a circle of flame or deer horn. He watched it for a long time, until his heart seemed made of that sweet light, and he felt that at any moment she might step out of the faceless shadow on the wall into his world.

He heard her voice, distant, silvery, pure, like her hunting horn. *Talis*.

"Yes," he whispered, and again, "Yes."

She said nothing more. He watched until her shadow reached out everywhere, pulled him into night.

Five

The boar and the bolt of lightning leaping out of the keep made Talis' name a kitchen word for a day or two. The hall-servants told the tale of the burrowing, deadly sorcery, the frenzied dogs, the spilled cups, the furious king, each a different way, as if each had seen a different light. The other tale came piecemeal from the hall: Something had happened to the prince. He had fallen off his horse. He had broken a leg, he had broken a rib, he had broken any number of bones. He had been dazed, he hadn't heard, and then there it was, coming at his back, and he turned, and next thing, they were pulling his silver spear-point out of the boar's heart. It wasn't magic; it was all as he had been taught, just as his father had done in his time, and for that instant, with his hair and his shoulders, he had looked just like his father.

Saro, deep in her wash water, heard his name echo around the iron cauldron. It was one more kitchen noise; if he had called her name to fetch a dirty pot, she might have put the name to his voice. Princes were no more real to her than roses or gold or a living boar, or the world beyond the kitchen garden. Anything could exist in that magical "beyond," except Saro. The prince's name was simply a word she could ignore, since it had nothing to do with pots. So she scrubbed and did not think, and gradually the dancing flame that was the prince's name grew still and, unfanned, became an ember of memory. The day Prince Talis . . . The day when the light . . . When he almost killed the King, and then was almost killed himself . . .

And then, unexpectedly, the ember flared again, became an argument, scraps of which Saro heard as she picked up dirty bread pans from beside the ovens. The hall-servants, gathering for the midday meal, flurried around the kitchen, feathers rustling, preparing for flight.

"I'm not going."

"I'm not going. It's not our place to be asked to go up there."

"Up all those steps. Let the guards take it. They're used to it."

"It's not just the steps, it's — "

"Pitch-black. And ghosts wander. Hungry ghosts. You'd have to be mad to go among them. It's one thing for Prince Talis; he's got his magic, and the guards are armed, but — "

"And when you make it past the ghosts and up all those stairs, then where are you? Face to face, so I've heard, with a Thing in the door opening its eyes and glaring at you."

Saro, loaded with trays, set them down beside the cauldron. A mincer darted to her side, grabbed a misshapen dove left on the tray, and vanished under a table. Bending, she began to scrub, and heard little more for a while than the slosh of water, the scrape of metal on iron, her scrub brush on stubborn grease.

"Saro!"

She pulled herself upright, turned to the iron stoves, where an undercook had scorched a sauce. Carrying the hot pan carefully, its long handle wrapped in her skirt, she edged around an argument between the tray-mistress and the head hall-servant.

"It's not my job," the tray-mistress said roundly, "to find a tray-bearer for Prince Talis in this muddle. Who should I send?" Her fingers pinched, crablike, caught a peeler's small, translucent ear. "Him?" He squinched his eyes shut, knife in one hand, potato in the other. He looked as grimy and knobbed as a new potato. "Boy, take a tray to the prince in the great keep." His mouth gaped; he endeavored to disappear down his shirt. "How far do you think he would get with it? Two steps into the dark and he'd flee, leaving Prince Talis' meal to the mice."

"It's not our job to go among ghosts and cobwebs," the head servant retorted.

"Well, it's none of mine, either." The tray-mistress glanced at the ear in her fingers, as if wondering how it got there, and loosed it distastefully. "If he's a mage, Prince Talis, why can't he levitate his meal from here to there?"

"He's busy with his other sorceries," the head servant said portentously. "And making a new lens so he can read his spells."

The tray-mistress breathed heavily through her nose. "It's your problem," she said, and turned to add linen in a gold ring to the tray under dispute. Saro heard the head servant's voice rise as she left them behind and eased around another obstacle: two apprentices coming to a boil over spices in a pudding. She dumped the scorched sauce down the drain and added the pan to her pile.

"Saro!"

She threaded her way through the servants and cooks, hurrying now, as they drizzled a latticework of chocolate sauce on a stewed pear, and placed walnut halves on small tarts of egg and cheese and finely chopped mushrooms. She collected the empty tart pans, and then the saucepans, added them to her pile, which was beginning to teeter. Working quickly, she had twin towers, one dirty, one clean, before she heard her name again.

"Saro!"

The voice belonged to the tray-mistress, who, scowling with frustration, dropped a fresh lily on a tray and handed the tray to Saro.

"Take this to Prince Talis in the keep. All she thinks about is pots," she added to the head servant, who looked battered but victorious. "Nothing else penetrates. She won't know enough to be afraid. Go," she added to Saro, who was adjusting the heavy silver tray in her slippery hands. "And quickly, before it cools entirely."

The head servant wrinkled his nose fastidiously. "But not through the castle. Not looking like that. Go around through the kitchen garden. Is she mute? Or just dense?"

"Both."

"Then how will we know if she actually makes it to the top of the keep with the tray?"

The tray-mistress rolled an exasperated eye at him. "Follow her," she snapped, and showed him her back.

Saro, who hadn't seen the woodpile and had scarcely seen the sky since she was found, ignored both on her way to the keep. She dodged gardeners, dogs, guards, as easily as she dodged elbows, tossed spoons, and mincers waving mincing knives at each other. One world was no more perilous than the other, for there was only the task at hand. All else could be ignored, as long as she herself was. And even the guards who thought to question her forgot the questions as they looked at her blank face, and then forgot her face. It was only when she opened the door to the keep and stood in the thin fingers of light falling from the narrow archers' windows along the stairs that she stopped, midstep, in the middle of her task. Something was happening inside her head. It seemed as if she saw two things at once: the broken, shadowy, mysterious keep, cloudy with owls in the upper rafters, and another tower, rising through it, at once solid and transparent as a dream. This tower had walls through which roses bloomed, and a broad sweep of ivory stairs that led to . . . something. Someone? Her pale brows crumpled; her lips moved soundlessly. Who was it at the top? She moved again, slowly, up stairs of white stone and stairs of dark stone, while owls did and did not swivel their heads to look at her through their great golden eyes. The door at the top was of dark, carved wood; the door at the top was painted white and gold. The door was always closed; the door was always open. . . . She moved through time and memory, scarcely noticing the endless steps, trying to make the picture clear in her head before she reached the door. The door was dark and limned by fire and guarded by a face. The door was always open and someone came to meet her, smiling. . . .

The door opened. Snow swirled out of it, and she glimpsed for one instant the terrible figure who had come to meet her. Something tried to leap out of her mouth. She brought up both hands to hold it back, and the tray crashed to the floor at Talis' feet.

They stared at one another, the prince and the pot-scrubber. Then they both crouched, picking up goblets, cutlery, broken plate, while the guards and the face in the door watched bemusedly, and Talis examined the remains of his meal.

"What had we here? Salmon swimming in gravy, roast beef on a bed of broken meringue . . . The bread is only slightly damp. And what was this?" He tasted a finger. "Too sweet. But it was pretty, whatever it was. Now. I only have to wring the salad out. I frightened you, opening the door so quickly after you braved ghosts and owls and endless stairs. You're not crying, are you?"

He looked at her. Then he touched his lenses and looked again. His eyes widened slightly, lingered on her face. He said softly after a moment, "You have the strangest face. It seems . . . to shift. Or blur. Something . . ." His own face did not; it was quite calm under her gaze. There was something odd about it she could not have described, except that it was the only face she had ever seen that made her want to keep looking at it. He asked, "What is your name?"

She averted her face abruptly, touched her mouth with one finger. He made a soft sound. She stood swiftly, her face still turned away, for she was not used to being visible. "Wait," he said, and she did as she was told.

Something appeared in her line of vision: the white lily on the tray. "Take it," he said. "I want to give it to you."

She stared at him. She did not take the flower, but she felt her face rearrange itself in a very strange way and realized, as he smiled, that she was smiling.

She thought of him all the way back to the kitchens. She found his face at the bottom of every pot she scrubbed, between her eyes and every face she looked at in the kitchens. It was still in her mind after supper, even while she cleaned the great mess of pots and pans and kettles, to clear the cauldron for its nightly dreams. Pausing between pots, she touched her face once, in curiosity, tried to see it in the water. She only saw dark cloud with suds floating around it.

And then, unexpectedly, Talis' face formed instead, as if the cauldron had taken the thought out of her head. She blinked, for he no longer looked calm; he was not smiling, as in her memory. He was seeing something, trying to move away from it without moving. She leaned farther into the cauldron, trying to see what he saw. His face grew small then; he acquired a body, surroundings. Fire behind him illumined the tangle of oak boughs above his head. As she stared, a young woman flung herself toward him. Her hair was long and tangled, her face wild in the light, strained with fear. She cried something: Fire flashed out of her mouth, then diamonds, then a small black bird of horror. And then an arrow of white streaked out of nowhere, passed between them and shattered the lens over Talis' eye.

Blood spilled across the black moon rising among the oak boughs. The boughs turned into horns, moving slowly into Saro's vision, lifting the moon higher until its bloody face filled the cauldron. Then it waned upward out of her sight, until she saw the face beneath the moon. The eyes, masked in pelt, moon-black, seemed to stare back at her through the dark water.

And then it was her own face, a dark, vague cloud, rippling now with her quick, terrified breathing. The tray-mistress, passing behind her, said, "Wake up and finish, girl, before you fall in."

She left the pot where it stood.

This time she saw only one tower, and it was dark and full of owls, questioning her when she disturbed them. She felt her way up with her hands. The steps seemed endless, but she was used to having no end in sight. She could not think; over and over she saw the white fire strike, the prince flinch back as the lens shattered. And then the terrible, inhuman face staring at her through water, as if it were scenting. . . .

She saw the door finally, impossibly far above her, a blackness outlined in fire. She climbed higher; it jumped closer, closer, the face on it awake and watching.

She ignored the face, and the guards who were making meaningless noises as she pounded on the door. It opened abruptly. The prince gazed at her, one lens sparking, the other oddly empty, she saw, as if it had already shattered.

He quieted the guards with a gesture, and asked gently, "How can I help you?"

She realized then that, with no words and no voice, she could tell him nothing.

Six

The White Wolf dreamed.

He was writing a book in the ancient school at the edge of the forest on the highest peak of Chaumenard. A book of spells, for beginning students. One spell in particular he needed to put into language, clearly and unambiguously, for the student who wore the lenses. He was working in the next room; the door between them stood open. The mage heard a page turn, murmurings, water poured out of a beaker. The spell the student worked was twisted, dangerous; its words would explode in his hands, for they meant other than what they said. The mage, trying desperately, could not remember the true words. Water hissed into fire; gold leaf melted, dropped in tiny, metallic tears onto a mirror. The mage tried to speak; he could not find the word that meant: *Stop*. *Rain*, he found, and *moon*, *horns*, *heart*. *Hart? Dark. Drawkcab*, he heard, very clearly, from the next room. And then there was a sound like air ripping apart.

He dropped the pen, rising. Steps came toward him from the next room before he could move. *Drawkcab*, a strange voice said. And the night-hunter of Hunter's Field stood at the threshold. His face was masked in fur, his mouth black with blood; the dark moon rode through his fiery horns as through cloud. He raised his hand and said:

Xirta Eflow.

The mage woke.

His heart was pounding; even awake, he stared into the dark, listening, trying to separate the Hunter's face from the night. He was alone in his quiet cottage; the dark hunter had been a dream. Still he lay tensed, incredulous, alarmed without knowing why. *Danger*, the dream said. *Warning. Drawkcab.*

He remembered the spell in the book.

He sat up, murmuring wordlessly, hands pushed against his eyes. The spell . . . Which was it? Something simple. Repeat these words thrice. *Ecirht*. Backward. He had buried the spellbook in solid granite beneath the stone cellar under the school.

Behind every spell, within every word, lay the name of the maker.

Xirta Eflow.

What, he wondered suddenly, intensely, had the young man who had climbed the mountain been doing in his dream? He could not possibly have found the book; he could not be awake now, within the dark, sleeping school, trying to work the simple, dangerously twisted spells within the book. It was a dream, he told himself. A nightmare. Nothing. No thing.

Drawkcab, the strange voice reminded him.

He rose and dressed.

As he stepped outside, he smelled stone in the still air, the moon-frosted peaks above him, and the scent of the earth, like some vast, sleeping animal. He yearned to shape the wolf, run across the plane of night beneath the stars. But if the dream was no dream, then he had no time, and if it was nothing but a few random fragments of memory pieced together, then he had no magic for things he had loved.

He thought of stone, and, for an instant, became stone, crossing distance as if it were not time and place but simply memory. He stepped forward into time, and backward into memory, and stood in the hushed, enclosed blackness beneath the school. He dove into stone as if it were water, seeking what he had hidden twenty years ago, before he had run out of the world.

The book was gone.

Stone was stone; it held his name, his words, nowhere. He drew back into his body and grew still, scenting the night again, calming his perturbed thoughts, to find, beneath them, a simple answer. One of the old mages must have noticed the book, a seep of its magic out of the cellar floor, and had brought it up. He would have buried it again in the library where, nameless, it had been ignored for years, until perhaps one of the beginning mages had looked into it for help.

He had only to find it, bury it again, and go back to bed.

He searched the sleeping school, silent and invisible, a shadow in the night, looking through dreaming chambers and finding no one awake, looking on shelves, in the library, growing more and more uneasy, until his dream became a subtle heartbeat, a cold rill of blood running through the stones, through someone else's dream. He saw a star of lamplight move down a long corridor toward him. He grew as still as stone, and as unremarkable. But the bearer of the lamp, hunched and slow, simply stopped in front of the blank stone wall and said, astonished:

"Atrix Wolfe?"

He drew himself free, reluctantly, shaping the mage whose name he had not spoken in twenty years. He said, "Hedrix." The light trembled in the old mage's hand. Atrix took the lamp from him. "I didn't want to wake anyone."

"I dreamed of you," Hedrix said, "and woke." His owl's tufted brows were lifted as high as they could go. He touched Atrix, held his arm, as if he might vanish back into the dream. "What are you doing here? Have you come back to stay? Why did you come so quietly in the dead of night? Why didn't you tell me you were here? Have you been with the wolves? Is that why you were reluctant to come among — " Hedrix stopped himself abruptly, studying Atrix, his own face quieting now, in a way that Atrix remembered, as he focused his thoughts. "You're troubled. How can I help you?"

Atrix lowered the lamp, sighing noiselessly. "I'm looking for something. I hoped to come and find it and disappear again, with no one knowing I had ever been here."

"But why?" Hedrix breathed. "Is it so terrible for you to be among humans now?"

"No. Only among mages." Hedrix was silent, astonished again. Atrix turned restively. Stone walls met his eyes everywhere, and he could not leave in any shape without finding the book. His mouth tightened. He said finally, dream-driven and trying to remember patience, "Let me talk. If I can remember how mages speak to one another."

The hand on his arm tightened. "Come with me," Hedrix said, and led him, with brittle slowness, lest their sorcery disturb more dreams, to his chambers. He sat down; Atrix put the lamp on his work table, and let his mind prowl a moment among Hedrix's things. The book was not among them.

He went to the window, drawn to the pale ghost of stones rising up to meet the setting moon behind the thick leaded panes of glass in the window. He let his face fall against the cold glass.

He said, "Has no one ever guessed that I made that monster on Hunter's Field that killed the King of Pelucir?"

He heard no sound behind him, not even Hedrix's breath. He turned, suddenly afraid for the frail old mage, and found Hedrix staring at him, his eyes as wide and luminous as a child's. Hedrix said, his voice shaking again, "No. Why would we?" He tried to pull himself up then, failed; he still stared. "You?"

"Yes."

"Well." Hedrix blinked finally. "That explains so many things." He laid a hand over his heart; Atrix moved toward him quickly. He knelt at Hedrix's feet, took his other hand, felt the shocked blood pounding through Hedrix, and the pain pushing against his heart.

He quieted his thoughts, letting the pain flow into his own heart, where it belonged. "It's over and done with," he said. "So is my life as mage. Except tonight. I have something simple to do, and then I'll leave you again. Hedrix. Don't take it so to heart — "

"Why — "

He heard the question struggling out of Hedrix, and tried to answer, speaking slowly, more gently, feeling his blood, or Hedrix's blood, beating with thin, frantic hummingbird wings. "I wanted to end the siege — "

"You should not — "

"I know," he said. "I should not have acted on that field. But I was afraid for Chaumenard. I lost my temper. I tried to stop a war, and made something more terrible than war. I made death to stop death." He had trouble finding air, suddenly. He closed his eyes, calming Hedrix's pain at the word, breathing deeply, evenly. "Hedrix. I need your help."

"Yes — "

"I made a mistake on Hunter's Field. And, when I came here afterward, I made a second mistake."

"You did not speak."

Atrix opened his mouth, closed it. He heard Hedrix's breathing then, harsh, but steadier. "No," he said finally. "I wrote, instead. That was my second mistake." Hedrix made a soft noise; Atrix looked at him. "My silence was a lie; the words I wrote were lies. I buried the book."

"You should never have gone to Pelucir," Hedrix whispered.

"Then that was my first mistake. But in wolf shape, I dreamed of that war. Of danger to Chaumenard. I did not stop to think."

"That you could be more dangerous than the army of Kardeth?"

Atrix bowed his head. "I take the shapes I am drawn to: On that field, the only shape of power I saw was death. I did not stop to think. . . ." The pain they shared lessened, dwindled finally into memory. Atrix rose, went back to the window. Staring at the moonlit peak, he saw only snow and black wind, and the vast raven's wing of night. "Tonight I dreamed again," he said. "I dreamed of that book opened, being used. I saw the Hunter's face. He spoke my name. So I came back here looking for the book."

"It was a dream," Hedrix whispered.

"Dreams speak, when the language of power remains unspoken. That much I have learned in twenty years."

"You did not find the book."

He turned, to look at Hedrix. "No."

Hedrix breathed quietly now, Atrix saw, though his hands gripped the arms of his chair, and his eyes had lost their bright, innocent pain, had become hooded, opaque. He lifted one hand from the chair arm, laid it across his eyes, as if he saw too many confusions at once.

"Why didn't you tell me this twenty years ago, when you came here after the battle?" Hedrix asked. "Why did you let us all think you had been among the wolves until then? We spoke of nothing else, when we heard the news from Pelucir. How could you have stayed silent, while we tried to guess who had done such a terrible piece of sorcery?"

Atrix shook his head, wordless again. "There seemed no words," he said finally, "for what I had done. Words were too small, they did not mean . . . They would crack like glass if I tried to fill them with this. All I could see then was what I had made. I brought the Hunter here with me. I tried to work; I saw him in every spell I wrote. I saw him behind every door I opened, between me and every mage and student I spoke to. You spoke to a mage who no longer existed . . . So I buried the book with its flawed magic in solid stone beneath the school, and I buried my own magic with it. I could do nothing but that." He shrugged slightly. "I could have gone to Pelucir, let Burne Pelucir kill me. But this seemed more appropriate and harsher than human justice."

"What did?" Hedrix asked uneasily.

"Relinquishing power. Burying it, as I buried the book. Since I no longer knew my name, it did not matter what I called myself. For twenty years, I have lived without magic. I do not change shape. I move in human time. I am no longer Atrix Wolfe. I am no one."

Hedrix stared at him, frozen in his chair; Atrix wondered if he still breathed. Then he saw Hedrix swallow. "What have you done?"

"I am a healer. I roam the mountains collecting herbs and mushrooms and wildflowers—"

"Wildflowers."

"I heal animals. I use no magic; I do not touch people, who might die if I refuse to use power. I make fire with wood, I move stone with my hands, I live as simply as it is possible to live. I am no longer a mage named Atrix Wolfe. I am a healer, and that is the only name I need—"

He stopped. Hedrix was rising, with an effort, clinging to the chair. Color had flushed back into his face; his eyes were wide, bright with some sudden, strange emotion.

"Atrix," he said, his voice shaking. "What have you done?"

Atrix was silent a breath, gazing back at him. "What was necessary," he said at last. "What seemed just. I removed a dangerous mage from the world."

"That," Hedrix said, "was your third mistake." He moved slowly to a small table, poured wine into a silver cup and took a swallow before he spoke again. Atrix, motionless, waited. "So the Hunter vanished, and Atrix Wolfe vanished, and we are left with you, picking wildflowers on the peaks of Chaumenard. What we do not have is any kind of truth. You are still the Hunter and the Wolf, and how will you be guided when you find yourself once more on a winter battlefield with no temper left and all that enormous power?"

"It will not happen again," Atrix said succinctly.

"How do you know? How can you know that? Only your death would prevent it, because that is all you understand of this — you make death to stop death. So. You used all your power to destroy Atrix Wolfe. You are still your own dark making."

Atrix closed his eyes, touched them. "Hedrix. The mage destroyed himself. I am a healer. Nothing more."

"Then why are you here?"

Atrix looked at him. The Hunter seemed to form out of lamplight and shadow between them, loosed from an opened spellbook that had been hidden within stone. "A small thing," he said patiently, but doubted it, suddenly: that he would find the book and bury it and return to the high cliffs and meadows, nameless and without a past. He moved abruptly, poured wine and drank it. "I must find that book. That's all. That's all, at this moment, that I understand." He turned abruptly, spilling wine; the stiffness in his face broke into hair-fine lines. "I should have gone to Burne Pelucir," he said tightly. "Walked into his court at dawn twenty years ago, and let his warriors kill me."

"I don't think," Hedrix said, sitting down, "that's what you should have done to Pelucir."

"I was afraid."

"Of dying?"

"That out of fear they would do nothing. What should I have done?"

"I don't know," Hedrix said uneasily. "I only know that power unused is power uncontrolled. You turned away from it, but it did not vanish; you simply do not know, anymore, what you are doing with it. Or what it is doing to you."

Atrix sat down. "It makes me dream," he murmured wearily. "I thought that was harmless enough."

"Tell me about the book. What does it look like?"

"Big. Very plain, bound in undyed leather. There is no name on it."

"Why?"

Atrix shrugged. "The spells were so simple, things any mage could have written, with a little care and patience." He drank again. "Perhaps I knew the name would be a lie. As the book is."

"You looked in the library."

"I looked everywhere. It moved itself out of solid stone, or a mage moved it. No one else could have."

"No one spoke of finding it. . . ." Hedrix's voice grew small suddenly, dwindled away. Atrix was silent, very still, watching Hedrix change in front of his eyes, gather himself into himself, it seemed, as if at the threat of a wild, imminent storm.

He said, his voice inflectionless, "You know where the book is."

"One of the younger mages asked me for it. He sensed something in it — "

"Where did he find it?"

"In a closet, he said. On a shelf. I had no idea what it was. I let him take it with him out of Chaumenard —"

"Out of Chaumenard? Where?" Atrix rose suddenly, alarmed at the odd expression on Hedrix's face. "Who has it?"

"Talis Pelucir."

"Talis —" He stared at Hedrix. Then he heard himself shout. "That book is in Pelucir? With a prince of Pelucir? In the castle on the edge of Hunter's Field? Hedrix — Does he wear lenses?"

He saw the answer in the mixture of fear and astonishment on Hedrix's face just before the White Wolf began to run.

Seven

Saro listened.

Sound in the kitchen had always been a constantly changing tapestry woven for a moment, frayed, rewoven, with threads spun from the spattering of onions over the fire, the rhythm of mincers' knives on hardwood, the head cook's brittle impatience, the undercooks' feverish hysteria, a peeler wailing, the tray-mistress's exasperated sibilants, milk scalding, meat spattering down into the fires, wood snapping and groaning, the changing voices of fire as it leaped into new wood, hungry as a spit-boy, or, sated, caressed darkening coals and murmured.

Everything had a voice; even the dumb, plucked, headless fowl turning on the spits spoke to the fire. So Saro heard everything as the kitchen's voice. Having no voice, she did not distinguish the sound of the chopping blade from the sound of human voices, unless the particular sound of her name caught her ear. She gave no thought to what might have come out of her own mouth if she suddenly spoke: It might as easily be the thump of kneaded dough against wood, or the clank of a scorched pot kicked across the stones, as any human word.

But she had a task to do, a pot to scour, and what stuck to the bottom of this particular pot was death. Death appeared constantly in the kitchen: swans and peacocks with their long necks snapped, boars skinned but for their heads, the tusks still bloody from combat, spring lambs, calves, pigs, among the woodland kill of deer, hare, squirrel, doves, quail, grouse, lark. Some came with an arrow in the heart or in one eye; the spit-boys fought the smaller pluckers for the arrows.

She could not scour this pot clean with a brush. Clean it as she might, the image remained at the bottom: the prince with an arrow of fire in one eye, killed like an animal by a hunter crowned with horns and a black, bloody moon. She could not grasp the image whole, peel it away from the pot, carry it in her hands to show to anyone. It existed only in her head, and to get it out of her head into someone else's was the urgent task at hand. A pot needed to be cleaned. What was in her head must come out.

Language did not immediately suggest itself. Like all the lesser minions in constant turmoil subject to the whims of sounds, she responded to anything. Her name was the one necessity. Other words had temporary value. She matched the sound of a voice with the face which needed her: A blackened pan, an expression, told her everything she needed to know. Of the flurry of words that accompanied the pan, one or two might be useful. An outstretched hand with a hot roll out of the oven — a dove that had not kept its shape, or had lost its currant eyes — spoke. An upraised hand, spoon, knife, spoke. A sidelong glance out of a spit-boy's fire-seared eyes spoke. Everything spoke. She heard what she needed to, in the crook of a finger, the angle of an elbow. It was a language she could speak.

But nothing the kitchen ever said resembled the vision she had seen in the pot. Nor did the human language, scattered constantly throughout the kitchen, suggest the death of princes. She knew vaguely of the various portions of beef or cooking wine, of herbs and greens and roots; the wood-boys spoke of chopping birch and oak and of every

kind of weather; musicians spoke of split reeds and ancient
fanfares; she knew the names of limp birds, their plumage
bloodied, their eyes misted with something they saw, that
were tossed in a heap at the pluckers' feet. She understood
the arrowhead snapped off in the breastbone, the still distant look in the eye. She could have pointed to prince and
arrow and eye. But no language she had ever heard had
formed a warning in the dirty water at the bottom of a
cauldron, and it was that language, she sensed, she needed
to speak in order to be heard. A language of wonder and
horror that not even the kitchen fire in all its phases ever
spoke.

So she listened. For the first time in her kitchen life she
picked out the threads of human voices in the ceaseless
warp and weft of sounds. She listened for a tone, a single
word, anything which might have bubbled up out of the
bottom of a pot filled with dreams, anything which had not
been tossed around in the kitchen, day in and day out, since
she had come to life beside the woodpile.

She collected scraps, much as the dogs and the peelers
did, as she followed the thread of her name through the
maze of sounds. The undercooks, when they had time between meals, seemed to talk of nothing but food.

"I grated the barest fleck of nutmeg into the raspberry
sauce," the sauce cook said, as Saro dragged a pot past him.

"A clash of tastes. A brawl," the pastry cook said.

"No, no. It encouraged the sweetness of the raspberries. A daring thing, but I chanced it."

"So I boiled the boar's head in a stock of onions and
pepper and rosemary; salt I added later, and garlic," a stew-
cook said to another, as Saro came for her stockpot. "I
debated raisins and cranberries, but decided on garlic instead, and tiny onions and tiny red potatoes. The brains and
tongue are simmering with leeks and cloves."

"Twenty-six quail," the fowl cook said, counting a pile for the head cook. "Eighteen woodcock, thirty grouse, eleven lark, thirteen wild duck."

"Pluck them," the head cook said. "Spit the grouse and woodcocks, braise the lark and quail in butter, stuff the duck with sliced oranges before they are spitted. They will be served with an orange-and-brandy sauce."

"Saro!"

Saro wrested a pan full of burnt butter and sugar from a couple of kitchen dogs. She ate the candied walnut the dogs had missed, before she filled the pan with scalding water. At a vast sink nearby, the plate-washers dipped plates rimmed with gold so gently into water they never splashed. Their hands moved slowly underwater like strange plants in a current that barely rippled the surface as they felt with their fingertips for stains. Unlike Saro in her puddle beside the drains, the plate-washers stood on dry floor; even their skirts and elbows stayed dry. Concentrating, they loosed words as carefully as they loosed plates to the dryers.

"So he took me into the keep, because no one goes there but the prince."

"No. Never the keep."

"It was dark and an owl flew at my hair. And then he kissed me. He smelled sweet, like almonds, instead of like smoke and fat, like the spit-boys. And his hands were so soft and smelled of almond oil. He was pulling my skirt up, when something moaned behind me. 'Ghosts!' he cried, and left me standing there trying to put myself back into my bodice before the ghosts did it for me. Then I heard the ghosts giggle. I stood still as an owl until I saw them against the open door. And then I screeched and chased them into the kitchen midden."

"Who were they?"

"Pair of mincers. So I don't know. He'll never ask me again, surely. He has wonderful eyes. Like bits of spring sky. I might have gotten a coin out of him, but for the brats."

"Or maybe not. They speak nicely, some, and they smell like flowers, but they take what they want, and then their eyes never see you again."

"Old Ana says she has a charm for that. You mix rosemary, lemon verbena and rose petals, and sew them into a velvet pouch and then you put it under your pillow and dream of him. And then you slide it under his pillow and he'll dream — "

"His pillow! How could I get near a hall-servant's pillow? They live up in an aerie somewhere."

"You bribe — "

"With what?"

"All right, then. You make a tiny doll of cornhusks, and steal something of his — a thread, a hair — and knot it up in a ribbon around its legs. And you say, 'No one shall untie this knot but me.' And then you bury the doll in a bowl of dried lavender. Every night for seven nights you dip your hands in the lavender and hold the doll and say that. And he'll come looking for you. He'll come. Because there will be no one else to free his legs but you. And he'll know you by the smell of lavender, which he breathes into his dreams."

"Saro!"

She found the face behind the voice at the far end of the kitchen, and she hauled a great soup kettle slowly past six vast hearths with the spit-boys crouched along them, faces red with heat and sweating, turning birds on the spits and dipping into the dripping pans to baste them. They rarely saw Saro; their eyes were for the washers and dryers, the pluckers with swans' long necks lolling across their thighs. They were wild things, living close to fire; they ate fire, sometimes, when no one was looking. Sometimes they ate birds whole off the spit, and were beaten.

They spoke tersely, voices at a pitch to carry low and clear from hearth to hearth through the babble above them.

"That one."

"Who? The bone-bundle? Her you want?"

"No, not Saro, you gizzard."

"Saro's a scrub brush. She's nothing real."

"No one's talking Saro."

"Who, then?"

"Her. Washer. Look at her hair. Golden as a duck on the spit."

"Honey."

"Honey in the mouth."

"Her. Her with the black hair."

"Boner?"

"Watch her hands, boning that hen. Watch her lift a thigh. Turn it. Twist it. Bend it back. And forth. And back. And then back, and back and back and there—thigh's loose and sliding in her hand and those fingers holding it."

"She's cutting it."

"Watch her face. Stare at her and she looks up. Eyes like smoke."

"She clouted me once with her knife handle. She's too handy with a knife."

"What'd you do to her?"

"Nothing. Just staring. Maybe I dipped my finger in the dripping. Maybe I licked it, staring at her."

"Her."

"Which?"

"The plucker."

"The skinny one? With her hair like it's full of dripping?"

"You can't see her eyes under her hair. They're like fire. She's an ember now, but she flames. She flames. And she doesn't care about ash on your fingers. The others —"

"Most others —"

"They all watch the fine clothes. The flower-eaters from upstairs. The ones who get to see the back of the King's head when they serve."

"The back of the prince's head."

"That was his boar we spitted yesterday. Big. They found his silver spearhead in its heart."

"He does magic, the prince."

"Up in his tower he does magic."

"He could have all of them. Every one of them. Even the tray-mistress."

"You gizzard."

"What magic?"

"Spells. He has books. Words he reads and then makes them into magic."

"I know what I'd do with a spell."

"Every one of them."

"Her?"

"Saro. You gizzard. Saro is a spell."

Saro, bending deep into the great wash cauldron, soapy water roiling and echoing around her as she scrubbed, found the odd words echoing in her head. *Saro is a spell. Saro is a spell.* The rest of what she had heard from the spit-boys made little more sense than the water did, sloshing in the cauldron. The washers were slightly less bewildering. Words hid something, danced around something, slid up to it and away. Something everyone knew but Saro. And whatever it was, they would not say the word for it. They said *lavender* and *ribbons*, *charms* and *spells*, *bodices*, *boning knives* and *honey*. *Chicken thighs*, and *fire* and *dreams*. But they said no word for the look in the spit-boys' watching eyes. Something lay beneath words. Something that was not a word, but which made words.

Something like her dream in the bottom of the pot. There was no word in what she saw: It made words necessary.

Saro is a spell.

Up in his tower he does magic.

He has books. Words.

Spells.

Saro is a spell.

She almost lost her balance, fell headfirst into the cauldron, trying to see herself out of the spit-boys' eyes, to see herself watching Saro, the spell. After a while the words seemed just another noise the kitchen made. But other words she kept: *Books, words, spells. Up in his tower he does magic. Out of his tower he will die.*

Up in his tower he has words.

"Saro!"

She pulled herself up, trailing water, and followed the reedy voice of the sauce cook, who had emptied the dripping-pans. He shoved the greasy, soot-coated stack at her. They were still hot; she wrapped her hand in her skirt and, hunched down, dragged them by the lowest handle. She took odd routes, under long tables, so that the cooks and the hall-servants in their purple silks, and the musicians in their reds and blacks, would not trip headlong into duck fat. Pluckers and peelers, idle for a moment, and huddled under the tables, showed little surprise at her passing. Most of them were nibbling: a pared apple, a roasted potato black with ash, a stray bone, a heel of bread. They shifted out of the way of Saro's pans, but never so far into the light to catch the cooks' attention. They spoke randomly of everything.

"My mother was a hall-servant," a thin blond girl with no front teeth said dreamily.

"She was never."

"She was. She was rich, and she was beautiful. But she died when I was born, and they didn't have room for me upstairs, so they kept me down here on the hearth. And then they forgot where I belonged. So I got lost down here. But I really belong up there."

"Saro was born in the woodpile," a boy with a runny nose said. He slapped another boy lightly. "Move your feet, you gout, let her by. Those pans are hot."

"Saro was carved out of wood," the blond girl said. "That's why she's put together like that. All clumsy and knobby. And why her face isn't finished."

"Why?" the boys demanded. There was a story in her voice, in her slowed, lilting words.

"Because one day the woodcarver, who used to be the sweeper here, but his back got so gnarly and crooked his chin sank down to his knee and he could no longer see where he was going and where he had been — one day he had a visitor."

"A what?"

"A stranger came, who stopped by the woodpile. The woodcarver couldn't see him; all he could see was his own face in shiny leather boots. But the stranger's voice was sweet as honey. 'Give me the doll you are carving, old one,' he said. 'I want to take it home for my child. I will give you money for it.' But the woodcarver wouldn't. 'You have a child,' he said to the stranger. 'This is all I have. And anyway I'm not finished with it.' And so the stranger got very angry — he was a great mage — and he said, 'Then I will give you a child of nothing, old man, since you gave my child nothing.' And the wooden doll came alive, all unpolished and knobby, with part of its face still birch bark, and that's why Saro looks unfinished."

"Ballocks," one of the boys said, after some delibera-
tion. "Tray-mistress says a milker left her there in the woodpile. Naked."

Saro tugged the trays out of the chorus of snorts and
hiccups, into an oblong of light between tables. The tray-
mistress, her shadow flung between the tables over Saro,
turned abruptly, a red rose between her teeth. She gestured
at one of the hall-servants, who nearly stepped in the
dripping-pans before he saw Saro crouched, hauling them
behind her. He drew back in horror from the grease, and
waited until she disappeared beneath the next table.

There she crawled through a game played with candle
stubs and the knucklebones of pigs. They were rolled sur-
reptitiously across the floor toward a target — the foot of an
undercook or a hall-servant — and whoever got closest won.
Whoever touched the target lost, especially if it was a hall-
servant's shoe, for then the players were usually routed, and
stubs and knuckles flew everywhere. The players, mincers
mostly, and on the edge of turning into spit-boys, waited for
Saro to pass, shaking wax and bones. They stared longingly
into her pans; some scraped crusts into the cooling grease.
They spoke little.

"Him. Pastry. He's still making diddles out of cream."

"Hit him, we're dead."

"Don't hit him, then," the player breathed. "Throw."

"Wait for Saro. She's in the way."

"Wish they'd eat and be done. I could eat ham the size
of a chair. A whole cow."

"An ox."

"They never leave much on the bird bones."

"There's stuffing. Sage, onion, liver — enough to fill a
barn."

"I could eat it all."

"Throw."

The knucklebone came within a thumbprint of the pastry cook's soft leather shoe. Saro heard their breaths gather and still, then fall again, together, as the cook, festooning a cake with loops and swags, shifted and kicked the bone away, never noticing.

"We could all die."

"Him?"

"Head hall-servant? Hit his velvet shoe with a pig knuckle? We'll all die."

"He'll swoon first. Throw."

Saro emerged into a huddle of musicians. "Fanfares," they said, "first and second, and third, the one Lefeber wrote, and then, with the first wine, the ancient fanfare of the House, and with the second wine, the Silvan fanfare, which you always take too fast, and there is a rest before the second cadence. Then — " Then they noticed what Saro pulled and they scattered hastily, draping the pennants and ribbons on their long golden horns carefully over their arms.

She reached the drains finally. She poured scalding water into the dripping-pans, and finished the soup kettle while they soaked. Nothing in its dark, wet hollows revealed anything but more dark iron, more water. She tipped it at last, poured the water down the drain, and set it to dry until it was needed. She turned to begin the dripping pans, and, bending, found herself eye to eye with the sweeper.

Hunched and shrunken, he seemed in danger of turning into the woodcarver in the plucker's tale, who had carved Saro out of birch. He seldom spoke, only nibbled what he could salvage out of her pots. His broom, a knobby, crooked staff with a fan of straw on one end, seemed a part of him, worn down to the bone and shiny with age.

He spoke. "You're coming alive," he said. "Your eyes are listening." He touched his fingers to his lips. "Don't let them see. You're someone's secret. Don't let them find you alive."

He helped soap and water and debris down into the drain and swept on. Saro stared a moment into water, looking for her listening eyes. Seeing only the task at hand, she put her hand to the task.

Eight

Talis rode into the green wood.

It was morning; gold light poured among the trees. The leaves hung still, shining green flames; if a wind rose, it seemed they would ring together like fine glass. Sun laid soft, warm hands on Talis' hair; he lifted his face to it blindly, felt light like sweet wine on his lips. He whispered, "I don't know your name." The leaves did not speak. She was there, he felt, flowing ahead of him in the light, fading into shadow just as he glimpsed her in his unbroken lens. Crossing a stream, he saw the reflection of her face among leaves, just before his horse's hoof broke the reflection into a thousand crystal pieces. She had been there, in the oak's shadow; there, beside the slender, graceful birch.

He could not find the place where she had appeared to him; every sunlit glint of water, every outstretched oak bough seemed to promise her. He rode slowly, aimlessly, wandering through light and shadow, seeing one clear world and one blurred, and her in neither of them. He did not know if he rode deep into the wood, or circled near its boundary; he did not care. He had not been in the wood since he had killed the boar. Movement still strained him; until then it was all he could do to climb the stairs in the keep and look for her there, among the shadows, though she did not come again. But he had dreamed of her that morning, standing in a ring of birch, saying his name. He felt her touch and woke, and her hand turned into light.

He rode with the sun until noon. The still trees rose aloof and solitary around him, holding secrets, he sensed, but they would tell him nothing. He heard horns, from far away; he recognized the fanfares. Wind rose, blowing out of his own world, breaking the enchanted silence. He turned toward the horns, rode out of the wood onto Hunter's Field.

He did not go to eat in the hall; he went up into the keep again, limping a little, haunted by her shadow. Someone noticed his absence: He was interrupted by game hens seasoned with rosemary, tiny potatoes stuffed with mushrooms, soup of leeks and cream, a braided loaf of dark sweet bread, a compote of cherries in brandy. He recognized the girl who brought it.

"You didn't drop it this time," he commented. She didn't smile. He studied her face a moment. The guards standing beside the door glanced at her, puzzled by his interest, then looked disinterestedly away. She was wax-pale, chafed with water. All the joints in her fingers seemed to be in odd places, out of proportion to one another, and far too long. Her face, without changing expression, seemed to change constantly, as if the position of her features was never quite fixed, never quite aligned. He tried to see the color of her eyes and failed, since her eyes had moved beyond him unexpectedly, to look through the open door.

He glanced back, wondering what had drawn her attention. A shadow had crossed the wall, he guessed. Or, on the table, the tiny diamonds in his grinding cloth had caught fire.

He said impulsively, "Set the tray on the table."

He followed her in, watching her face turn slightly, her attention drawn here, there. The window moved as she set the tray down; light spilled suddenly over it. She did not seem surprised by that, or by the restless ghosts roaming in and out of the whitewash. Perhaps, he guessed, nothing surprised her, or everything did. She turned her head suddenly, surprising him: She caught his eyes in an intense, unblinking gaze that was like a question in a private language.

Her lips moved a little; she turned her head swiftly, her face hidden again. He realized that she had stared straight at him, and he still could not remember the color of her eyes.

She went out again, quickly and noiselessly, left him staring at the door.

"I'm seeing things," he murmured, "without my lenses."

Several hours later, he was interrupted by the King.

He heard Burne announce himself, cursing the stairs before he entered. Talis fitted the new lens into the frame and slid the lenses on. His brother's face, distinct in one eye and imprecise in the other, seemed relatively calm in both.

"I came to see if you were still alive up here," Burne said. "You've been far too quiet. No lightning bolts, no explosions. The physician said he had not seen you today."

"I went riding," Talis said. "And then I came up here to finish my lens."

"I don't know why he bothers to give you advice, when you don't even listen to me."

Talis eyed him. He pulled the lenses off, cleared a place on the table and sat. "I listen to you," he said mildly. "Now what have I done?"

"You're spending all your time in this place, for one thing. It's stifling with memories. Look at that." They watched silently as the shadow of a boy with a torn cloak and a handful of arrows edged to the window and knelt to shoot. "I don't," Burne said tightly, "know how you stand it up here."

"They're not my memories," Talis said gently. "I only see the magic."

Burne averted his eyes from the walls abruptly, afraid, Talis guessed, or recognizing one of the figures. He frowned down at his lens, wishing he could share some of Burne's past instead of only his memories: the ghostly king Talis had never known, the horror of Hunter's Field. Burne had told him tales, as everyone had. Someone living, he realized early, who had not been scarred by the siege or haunted by memory, was valuable to the storytellers. Having no memories of his own, he became their receptacle for memory, and, with his untroubled past, for hope. He waited silently, knowing what hope Burne had in him now.

"They never found who did that sorcery?" Burne asked, still troubled by the keep. "Not even the mages know, in Chaumenard?"

"No."

"Some stranger, then, hired by Riven of Kardeth."

"Maybe. But it was a very powerful piece of sorcery. Mages that powerful don't bother to hide their names."

"An evil mage might," Burne suggested.

"But where is he? She? Why would an evil mage not use such power again, or a good mage use it in the first place?"

Burne shook his head. "No good mage would have done it. Mages' lives are not separate from their magics. Isn't that what they teach you at the school?"

"Which explains my accidents," Talis said wryly. "I lead a reprehensible life."

"You know what I mean. Anyway. Outside of trying to kill me now and then, the life you lead is far too respectable. This house is full of company, and you're shut up here in this keep ignoring half a dozen young women who didn't come to look at my greying hair. It's high time you married."

"I just came down and killed a boar for you," Talis protested. "And broke my lenses. Isn't that enough to ask of me for a while?"

"I won't have heirs," Burne said. "You'll inherit Pelucir, and you need to give this house another heir. We lost a king when you were born; no telling, with our history, when we'll lose another."

Talis dropped his face in his hands, murmuring. He emerged almost as quickly, to gaze at Burne. "It was that boar. It frightened you, seeing me in danger."

"It terrified me," Burne admitted. "Seeing you spellbound, oblivious to shouts, hounds barking, horses, birds, trumpets, the boar splashing straight at you across the stream, and you in another world . . ."

Talis opened his mouth, closed it. Words filled his mouth. *Three white deer*, he wanted to say to Burne. *Three white hounds. Three white horses and the Queen of the Wood with her hair like dying oak leaves, and her voice like mourning doves* . . . He felt Burne's attention, focused, acute, as it could be when he sensed something concealed from him.

"Talis," the King said, and Talis slid off the table, still silent. A white fire caught his eye; he detached the new lens from the frame and picked up the grinding cloth.

"I met someone," he said finally, working at the lens. "In the wood."

"Who?"

"A woman. She distracted me. The hunt startled her away."

"Well, who was she?"

"I don't know. She didn't tell me her name. We barely talked. I fell off my horse and then I saw three white deer, then three white hounds and then three white horses. And then—and then she let me see her face. She was very—she was more beautiful than—"

The King grunted. "They always are," he said unexpectedly. "The women you meet in a wood, or a meadow, or beside water, whose names you never know. Far more beautiful than those you know too well."

Talis held the lens to his eye. "It wasn't like that."

"It never is." Burne met his brother's exasperated eye within the lens. "You may lose your heart to a dozen women in a dozen woods, but you will marry a woman with a name and a family suitable to your rank, not some nameless someone without sense enough to tell you to get out of the way of a charging boar."

"It wasn't," Talis said tensely, "a moment when common sense seemed applicable. And if you tell me such moments never are, I will pick up this table and throw it out the window. If the window stands still long enough." He ground the lens furiously a moment; Burne watched silently. Talis' hand slowed; he said finally, without looking up, "What does it matter? I killed it, anyway."

"And I sent you away for two years to learn to think like that," Burne marvelled. He dropped a hand on Talis' shoulder. "I don't know who you met in the wood, but she sounds dangerous. Dangerously feebleminded, if nothing else. Tomorrow, I want you to join us for the hunt again. And stay with it this time."

"All right." He listened to Burne linger a moment, then cross the room, open the door, before he raised his head. "Burne." The King looked back at him. "It really wasn't like that at all. It was like nothing I have ever known."

He heard his brother's answer in the silence Burne left behind: *It always is.*

He finished the lens as the sun setting beyond the yard and the rampart wall flooded the window with light. The light faded; the window moved, showed him the green and dusky blur of wood upon the hill. He put the lens to his eye, saw the wood clearly, a shadowy, secret place in the twilight. He looked at it for a long time, until the trees began fading and night rode toward him down the hill. He lit lamps, then, and fitted the glass into the thin gold frame, slid the finished lenses on.

He went blind suddenly, both lenses filled with black. Wind rose within the tower, a strange, fierce whirl that nearly blew him off balance. He heard papers fly, books snap open, pages riffling and tearing. The black wind grew stronger; things of glass and wood crashed, broke. Something struck him. He stumbled, still blind, swallowing blood, and brought himself up against a corner of the stone hearth. Bewildered, shaking, he pulled the lenses off.

His eyes filled with fire. Then he saw the horn woven into the flames, and the black moon of a hundred tales riding among them. He backed against the hearth, a sound shaking out of him. His heart beat so raggedly, he could scarcely breathe. There seemed nothing human in the fur-masked eyes gazing back at him. Hounds, enormous and shadow-black, swarmed around the Hunter; their noiseless claws struck sparks on the stones. Still holding Talis' eyes, the Hunter lifted a fistful of torn pages to his teeth, bit into them. Blood ran down his mouth, as if words bled. Talis swallowed, his throat paper-dry. All the sorcery he had ever learned seemed crumpled in the Hunter's hand, all the words he knew. He found one, as sweat from the flames burned down his face, and only the stones against his back held him on his feet; the word itself sounded choked, barely distinguishable. "Why?"

The Hunter raised his hand. "Drawkcab," he said. A book as ancient as Pelucir and heavy as a stone flew past him and slammed into Talis. His head snapped against the hearth; his lungs filled with fire instead of air. As he slid to his knees, he felt the Hunter's hand in his hair, pulling his head back. Desperate for air, he breathed only words, dry, torn parchment, spells he had spoken forced backward into his mouth, until he grew blind again and winds roared through him, though he could not find a thimbleful of air.

Then a wind out of nowhere, as fierce and wild as if it had blown down from the mountains of Chaumenard, dragged him to his feet. Scraps of words flew out of him; his eyes flickered open. He saw the Hunter blur and flow into black flames of horn and hand and waning moon; the wind, singing like a wolf, flattened the hounds into shadows among the ghosts. Outside, guards clamored at the wind, heaved against the door, pounded on it when it would not budge. Hands, barely visible, like windblown snow, gripped Talis, lifted him. He struggled and choked again, the keep reeling around him. The window, framing the green wood, rattled in the eerie whine and shattered; Talis, slumped in the wind's strange hold, felt himself blown through broken glass. He glimpsed the keep growing oddly smaller, sending a long trail of torn scrolls and parchment in the wake of the wind, while, from the broken floor below, a white mist of owls fled the opposite direction. Then he saw the vast twilight sky wheeling toward him, and he closed his eyes.

He woke again to birds crying. On his hands and knees, in a litter of dry parchment, he retched paper and words, then sagged onto his back, racked and sobbing for air. He felt a hand touch him and panicked, rolling wildly. Earth, leaf mold, scented the air; he opened his eyes, stared senselessly at the ground.

"Leaves." His voice, raw with pain, sounded hardly human. "I thought it was more words."

He heard a voice spun thin as cobweb. "Talis."

He lifted his head. A stranger crouched among the roots of an oak tree on the hill overlooking Hunter's Field.

He had white, shaggy hair, eyes an odd blur of light and dark. He wore a torn, grass-stained tunic; his feet were bare. He looked lean, craggy, weathered, both old and timeless, like a tree or a stone, and as wild as anything that lived among them. He had ridden the wind to rescue Talis from the keep: a mage, Talis knew, but no one he had ever met.

He straightened, and wiped tears off his face with the back of his fist. His fingers were locked around something; he opened his hand, amazed. "I brought my lenses." He put them on, and saw the expression change on the hard, worn face.

"You," the mage said grimly. He closed his eyes briefly, opened them, as if he expected Talis to disappear. "I thought so."

"Who are you?" Talis asked. "You know me. I don't know you." Then the answer came to him; he felt the spidery touch of wonder glide over him. "I know you."

"Yes."

"Atrix Wolfe."

"I saw you on the mountain," the mage said. "You were looking for me. You climbed too high and dropped your lenses."

Talis stared at him. "But you're here. In Pelucir. You saved my life."

The mage's face tightened. "Barely." He turned, gave a hawk's glance across the field. Talis shifted to kneel beside him. On the field nothing moved but the twilight trembling on it like a gathering army of ghosts.

Talis swallowed dryly; a word he had swallowed licked like fire at his throat. "Is he still here?"

"Yes."

"Do you know what he is?"

"Yes."

"He is the Hunter of Hunter's Field."

"Yes."

"He killed my father." Talis was still trembling, watching things drift, eluding definition, on the shadowy field. "I recognized him from tales. The black moon, the burning horns . . ." He tensed. "He is in the castle with Burne."

Atrix Wolfe shook his head. "The Hunter is no longer in the keep."

Talis looked at him. "You know him, too . . . What made you come to Pelucir? As if you knew I needed help."

"I knew you needed help," the mage said. He seemed to sense Talis' confusion, and turned his attention from the field. His eyes, the bruised grey of the twilight, met Talis' eyes. He studied the prince a moment, as expressionless as stone. Then expression welled into his eyes, like water breaking through ice, and he looked back across the field. "I was trying to find my spellbook. When I learned you had it, I knew you were in trouble."

"How —"

"Hedrix told me you had it. After I dreamed that you were using it. A young mage wearing lenses . . ."

"You dreamed —" Talis' voice sharpened with amazement. "But why? You've hardly been seen since before I was born. Why did you appear twice out of nowhere to help me?"

"I don't know. Our paths keep crossing. I used magic for the first time in twenty years, to show the wolf to you on the mountain . . . And again, today . . . I came a long way to cross your path in Pelucir."

The wood was soundless now, leaves as still in the twilight as if they were spellbound. The full moon, rising among the great, tangled branches of the oak, made Talis' throat close. He whispered, "He tried to kill me with words."

"He summoned me with them."

Talis shuddered. He touched his lenses, trying to see more clearly in the night closing around him. "Why you? Was he hidden in the keep all this time, or did he just appear there, knowing you would come for the book?"

"Where exactly did you find it?"

"In a mop closet."

The mage turned again to look at him. "A mop closet."

"We had been instructed to hide. I saw your book on the shelf and hid in it. Something about it made me curious. I asked Hedrix if I could take it with me back to Pelucir. You saw me," he added, remembering, "just before I left." He touched his lenses again; his hand shook, left them slightly askew. "Why did you keep the book there?"

"I buried it in solid stone," Atrix Wolfe said. "It found its way to you. And then to Pelucir."

Wordless, Talis watched the mage; the mage watched the field. Horns sounded into the twilight, bright, urgent, drawing Talis' eyes to the curve of battlement wall against the sky, the oblongs of fire spiralling up the round towers, the flickering wash of torchlight across the upper window of the keep, where someone within searched frantically among the ruins. He said softly, "The spells don't match the words."

"That's why I buried it."

Talis drew breath soundlessly, so not to disturb what was piecing itself so tenuously together. "Why?" The word, too, was soundless.

The mage rose beside the tree. Oak boughs rose above his head, the bright moon burning within them. Talis felt the blood flow out of his face, at a memory or a sudden vision. "Why are my spells so twisted?" Atrix Wolfe said. "Why have I hidden myself since you were born? Why was it you on the mountain, looking for me, you who found my book?"

He nodded, his eyes on the castle across the field. "I want and I do not want an answer to that. Why it worked its way out of stone to come here. To this place. To you."

He looked down at Talis, still kneeling, hunched over himself now, like an animal gathering into itself, avoiding the hunter's eye. Talis heard himself say calmly, though his skin felt taut, chilled in the moonlight, and his body had grown still as leaves, as air within the wood, "How do you know the Hunter of Hunter's Field?"

"I made him."

The words struck like a blow; for an instant Talis thought the sudden, sharp pound of his heart would send the birds crying into the air. But the wood was undisturbed around him. He rose noiselessly. The mage, all his attention suddenly riveted on the field, did not stop him when he began to run.

A horn, pure and solitary within the wood, sounded the beginning of the hunt.

Nine

The fanfare signalling the beginning of supper refused to sound.

The tray-mistress and hall-servants listened for it absently, standing beside steaming silver bowls of soup with tiny saffron biscuits shaped like fish floating in it. Behind them, undercooks took long loaves smelling of onion and basil out of the ovens, and wrapped them snugly in linens to keep them hot. Haunches of ham crackled and split on the spits, juices flowing into the dripping-pans; the spit-boys' lean cheeks were pouched with stolen bits of skin. Saro, deep in her cauldron, heard nothing but water sloshing and echoing around her. A small copper tower of saucepans stood at her elbow, some sticky with boiled frosting, others with congealing rice flavored with lemon and mint. She was washing them one by one, oblivious to the small fingers scooping rice or frosting, whichever she uncovered, from the top of the tower.

As she straightened to reach for a dirty pan, noises came clearer: a laugh from the servants, the tray-mistress's tart voice, the head cook snapping at someone, a squeal from an apprentice burning a finger. She scrubbed the pan, straightened again to lay it on the floor to drain. Silence, as if everyone were listening at once, was broken by a servant, and another laugh. She took a pan, and plunged again into water floating with rice kernels and bubbles. She flicked rice out, reappearing briefly. Silence again. She finished the pan, laid it on the floor, heard a murmuring and the head cook's tense voice.

"The soup — the soup! The fish will melt."

She reached for a frosted pan; the tray-mistress said grimly, "They're all here, they didn't hunt, so why aren't they eating? Unless the musicians forgot how to play."

Saro bent again, felt for the pan in the gummy water. More rice than soap floated past her face; the water was cooling. She finished the pan, laid it down.

"Someone should go," the tray-mistress said.

Saro turned, heaving against the cauldron. Water slapped over the side toward the drains. A mincer, his breath sugary, pushed with her, wanting to see the water spill.

"I'll go," the head servant said, straightening a gold-trimmed cuff fussily. "The musicians may know."

The head cook studied the fish biscuits in a soup bowl and groaned. The cauldron tipped; water poured into the drains. In the unaccustomed silence everyone, having nothing else to do, looked at Saro. Then their eyes moved to one another. The head cook threw a boning knife across the room. It stuck in a rafter above a spit-boy's head; the spit-boys, their chewing suspended, looked impressed.

"Beat them, someone," the tray-mistress demanded. "They're eating the hams."

"What does it matter?" the head cook asked fretfully. "No one else is."

"Be patient."

"Pah." He sniffed. "What's burning?"

An apprentice sprinted for the fires. Saro poured hot water from the kettle into the cauldron as the head servant came back down the steps. They all looked at him; the head cook made a sound like water about to boil.

"Well?"

The head servant looked bewildered. "Apparently the prince is missing."

"Missing!" the head cook shouted, and Saro stopped abruptly, hot water splashing over her hands, down her skirt. "He's up in the keep."

"No — "

"Then he blew himself away."

"No." The servant paused. "Well. Maybe. The guard — "

"What guard?"

"The keep guard. They said they heard strange noises. They tried to enter. The door was — impossible. Then some strange mage blew past them. The noise died; they were able to enter. The prince was gone."

"What of supper?" the head cook demanded. "The bread is cooling, the fish are melting, the — "

"The beans are scorching," the apprentice said, heaving pots off the fires. Then he flung open an oven door, peered into the blackness. "The swans are burning."

The head cook turned away, moaning. The tray-mistress hissed with fierce curiosity at the head servant, "Go back up. See what more they say."

Saro, moving more slowly than usual, stared into the wash-cauldron before she began filling it. She saw nothing but a few grains of rice clinging to the bottom. Habit moved her; she was not used to doing nothing. She poured hot water in it. Still she saw no sign, in the dark rippling, of prince or mage. She added soap, more water, and began to scrub again.

She had nearly finished the saucepans before the head servant returned. By then the head cook had flung a few more things; the mincers, peelers and pluckers had taken refuge under the tables; the undercooks had opened a bottle of brandy and were passing it back and forth.

"The mage," the head servant said, pale, "must have been taken, too. So the King says. The King is baleful."

The cooks and undercooks stared at him. The tray-mistress reached for the brandy bottle. "What," she asked ominously, "do you mean 'taken'? The mage took, he wasn't taken. The mage stole away the prince."

"The King says not. The King says — " He paused, drawing breath; the tray-mistress upended the brandy and swigged. "The King has sent messengers to the mages in Chaumenard. He bade them ride until their horses fell, then run until they could only walk, then walk until they could only crawl, but to get themselves to Chaumenard before they drew another breath. He is calling a hunt."

The head cook, morosely beheading black meringue swans, interrupted incredulously. "A hunt! At this hour? What can they hunt in the dark?"

"A woman."

They stared at him again, mute. The tray-mistress clutched the brandy to her bosom; the head cook's knife hung suspended over the charred curved neck of a swan. Saro, bent deep into her cauldron, heard the word echo oddly in the hollows. *Woman*, the eddying water whispered. *Woman, woman, a woman.*

"What woman?" The tray-mistress's voice cracked.

"The King said the prince came upon her in the wood. She held him spellbound until he was nearly killed by the boar he killed." At the hearths, the spit-boys exchanged glances, their eyes hooded, reflecting fire. "Nameless, she was. So Prince Talis told the King. And beautiful. The King said that word as if it meant everything but. So the wood is where he will search for Prince Talis tonight."

Still the kitchen was silent, spellbound by the tale. The woman herself seemed to waver in and out of light and shadow as all their dreaming gazes conjured her. Even the head cook saw her, in memory or in desire; her shadow fell over the tray-mistress's face. Saro, listening to their strange silence, saw only her own dark reflection at the bottom of the cauldron. The tray-mistress said abruptly, shaking them all awake, "Not everyone will hunt. After the King rides, those left here will want their supper."

"Such as it is," the head cook muttered.

"And those returning from the hunt later will want theirs." The head cook, his face loosening as he calculated two suppers, hot and cold, got to his feet.

"Reheat the soup," he commanded. "Remove the fish. Chop green onions to float in the bowls with a pinch of paprika."

"Choppers!" an undercook roared, and choppers scattered like mice from under the table.

The head cook's eye fell on the brandy bottle. "Take hot brandy and spiced wine to the hunters in the yard, and thin slices of apple and game pie — quickly!"

"Quickly!" the tray-mistress echoed, rattling trays. The musicians clustered, devising appropriate accompaniment to send off a hasty and desperate hunt. Saro, stacking the last of the copper pans, found her tower disappear as apprentices whisked away clean pans to heat the brandy and wine. Someone took the last pan out of her hand. She leaned a moment against the cauldron, wet, idle, listening for her name. Voices shouted of the hams, and the loaves of bread, and of eggs to make more meringue, of onions and bowls, trays and platters and music, but no one cried Saro. Weariness dragged at her bones; heat from the ovens and open fires laid heavy hands across her eyes. Still listening, for there was always another pot, she dreamed a little; a word echoed not through the kitchen but in her head.

Woman. A woman. Woman.

"Saro!"

Her body stiffened. But her eyes refused to open. She searched blindly, her face turning to catch the sound of her name. *Saro*, she heard again. But she did not recognize the voice.

She opened her eyes, her hands dropping to the rim of the cauldron to hold herself upright, for she was suddenly so tired that her body wanted to melt like water onto the stones.

The kitchen was oddly silent, dark but for beds of embers glowing, fuming fiercely in the hearths. It seemed empty, without even a mincer asleep under a table. She could hear, as from a distant room, or another world, the familiar, constant tangle of voices and noises, the nightly skirmish that produced the feast. In the shadows, something moved.

She stared, motionless, still gripping the cauldron. There was no kitchen-word for what she saw. The great crown of horns seemed to sweep the rafters with fire; though, as in a dream, nothing burned except the dark moon within them. The man's face was shadowy, indistinct; it was his eyes she remembered, staring at her out of the cauldron, seeing her. Huge black hounds swarmed restlessly around him, but made no sound. She felt her heart pulse in her throat; her head went back a little as he took a step toward her. But nothing else moved; all her bones were frozen except her finger bones, which gripped the iron cauldron like iron. She could not even blink; her eyes were strained wide, transfixed by the cauldron's dream coming at her across the kitchen.

"Saro."

She opened her eyes. She felt wet stone under her face, her hip, her hands. Someone held half an onion under her nose. She took a whiff and pushed herself up. She looked around, bewildered; faces ringed her: pluckers, boners, washers, the sweeper. The tray-mistress loomed over them. Her voice, small and faraway at first, broke some sound barrier and boomed abruptly.

"Give her soup, and some bread, and milk. She's forgotten to eat, she has not even that much sense. She'll work herself to death one of these days. Get her on her feet again; the pots are starting to pile."

A plate-washer and the smoky-eyed boner helped her sit, brought her food. The sweeper swept himself away, then swept back again and dropped a meringue swan, unburned but missing a tail, into her lap. The boner said sharply to the staring crowd around her, "Leave her be, or I'll bone you, you little gamecocks."

"But what happened to her?"

"She fainted," the plate-washer said. "It's a wonder she didn't fall headfirst in the cauldron." She patted Saro's shoulder as the crowd dispersed, snickering at the thought of Saro's legs dangling out of her wash water. "Poor shadowy thing. She's nothing but bones and skin, pale and damp like a mushroom. Yet she's always working like something demented." She was silent a little, she and the boner both were, gazing at Saro like cats as she ate, eyes like wood smoke, eyes like hazelnuts, fixed and unblinking. "Look at her," the washer whispered. "Look at her face. Things move around in it. She never looks the same twice."

"Like she's not meant to be looked at," the boner breathed.

"To be seen. Or not meant to be found."

Saro dropped bread in her lap. Soup would have followed, but the boner took it quickly, for Saro had begun to shake. She held herself, drew her knees up, pushed herself against the cauldron, her eyes flicking around the kitchen, searching for the night-hunter among the apprentices putting the morning's sweet rolls into the oven, among the scrawny mincers gnawing bread and bones under the table, among the spit-boys, their faces almost as wild and secret as the face in her vision. *Found*, she heard again in her head, and knew the word meant her as surely as her name. The horned hunter had isolated her from all the noises and bodies and words in the kitchen. He had looked at her and seen her.

Found.

"Eat," the washer urged, holding the bowl to Saro's lips. "It'll be a long night, what with the hunters out. You'll need to stay on your feet."

The first supper, shorter than usual and even more chaotic, ate up clean pots, spit them out dirty, as the head cook replaced, reheated, improvised. Saro scrubbed, rinsed, drew fresh water, scrubbed again. But nothing could wash away the dark vision in her head, the feeling that she no longer belonged to the kitchen, one of its familiars like the mincers or the cats, that no one outside would claim or recognize or even give a thought to. She belonged in the night-hunter's eyes. He had found her.

As he would find Prince Talis.

He would find her again.

She could feel her throat trying to make a sound; nothing came. She could not hide in the kitchen among the pluckers and choppers. They would fall into their dreams, leave her behind, alone, in the still dark hours when no one called her name. When not even the fire spoke. The kitchen began to calm itself behind her, musicians and servants, cooks and undercooks, eating wearily at tables, everyone else in a corner, at a hearth, under a table nibbling leftover ham, heels of bread, broken swans filled with fruit. But still she scrubbed, for there were pots, frying pans, dripping-pans, heaped crazily around her. Saro and her noises were the kitchen's voice, familiar, constant; no one paid attention to her clattering. Even the boner, eating bits of ham off the tip of her boning knife, had forgotten her. As they would forget her at the night's end, drift away and leave her to the shadows.

To the hunter.

"They're not back yet," a musician said fretfully, standing at one of the butcher's tables behind her. "I haven't heard the horns. They always sound the horns when they leave the wood, and again at the gate."

"If he's with a woman, the prince," another said wryly, "he might not be found until morning."

"If he's off chasing a dream through the wood, then what happened to the mage? What happened in the keep?"

Saro immersed half of herself and a half-dozen saucepans in steaming, soapy water. Then she straightened again, holding the sides of the cauldron, remembering silence, the smell of owls, the hint of secrets.

Up in the keep he does magic . . .

But he was gone. The keep was empty . . .

She reached again for pots.

She finished the last pot long after the plate-washers had finished. The royal hunt had not returned. The night seemed soundless, as if it, too, listened for horns. The pastry cooks finished the sweetbreads and butter pastry for the morning. Some left, others drowsed, or drank wine and talked. The spit-boys lay beside their fires, watching them, feeding them now and then, as aware as lovers of every changing mood, every shadow. The younglings had gone to sleep; the washers, waiting for the second supper, had fallen asleep at the tables with their heads in their arms. Even the tray-mistress drowsed, only grunting a little when Saro laid the last gleaming dripping-pan on the stack.

She turned and looked at the kitchen.

No one looked back at her. She was an iron cauldron, an apron, a table, something so familiar no one bothered noticing it, not even when it was stalked by a bloody moon above a hunter's masked face.

She would hear the horns from the keep, slip back into the kitchen before anyone could use a pot to want it washed. She would be safe within the prince's magical room; the hunter would never find her there.

A flame vanished into an ember, cast a shadow across a spit-boy's face as he raised it to see what moved in the night, what long hair, what skirt. But it was nothing, only Saro, and he forgot about her even before she faded out of the firelight.

Ten

~≈~

Talis ran.

At first he scarcely heard the hunting horns. They seemed echoes of a battle fought the night he was born, a call to the bloody hunt on Hunter's Field. He ran into a past that shaped itself around him into something living. All the memories of the siege were no longer shadows, ghosts, tales. The ghosts had names; they had feverish, bloodshot eyes; they had torn cloaks and worn boots and broken pieces of armor. They raised a tattered banner: the boar of Pelucir, tusks rampant, swords crossed above its head, a crown above the swords. His father rode among the ghosts. Burne rode beside him, and so did his uncles, his young cousins. Ravens followed them, and the Shadow of the Wolf.

He opened the gate, the survivors said, and we rode out behind him into the winter night to meet Riven of Kardeth. To rout him, or die in the field like warriors, not like starving rats hiding behind the walls.

He was tall, your father, like you. Dark-haired, like you. A web of silver over the dark. More like your brother in temperament. He liked movement, noise, the hunt and the feast. And generous: He liked to give, he took pride in his giving—a hound, a fine hunter, a blade, a piece of land.

The Queen—she was the one for the music and the books. She never cared to hunt, but she loved to ride. She played a little pipe of rosewood and gold. She died, almost to the moment, when he died. They saw him fall, and then they heard her give a great cry of sorrow and she died, there, with you beside her in the bed.

You have her gentleness, her smile. She gave your brother her fair hair, and you her eyes. They loved her, your brother and the King. Their eyes followed her. Light-moving, she was, like a bird, and graceful as water. Water never makes a movement without grace.

The Hunter rode with ravens on his horns.

His mouth ran with blood. He ate the last words of the dying. He harvested their names, so that when dawn stretched across the field, taut with silence, like an unbeaten drum, the dead were unrecognizable.

They watched us from the wood, until we brought in our dead. And then they came down and got their own. What they knew was theirs. They were gone by nightfall. The rest, the snow and the hungry animals got.

Your father died. That's enough for you to know.

He died on Hunter's Field.

We brought him in as we fled inside. We were able to recognize him. All night we watched.

By dawn there was nothing alive on Hunter's Field but ravens.

The Hunter vanished with the moon. As if he had been a dream. No one knows who made him.

Riven of Kardeth paid some sorcerer to make him. He could find no honorable way to defeat Pelucir.

There was a ring on your father's right hand that the Queen gave him. We recognized him by that.

She cried sorrow.

The Hunter killed him, and she cried sorrow and died. . . .

Talis sensed the Wolf behind him.

It was a power far stronger, more complex than his

own. It moved silently as shadow, a nebulous presence slipping from leaf to leaf after him; it knew his name. His body faltered; his knee twisted suddenly, throwing him off balance. As he fell he melted into his shadow, cast by the moon in a net of boughs. Shadow, he picked himself up and limped to an oak, then molded himself like bark around its trunk.

Talis.

The horn sounded again, still solitary, very close. He shifted upward along the curve of the first branch, clung there like some great dark moth. Something moved beneath him, shape pulling itself free from leaf and shadow and bark. At first he thought it was the mage. Moonlight struck it, and Talis nearly lost hold of both the tree and his shifted shape. What rode below was made of leaves, its upturned face layered and molded into fierce and elegant lines. One hand rested on a bare, pearl-black mane, the other held a spiral of silver; the fingers were long and graceful and green as birch leaves. Hair, rippling, heavy, the gold of dead oak leaves, shook back down broad oak-molded shoulders; eyes, shadowy green, seemed to pick Talis out of the bark.

He raised the horn and blew.

Talis dropped out of the tree, ran, half-man, half-shadow, deeper into the wood. The rider followed, a broken leaf, a tiny, snapped twig, a sigh of wind. Other horns sounded then, a distant weave of trumpet and hunting horn: the ghosts, Talis thought, of the One Great Hunt. No one else hunted at night. No one human. He felt himself pulling into human shape then, his eyes burning, his throat swelling, burning with horror. He put his wrist against his mouth to stifle sound, and heard his footsteps, beating through the dead leaves. *Atrix Wolfe*, they said. *Atrix Wolfe*. The name pursued him, ran beside him, casting its white shadow in the moonlight.

He cleared his mind stubbornly, dreading the touch of

the leaf-shaped fingers, the inhuman eyes, almost as much
as the White Wolf's charred-silver eyes. He pulled his
weary, struggling body around a huge rotting log, and then
lay among its ruins, half-shadow, half crumbled, lifeless
wood. The rider, a brush of leaves and moonlight, passed
him. Talis drew himself into a pool of shadow, then, under a
touch of moonlight, became a hare, frozen still, listening.
Trumpets sounded again, a bright, urgent fanfare of warning to the wood. He moved to the end of the log, turned to
hide within its hollow heart, and found himself face to face
with the White Wolf.

Talis.

Startled out of shape, he became human. He whirled to
run. Something caught his wrist — a human touch. He
stumbled, wrenched his knee again, and caught himself
against the the side of the log. He leaned against it, catching
his breath, one hand tight against his ribs, watching helplessly as the mage took shape in front of him.

"Talis," Atrix Wolfe breathed. Talis, his throat burning
again with too many words, tried to twist free; the mage
pulled him back, held him against the wood, held his eyes. "I
am not the only thing you have to run from in this wood,
and you are running blind. Listen to — " He disappeared
then, into all the words that Talis could not say, pouring out
of him in a sudden, furious flare of silver. Talis, amazed at
himself, straightened; the mage shaped himself out of light
before he could run again. "Talis — " He flung up a hand as
Talis shouted a silent question; light whiter than moonlight
parted against the mage's hand, scarred the trees around
them. Talis sagged against the dead oak, shaken by the
uncontrolled power; it held no answer, he realized, no language but a cry.

He found words finally and used them. "Why? Why
you?" He gripped the mage suddenly, and, stumbling off

balance, bore him back until a tree stopped them. "Why you, Atrix Wolfe?" Trumpets sounded at the name. Ghosts, Talis thought furiously; the mage, his face turning toward them, looked suddenly haunted. "Was it betrayal? Dishonor? What did Riven of Kardeth promise you in return?"

"If I had taken what he promised me," the mage said tersely, "your father would be alive, and both Pelucir and Chaumenard would belong to Kardeth." He slid like a shadow out of Talis' hands, left him holding wood. "It was nothing that simple."

"No," Talis said, staring into a tree bole. He turned his head, trembling, still clinging to the tree, searching the worn, powerful face for a hint of answer. "It wouldn't have been. Anything that simple." He heard horns again, an untuned chord, and realized suddenly that all the ghosts were in his head. He whispered, cold with horror, "Burne."

"Yes."

"Burne. He's hunting at night, here —"

"He is hunting you," Atrix said. He did not move, but something of him — a thought, an expression — reached between them in a silent plea. "Talis — Listen —"

"He will be killed!" Talis did not recognize his own voice. Birds whirled, crying, out of the trees. "Like our father!"

"Talis!"

His name shocked through him, like a voice cutting through a dream to wake him, silence him, focus him. He turned, still backed against the tree, wondering what he had roused with his last cry. He said tightly, more quietly, "I'm listening."

"Find Burne, take him out of this wood, back to the castle —"

"Across Hunter's Field? How many dead kings do you want on your mind?"

"What do you think I have been doing for twenty years?" Atrix Wolfe asked him. "I have been running as hard and fast as I could away from this. And here I am again, in the dark of night on the edge of Hunter's Field, while a king of Pelucir rides to meet my making. You brought me back into this nightmare, Talis Pelucir. You summoned the Hunter and the Wolf, out of twenty years of silence. He has haunted me every moment of those years. If I thought my death would put an end to him now, I would not waste another breath on my life. But I can't be certain, and I will not leave Pelucir to face him alone again."

Talis stared at him. "He's your spell. Under your power."

"I made him," the mage said tautly. "Yes. But I do not understand anymore what I made that night on Hunter's Field."

Talis was silent. He touched his lenses, trying to see the harrowed face more clearly in the moonlight. The hunting horns of Pelucir sounded again; they called his name with every note. He nodded once, his face bloodless, stunned expressionless in the silvery light. "I will take Burne out of here. But how will you fight this — How can you — What magic can you use against yourself? Where in all they teach in Chaumenard, do they teach you this?"

"It is the first thing you learn," the mage said wearily. "To see. To name. To become what you have named." He turned his head then, not toward the hunters but toward the still trees bordering the field. Talis lurched away from the log, his heart hammering. Atrix held up a hand: *Be still*, the gesture said, and Talis calmed himself, finding in the ancient, crumbling wood he left, a still place in which to think. "Go," Atrix breathed, and Talis said, not moving, as the mage eased into moonlight and disappeared,

"Where, in all of Pelucir, can we run from you?"

Moonlight shaped a stag running toward the field. Watching, still motionless, Talis heard horns cry a fanfare for the hart. His breath caught. The stag was white as moonlight and as silent; its horns seemed molded of gold. It cast a white shadow. Hounds slipped after it, night-black and crying fire, leaving bloody prints beneath the trees.

He could not see the Hunter. But he saw the horns of the white stag flame suddenly. It stumbled, caught itself, and ran on, crowned with fire. Trumpets cried again, bright, too close, slightly out of tune. Talis, swallowing horror like a bitter root, slipped into shadows, ran, a shadow of himself, toward the human company.

He heard the howl of the Wolf.

It cried as if to be heard across Pelucir, clear to the mountains of Chaumenard, summoning, warning. The desperation in the cry dragged at Talis. He stopped, bewildered with impulses. If the mage dies, he thought wildly, we are dead. Burne, and I, and the hunters of Pelucir. If I go to help him, I will be helping the one who made the thing that will kill us all. If I don't, we are dead. If I do . . . we are dead, he realized, calmer now, his hands clenched. There is nothing I can do. But if he runs away from us, and the Hunter pursues him, we may still live. . . .

He turned, slipped quietly through the trees to find the royal hunt, to flee the wood with Burne before the King understood what ghosts haunted Pelucir that night. What dark making. He heard the King's horns again, hesitant in the odd stillness, but ringing true. They were answered; the King's hunt spread raggedly in front of him, he guessed, and, taking his shape so that they would recognize him, he began to run again.

Moonlight flooded the wood, a silvery mist within a tiny clearing, a circle of birch, a disc of grass, a disc of starry sky. Talis ran into it before he realized that, like the hare in moonlight, he was visible to anything that chanced to look. But he reached the other side without setting hounds baying, without the dark moon rising in his path. Still, motion in the motionless wood snagged his eye as he crossed the edge of the circle: a figure emerging out of pale birch, pointing toward him with the gesture of windblown leaves. Moonlight, he told himself, as his head snapped back at it, and the cold sweat pricked his face. Moonlight, it seemed, and leaves: nothing more. Leaves sighed behind him and were still. He quickened his pace.

The King's horns sounded; he swung toward them with relief. Something brushed across his shoulder; he spun wildly, sound leaping out of him. Leaves, he thought, nothing but leaves. It did not reassure him as he ran, recklessly now, limping a little, in and out of the moonspun shadows. They rustled behind him and were still again. He looked back in spite of himself, and saw the shadows of three hounds, soundless, blood-red and flowing like fire after him.

"Burne!" he shouted desperately, wanting only to find him before the Hunter did. "Burne!" Only horns answered. *I'm mage*, he thought, fleeing hounds out of another world. *I can do better than this*.

Drawkcab, a voice said in his head, in warning, but he insisted, arguing with himself: Not every spell is twisted. Some things are simple. Some things are the face they wear. The name they bear.

He concentrated, but found no spells in his head for the problem, only crazed questions. If he became invisible, could the invisible hounds see him? If he became invisible and still, stopped moving, would their fiery shadows, passing over him, mold his shape out of air? If he stopped moving, he knew, he would simply fall, lie on the ground and hear nothing, see nothing, until he had found enough air in the world to breathe, and the pain stopped hammering through him. If he became invisible, would he still feel pain?

A horn called behind him. He looked back, not wanting to look back, knowing what he would see. Three horses as white as moonlight with shadows of moonlight galloped behind the hounds.

"Burne!" he cried again. It came out more plea than shout, but, to his astonishment, he heard his brother's voice.

"Talis!"

Talis, the wood murmured around him.

"I can't," he breathed in answer. He saw movement in the trees ahead, muted color, horses disappearing into shadow. The King's trumpets sounded again, a noisy, chaotic fanfare.

"Talis! Where are you?"

"Here," he called to the flickering riders, the odd spark of silver the moonlight struck on metal. The word held little sound. The hounds flowed past him noiselessly, effortlessly; he felt a chill at his back, the breath of a horse with eyes as pale as ice.

He saw Burne then, riding toward him down a long shaft of moonlight. "Talis!" the King shouted. "Talis!" He rode hard, close to his horse's neck, dodging trees; Talis saw him clearly, running just as hard, but the distance between them never seemed to shorten. Burne began to grow smaller as he rode, his voice more distant.

"Burne!"

"Talis!" the King cried, from a long way, a world away, as he galloped down the moonlight. Then he dissolved into a pale light. Talis, murmuring wordlessly with despair, stumbled and lost his balance. He saw the white shadow of hooves rising above him; the ground struck him before they did.

Eleven

Saro stood in the empty keep.

Something had happened, her eye told her. The light from the one unbroken oil lamp on the mantel showed her a broken bowl and torn books scattered in the empty hearth. What had been on the table lay in pieces all over the floor; the table itself, a massive block of wood with legs as fat as brandy kegs, stood on its head. A rafter had fallen, hung by one end into the room. Pages wrenched out of books covered the floor; the books themselves, spines twisted, bindings ripped away, lay in a pool of water spilled from smashed buckets.

She stood very still, scarcely breathing, trying to become as unobtrusive as shadow, as the door post beside her, cracked where the guards had broken the latch. The single window stared out at the full moon; moonlight limned jagged pieces of glass still clinging to the frame. She heard no sound within the keep; not even the owls spoke.

She took a step forward into the room, felt water lap against her bare feet. Words floated in the water, scraps of letters, sentences. A letter, graceful and tangled around itself, glinted gold in the light, floated next to her foot. She picked it up carefully, flattened it in her palm and studied it. It said nothing. But it was important, a key to things Prince Talis knew, a kind of magic in itself. She put it carefully into her pocket.

This was no place to hide. Something had swept through this room, tearing apart everything in sight. Even the gold and silver cups had been twisted, dented. Even the silver branch of candles lay flattened on the floor, among pieces of mirror and glittering scraps of the prince's cloth. There was not a single book left whole.

She took another step into the room. What came here once could come again. It had already found the mage and the prince, she guessed. It could find her, in this lonely wreck of a room. And no one would ever know that she was gone. At least, in the kitchen, they might cry her name before she was taken. Here, no owls were left to question anything.

A sigh of breeze through the window spun flame long and ragged through the air; something in what had been shadow caught her eye before the flame subsided. She took another step, another, mouse-quiet, trying not to disturb the water she walked through, while words floated to her feet and clung. There was a book. One book, still whole, in the litter of ripped pages, empty bindings.

Up in the keep he does magic.
He has books. Words he reads and then makes into magic.
Saro is a spell.

The book lay in the underside of the table. It was closed; its plain leather cover said nothing. Inside, it might speak of cows, or recipes for sauces. But it was the only book left whole in the devastated room. Maybe because it spoke of cows. Or maybe because the language it spoke was stronger than what had destroyed everything else in the keep.

She knelt in the mingling of water and lamp oil beside the table, and picked up the book. It seemed oddly light for its size. She opened it. It spoke on every page she turned. Sometimes there were drawings that spoke in ways she understood: herbs, flowers, an upside-down cup, an odd animal that the hunters had never brought back from the wood. Something in it, maybe, could tell her by any means — by fire, or ash, or water, by the position of birds flying across the moon, or the pattern of rings in the wood chopped for the woodpile — how to say her vision: the prince with his lens shattered by an arrow of light. How to speak.

She closed the book. A stronger breeze sent the light shivering, then extinguished it as she rose. She froze, the book held tight under her arm. The window shifted abruptly, left stone wall where the moonlight had been. She waited in the sudden dark, feeling her heartbeat in her throat, unable to move even to fall, though her bones seemed fluid under her skin, and waves of terror prickled over her. But nothing came. After a long time, the window shifted again, finding the moon. She followed the path of moonlight in the dark water to the door.

A voice cried from the hall, as she entered the kitchen again. The tray-mistress lifted her head from the table, stared senselessly down at it, as if wondering what it was doing under her face. Saro slipped the book beneath a cupboard not far from the cauldron, that held stacks of aprons, scrub brushes, towels, soap. The book had survived the fury in the keep; nothing in the kitchen was likely to harm it. Turning, she saw a spit-boy's eyes on her. But they were dazed, drugged with dreams: Saro, carrying a book into the kitchen, could only be another dream.

The tray-mistress rose, grabbed a tray and banged it with a wooden spoon. The undercooks, sprawled wearily among wine bottles, lifted pale faces; apprentices and wood-boys, called by the trumpets at the gate, slipped in from the night. The head cook followed them, tight-faced and alert, as though he never needed sleep. Apprentices kicked the mincers and choppers under the table; reluctantly they emerged, blinking at the sudden leap of fire as spit-boys heaved logs onto the drowsing embers.

A cold supper, the head cook said, for the returning hunters. Hams were sliced, and cold roast fowl, and long loaves of bread; a simmering soup of shredded beets was ladled out of cauldrons to cool. Lettuces and boiled potatoes and scallions were chopped and mixed with vinegar, pepper, rosemary and dill. Dark, dense cakes heavy with nuts and dried cherries, redolent with brandy, were pulled from the cooling ovens. Whipped cream and flaked, toasted hazelnuts frosted the cakes.

The hall-servants began to gather in the kitchen. Undercooks funnelled rosettes of minced pear onto the soup. Musicians, returning from the hall, picked at ham and fowl, and shook their heads groggily at the head-cook's questions.

No, the King did not want music at this supper.

No, Prince Talis had not been found.

The tray-mistress, arranging parsley around the ham, and wreaths of rosemary around the roast fowl, bade the servants grimly to find out what they could. Bewildered, disturbed, they piled news onto their trays along with dirty plates.

There was magic in the wood, that night. A ghostly hunt had ridden with the King's hunt, invisible, but calling with sweet and melancholy horns. A white stag with burning horns had fled through the trees ahead of the hunt. There was no sign of the mage. But the King had seen Prince Talis running toward him down a long shaft of moonlight.

And then he disappeared.

"Taken," the head cook grunted when he heard this. The tray-mistress sat down slowly, fanning herself with a tray. Saro, scrubbing the heavy soup cauldrons, scrubbed as noiselessly as possible.

"Taken!" the tray-mistress breathed. "By what?"

"The wood," the head cook said. The hall-servants glanced at one another. Trees, the shadows of trees, seemed to flicker on the kitchen walls.

"He was hunted down and taken," a servant said softly. "The King says by the woman in the wood. He says little else, except to curse her and the wood. All he can do now is wait for help from Chaumenard."

"And the mage?" the head cook demanded. "The one who rescued Prince Talis in the keep?"

The servant shook his head. "Gone. Or fighting in the wood, still. Some say they heard a strange howling, and saw flashing lights and other things among the trees. The King said it was not to the woman Prince Talis ran, but toward the King. She took the prince in spite of himself."

"And no one saw her?"

"Only moonlight, when he disappeared, and the wood."

"Where," the tray-mistress asked in bewilderment, "would she have taken him?"

The question lingered in a sudden silence. The head cook gazed at the tray-mistress speculatively. The spit-boys glanced at one another, sharing an unspoken thought. Everyone else looked in all directions: at the gleam in a copper pot, at fire, at dried herbs and cheeses strung across the rafters. Eyes smoldered, or grew vague. Saro's hands slowed; a kingdom of light and airy bubbles and undulating shadow seemed to shape itself in her water.

"There," the head cook said softly, "you have it."

"Have what?"

"The question. In a nutshell."

"Is that where she took him? Into an acorn? Into

moonlight? How will the King or the mage find him to bring him home?"

"I don't know. The mage will know." The head cook got to his feet restively, compelled by the King finishing roast meats and potatoes in oil and rosemary above them. "Send up the cakes and cheese. And more brandy," he said to the servants. "Not that he'll sleep tonight, the King." His mouth roiled suddenly over a word; he looked ready to spit it. "His father dead early, his brother lost, and him childless — sorcery is nibbling away at Pelucir."

"Prince Talis will return," the tray-mistress said in horror. "He must!"

The head cook, studying the cakes, did not answer. "Lay them in brandy and light it," he said to the apprentices. "Take the ham bones and simmer them overnight in cloves and bay for soup."

Saro finished the last of the cake pans, from which the sweeper had picked cherries clinging to the bottom. Her hands felt cold, even in the hot water; her heart pounded raggedly, trying to say something. Prince Talis, lost in the wood . . . The prince with the oak behind him, in her vision, the tangle of boughs, the tangle of horns . . . *Now*, her heart said urgently. *Now. Now. Now.* Her hands sped through pots; she moved to the cries of her name so swiftly that under-cooks, finding her suddenly beside them, blinked in surprise and almost saw her. The King sent down for more brandy. Servants brought back half-eaten cake. Mincers, pluckers, boners, choppers, stood around the tables, eating scraps with their eyes shut. Servants brought down the last of the plates, the last of the news.

The King, they said, will hunt again. Tomorrow, and the next day and the next, and every day after that until the prince is found.

Slowly the kitchen quieted. The head cook sat up late

with the tray-mistress and the head servant, sharing a bottle of brandy in which a pear, like some great golden pearl, hung suspended. The spit-boys slept at the hearths, waking only as the flames dwindled under the soup stock, and the simmering in their dreams began to fade. The small children had disappeared with the dogs under the tables. Saro, scrubbing the spits clean, and the sweetbread pans, worked quietly, listening to murmurings behind her as the brandy bottle tilted, and the brandy's slow rich ooze spoke of pears and liquid gold.

"Terrible," the tray-mistress breathed. "Terrible. It brings to mind that dreadful winter. The tales that came into the kitchen then . . ."

"That's what they say up there." The head servant sipped his brandy. "That's what they thought attacked the prince."

"But the mage killed it," the tray-mistress said anxiously. "Didn't he? So it can't have been."

"It was a spell of the prince's that caused him trouble. And they say the wind that rescued him leaped and howled like a wolf. Like the wolf the hunters heard in the wood."

"Atrix Wolfe," the head cook said abruptly. Then he shook his head. "No. Not in Pelucir."

"They say that's what the King saw in his cup before the hunt. The monster of the winter siege. But it came out of the prince's misbegotten spellbook. And a woman taking Talis is far different. Trouble, yes, but not the nightmare the King feared."

"A terrible winter," the tray-mistress repeated. Her elbows thumped on the table; a joint in her stool shrilled. "That head cook left at the end of the siege. He was a broken man, having to cook up feasts of beans and roots, and boil soups out of bird bones so empty they whistled. I washed plates, then. I did everything — the kitchen-brats fell ill with hunger and did nothing but cry. The spit-boys all left to fight. There was little for them to spit, and little more than that to burn. And then to win, and lose so much at once . . . It was a bitter victory. Bitter as the winter, but for the new prince, who only cried once, they said, and then grew calm and sweet, with his mother's eyes, watching everything in wonder. To lose Prince Talis would be — He's all the King has, now."

"There's two," the head cook said precisely, pouring more brandy. "You've got to keep that in mind."

"Two what?"

"Sides. Two tales. Two to keep track of."

The head servant nodded solemnly, his eyes wide, bloodshot. "The mage may already have dispatched the prince's spell. Leaving us with the prince and the lady in the wood. Which — "

"Which is a different thing to look at than a deadly spell," the head cook said. "There's the mage and the prince's spell. And there's the prince and the lady of the wood. Mage and spell will take care of themselves: We don't need to worry about that anymore."

Water, heaving onto stone, whirling into the drain, pulled their eyes to it, and then to Saro.

"She's like a . . ." the tray-mistress said; her voice trailed away. The head cook nodded.

"Not quite . . ." He yawned. The head servant finished looking at Saro and stared down at the table.

"Like a thing made, not born. Made to scrub pots."

The tray-mistress tapped her temple significantly. "Pots," she said, "are what she understands. Not feelings. Or words. Not dreams and restlessness and hankerings, like the other girls. Not rising above the kitchen. She barely knows where she is. Nor does she care."

The head cook grunted, losing interest. Saro let the

cauldron stand upright, her eyes on the shadow under the cupboard where the book lay hidden. She sat down near it, tilted her head back, watching fire under her eyelids. The voices soothed her; as long as she heard them, she would not see the night-hunter stalking the kitchen. But as long as she heard them, she could not open the book. It was not a pot, it did not belong in her hands, it belonged to the prince in his keep. They would take it from her, she understood clearly, for it was not a pot. Not what they were used to. She sat quite still behind the cauldron until voices finally ceased. Chairs spoke to stone; shod feet to stone and stairs. The door opened; night stood a moment at the doorway, dark and crowned with stars. Then the door closed.

She drew the book from the shadows.

The fire spoke; wood snapped, pitch hissed. A spit-boy snored. Someone under the table whimpered with dreams. A dog barked in the yard. The soup bones simmered; the candle in the sconce over Saro's head fluttered in a stray breeze. Everything spoke, it seemed, except the book, which remained, under her searching eyes, completely silent. Still she studied it, turning its pages as gently and carefully as the washers handled the King's gold-edged plate. Some of the paper crumbled under her fingers, so thin and delicate were the broad pages that survived the windstorm in the keep. But none of the writing crumbled. It was dark and clear, in neat rows on every page, and what it said she could not imagine. She held the writing up to her ear and listened; she stroked it with her fingertips. It remained as mute as she.

Fire guttered, drew shadows around her. A spit-boy woke, murmuring to the fire, shifted to drop a piece of wood on it, his eyes still closed. Still the shadows remained; night gathered itself in corners, in pools of darkness. Saro swallowed dryly. Something pricked behind her eyes. A word she could not say burned in her throat. What pricked in her eyes rolled down her face suddenly. She caught it, startled. Mincers did this, when spit-boys batted at them with scarred knuckles for coming too close to their fires. Plate-washers did it sometimes, silently dropping pearls of water from their eyes into the wash water. Another drop fell, to her horror, on the page; a word blurred under it. She blotted it carefully with her hair, everything else being, as always, slightly damp. The word had not changed shape.

She wiped her eyes. There was a task at hand, and this was the task: to learn to speak the silent language of the prince's book. If its words were spells, and she, Saro, was a spell, then maybe she would find herself within these neat lines. She must learn to say magic in magic ways, since she had no other voice. Or perhaps, in those incomprehensible pages, she would find a voice.

She might find anything at all. She felt another odd thing inside her, as if she had swallowed the light from the candle, and it shone for a moment through her: For that moment she saw beyond the pots. Then she bent over the book again, felt it slowly become familiar, as all the ceaseless random voices in the kitchen. It became simply one more voice that called her name.

She sat with it until the moon set beyond the high kitchen windows and the candle guttered out. Then she slid the book back among the shadows. With one hand stretched out toward it, like the spit-boys slept beside their fires, she curled on the stones behind the cauldron full of odd whispers and visions, and fell asleep.

Twelve

Atrix fought the Hunter until he vanished with the moon. The Hunter pursued the White Wolf through the wood into the open field; the Wolf hid among the ghosts of Hunter's Field. Now he was a sword in the hand of a warrior, until the warrior fell, and the sword dropped to the ground, and the moonstruck blade reflected the Hunter's searching eyes. The mage became fire clinging to the bloody rag wrapped around an arrow flying toward the highest window in the keep. The window became an eye; the eye blinked, shifted. The arrow struck solid stone, dropped into the snow. The ghostly flame went out; the mage fled. Remembering the living, he lured the Hunter again and again away from the castle. As raven, he tried to fly toward Chaumenard, draw the Hunter after him. The Hunter's hounds became ravens, drove Atrix back onto the field, back toward the wood.

The Hunter refused to be driven from the field, and Atrix refused to leave without him. He harried the Hunter constantly out of shape, so that those within the castle would not see him. When Burne Pelucir's hunt rode slowly out of the wood near midnight and blew a weary fanfare to the gate, the Hunter and his horse and hounds were night-shadows, pinned motionless and paper-thin, on the ground the hunters rode across.

Talis was not with them.

The Hunter would not speak, nor would he let Atrix past his raven's eyes into his mind. When the moon grew small and cold among the stars, his hounds fanned the field, hurried the mage across it. Atrix, trying to see into his making, find a name for it behind the Hunter's eyes, saw only the most bitter of memories: the King of Pelucir, the shaft of the banner of Pelucir driven through his heart, dragged down among the hounds.

"What are you?" he cried, losing his hold of the Hunter, who seemed to have no substance but power. But the Hunter did not speak until the moon set.

Then his dead moon-eyes held Atrix's and he said, "Sorrow," and vanished.

Atrix, driven uphill to the edge of the wood, took his own shape, trembling with exhaustion. His own shape refused to do anything for a while but lie on the oak leaves. He waited, but the Hunter did not return. He listened for Talis, scented the wood like a wolf, searched it with his mind.

The wood was empty.

He closed his eyes and saw Talis' father fall, the dark hounds gather over him. "Sorrow," he whispered, and rose wearily, and carried that word with him to Burne Pelucir.

He found Burne sitting alone in the empty hall. Guards stood at every door. Guests looking as haggard as the King murmured in the corridors beyond, red-eyed, drinking wine, casting fretful glances into the silent hall. Servants hovered in doorways, waiting to be summoned. Atrix appeared out of torch smoke, as dishevelled and worn as the hunters. The guards shouted sorcery; the hunters raised what came to hand, but without conviction, since Burne, sitting hunched at a table with his chin on his fist, only stared at Atrix dourly.

"Who are you?"

"Atrix Wolfe."

Burne's brows rose in amazement. He stood after a moment, quelled the noise behind him with a shout. He added another shout to the hall-servants. "Wine! Sit down," he added to Atrix. "We may be suspicious of sorcery in Pelucir, but you have a name as ancient as gold. Did you just come from Chaumenard? Or are you the mage who blew into the keep to help Talis?"

"Both," Atrix said. A servant brought wine, cups; behind him the doorways and corridors were soundless. Atrix touched the cup poured for him, did not pick it up. "I came to tell you something. I told Talis last night. He — "

"Did you find him?" Burne interrupted.

"I sent him to find you, after I took him out of the keep. We heard your hunting horns in the wood. You never saw him?"

"I saw him," Burne said, "but only for a moment." He lifted his cup, drank deeply. Atrix stared at his own dark reflection in the polished wood, waiting, motionless, unblinking, until he heard the metal hit wood, and then he closed his eyes.

"And then what happened to him?"

"I almost reached him." Burne sighed. "Almost. He was running toward me, down a shaft of moonlight. But he fell, and the light closed over him, and he disappeared." Atrix opened his eyes. "She took him," Burne finished grimly, and drank again.

"She," Atrix said blankly.

"The woman he saw in the wood."

Atrix moved his gaze from his shadow to the King's weary face. "What woman?"

"Beautiful, he said she was. Beautiful," Burne repeated sourly. "Nameless, coming out of the trees, she cast a spell on him and nearly got him killed."

"Last night?" Atrix asked, his thoughts tangling

suddenly in moonlit paths, nameless woodland enchantments, dangers that had nothing to do with him.

"No — days ago. He's been dazed ever since. And now she has him."

"Who has him? Has him where?"

"How would I know? I hoped he had hit his head when he fell off his horse and imagined her. But no." He brooded at his wine a moment, then at Atrix. "You," he said hopefully. "You know all the paths and ways of magic. You could find him."

"I don't understand," Atrix said. He had grown tense, struggling to envision ways and paths of magic that did not end in horror on Hunter's Field, but went beyond it to unnamed realms, into which a prince of Pelucir had vanished. Light and shadow shifted within the hall; an unlit torch flamed suddenly; tapestries on the walls stirred and settled. Beside him, Burne had stopped breathing. "Talis wasn't running from a woman, last night. He was running — "

"He ran from her," Burne said. "And she took him." He spoke carefully, his eyes on the unpredictable shadows around him. "That's all I know. The winter siege of Hunter's Field did not leave me much besides Talis. If I lose him, I lose — I will not lose him. I cannot. You came out of nowhere to rescue him last night from his own sorcery. I'll give whatever you ask, if you'll rescue him again."

"I don't — "

"That's what it was, wasn't it?" Burne interrupted. His hands locked suddenly around his cup; he did not look at Atrix, or at what Atrix's thoughts disturbed around them. "In the keep? Just one of his dangerous accidents."

Atrix grew still. He felt the tension in the silence behind him, then; he scarcely heard breath or thought. In the uncertain mingling of light and smoke and shadow, something threw its own shadow across the hall. Atrix watched it form, nebulous and imprecise, out of all the fears that the strange magics and mysteries had aroused. They felt the Hunter's presence, he realized. They knew, and they did not want to know they knew, what they feared. They wanted Atrix to tell them anything but that, anything but legend, terror, mystery, death, anything but that the tales spun out of Hunter's Field had no ending yet. Burne stared into his cup, waiting; his fear lay like a streak of dark between them, cast by nothing visible.

Atrix relinquished truth for the moment; the air grew brighter, calmed itself, shadows attached themselves to visible objects. "Talis brought a book of mine from Chaumenard."

He heard the King's breath again. "Yes."

"It seems simple, but it's very complex, and very dangerous."

"I knew it," Burne said, his voice loosening. "I told him so." His hands loosened around his cup; he drank. Atrix heard movements, murmuring again behind them. "He's had other accidents; he nearly — Never mind." He looked at Atrix finally. "What did he conjure up? They say it tore the room apart."

"Something he could not control."

"But you can. If it's still around."

"Yes," Atrix promised flatly. "I will control it. If it's still around. But the sorcery in the keep has nothing to do with a woman in the wood. I don't know how to rescue him from moonlight."

"It's like him," Burne sighed, "to leap from the bog into the morass. He didn't seem to fear her, though; he seemed — under some enchantment. It was impossible for him to be reasonable. Even to admit she may not be real."

"Real."

Burne shifted, his mouth tightening. "Human," he said

reluctantly, as if to say what she was not somehow made her real. He shook his head. "Such things don't happen to princes of Pelucir."

"And yet," Atrix said, watching the King's expression, "you have seen her."

"I have not."

"You don't question her existence, even though she may be living in light."

The King shifted again, uncomfortable with wonder, or with memory. "There are always tales . . . Besides, I saw him vanish."

"Do you remember anything else he said about her?"

"Other than that she is as beautiful as the sun and the moon and the stars? No. I wouldn't listen to him. I didn't want to hear such things from him. I need him to fall in love with someone human, highborn and healthy, to give Pelucir heirs. Not a woman who wanders around in a wood without a name, who lives in moonlight and is probably as ancient as the moon. Something about deer."

"What?"

"White deer. And three white hounds. She was hunting, too, that day he saw her. And three — " A sound came out of Atrix, and the King stopped.

"Three white — " He stared at Burne, seeing the wood again, not the terrible, leafless wood he knew from the winter siege, but the sweet, secret green wood of his dreams. "Three white deer, three white hounds, three white horses, and the woman — "

"Yes," Burne said sharply. "What is it? A song?"

"A dream." Atrix shivered a little, chilled with wonder, remembering the empty oval of her face, the arrow striking his heart, so that he woke suddenly before he dreamed of pain. "She rides through my dreams. But I have never seen her face."

"Talis did," Burne said grimly. "He wasn't dreaming."

"There's always a shadow where her face should be, though her hair and her voice are beautiful. She raises her bow and cries 'Sorrow,' and shoots me."

"She does what?" Burne stared at him. "She shoots you? Does she kill you?"

"I don't know. It's a dream — I haven't died, yet."

"It's not a dream, and Talis is in it, too." The King's voice was rising. "Did she shoot him, too? What is she? Some nightmare out of the wood?"

Atrix rose restively. "I don't know." He paced a little, aware of men moving out of the path of his shadow, in case he kept his sorcery there. He came back to Burne's side, leaned against the table, trying to find his way back into the dream without dreaming. "She is not a nightmare. No. She is a mystery . . ." His voice faded; he heard the Hunter again, just before he had vanished at dawn. *Sorrow*, he had said, and then the moon set.

The hall had grown soundless again around Atrix. He stirred, seeing but not knowing what he saw, and quelling the terrible, urgent impatience he felt at his ignorance.

"What is it?" Burne asked tautly.

"I don't know . . . I need the prince's lenses."

"He saw her face through them," Burne sighed. "I knew she meant trouble. Help me. Please. He is all that Pelucir has left."

"I will find him," Atrix said. He stood silently again, trying to remember, past one night too full of sorcery and twenty barren years, what nameless shapes of beauty and mystery he had encountered that might point toward an undiscovered land. He saw the wood again in two worlds: one lifeless, dark, blanched with winter, the other drenched with light, green leaves trembling in a sweet, soundless wind, and both on the edge of Hunter's Field.

Burne seemed to glimpse them, too, as if Atrix's dreams and nightmares fashioned themselves just beyond the morning light. "Why," he asked slowly, "would you dream in Chaumenard of a wood in Pelucir?"

Atrix shook his head wordlessly, having no answer Burne wanted to hear. "I will find Talis," he promised again. "But it's her wood, not yours, I must enter, and I do not know the way."

"You'll find it," Burne said. "You can do anything. You are Atrix Wolfe."

He turned in his chair, gestured to the waiting crowd, and they entered, tentatively, uncertainly, to meet the legend of Chaumenard who was, when the King turned back to him, no longer there.

Thirteen

Talis woke.

He woke in a dream of the wood, he thought dazedly, raising his head. No true oak grew that shade of gold, though that gold was what the eye looked for in the golden oak. No true grass felt so silken, no true shadow laid a swath of such dark velvet across it. No true leaves burned that tender and fiery green in the morning light. The long grass glittered under a web of jewels. He moved his outflung hand, touched a jewel and it melted down his finger like a tear.

Three white hounds.

He stared at the tear of dew, remembering.

Three white horses.

One white stag with golden horns, trying to outrun the fire in its horns.

The black moon rising in a crown of horns.

Atrix Wolfe.

He rolled onto his back, blinking at the sudden light glancing across his lenses. White birds soared out of the oak into light. He dropped his lenses on the grass, hid his eyes in the crook of his arm and watched the Hunter, blood running from his mouth, eating the page out of a book.

Eating words.

For a moment, Talis tasted the dry, cloying parchment again in his own mouth. *He tried to kill me with words....*

He heard horns.

He recognized them immediately: Burne, hunting again after last night's wearying hunt. How had it ended? Moonlight . . . Burne riding toward him down a long shaft of moonlight . . . Something had happened; he had fallen; Burne had missed him in the dark. So the King had returned to the wood.

Talis slid his lenses on and rose. He felt, and knew he looked as if he had been dragged for a mile or two behind a horse. The horns sounded close. He waited, standing under the oak, searching the wood for movement, color. An arrow, snicking past him, struck the tree above his shoulder. His brows lifted; his lenses slid. The tree gave a sudden shudder, leaves rustling, whispering. Talis ducked behind it. The deer the arrow hunted burst out of some bushes, ran deeper into the wood.

He saw the hunters then, fanning out in front of him, some pursuing the deer, others searching the wood. As he stepped out from behind the oak, he saw Burne.

The King rode toward him; he stepped clear of the tree's shadow, calling urgently as his brother rode past him: "Burne!" The King turned his mount abruptly beneath the oak. Talis saw his expression, a mingling of hope and confusion, change as he circled among the flickering shadows. He said wearily to their lanky, fair-haired cousin Ambris, who reined his mount where Talis had stood a heartbeat earlier,

"She must have some reason for taking him. Surely she'll give us some sign, some message. She wouldn't just take him, for the sake of taking something human. Would she?" He sounded unconvinced. Talis, standing between the horses, said through clenched teeth: "Burne."

"I don't know," Ambris said heavily. "Didn't the mage tell you?"

"He didn't know, either. All she ever did was shoot him, in his dreams."

"Burne," Talis said, amazed; his voice shook.

"Well, then," Ambris said. "She might have taken him for any reason. Any reason at all. He's young and likely looking, it's spring —"

"Ambris," Burne said irritably.

"Well, you asked. I don't quite understand what you think she is. If you're thinking she is what I think you're thinking, and she took him lightly and carelessly as they take humans, then we might be old men before she tires of him."

"Burne," Talis whispered. Not even the King's horse flicked an ear in his direction.

"Fine," Burne said explosively. "As long as she sets him loose before I die. What are you saying? That I shouldn't bother looking for him?"

"No, but —"

"I warned him. I tried to. You don't offer your heart to what shapes itself out of water or light or white birch. But would he listen?"

"They never do," Ambris said, and Burne's face reddened; his mouth clamped shut on a word. Ambris added hastily, "It's likely she wants Talis for some important purpose, and she'll give us a message. Or he will. She is not a monster, the mage told you, but a mystery."

Talis felt his bones melt into air and light with horror. "Burne!" he screamed, trying to hold the King's reins. "Am I dead?" He might have been the leaves talking above Burne's head, the wind trying to grip the silver-scrolled reins. *I'm a ghost*, he thought, cold with terror. *Like the ghosts of Hunter's Field. This is how they feel . . . Except that they must remember dying, and I can't remember. . . .*

"What exactly did Talis say about her?" Ambris asked.

Message, Talis thought desperately. *Message*.

"She was more beautiful than dreams and that was why he didn't hear the boar charging him, or the hounds, or the horns, or all of us shouting at him to move."

Ambris grunted. "So that was it. She could have warned him. Did she want him dead?"

"How do I know?" Burne shouted. "Why would she want Talis dead?"

"I don't know," Ambris said. "Why would she ride without a face through a mage's dreams? I don't understand any of this. I'm just trying to —"

"Do you think she was luring him to his death?"

"I don't think," Ambris said carefully, "we should assume anything beyond what you saw. He ran down a shaft of moonlight and was taken by the wood. He must be here somewhere."

"Do you think," Burne said starkly, "it's because of all the animals we kill?"

"No," Ambris said emphatically. "I don't. Nor the trees we cut and burn. So don't ask that."

Burne's face lifted toward the leaves that rustled now and then, like slow, ancient breathing; boughs creaked like old bones. "Do you think — " Talis heard him ask tentatively as he knelt on the ground in front of the King's horse.

"No," Ambris said again.

Stones could speak, if he could hold them; the ground could speak, if he traced his name through dead leaves. He brushed at them; they moved, responding to his touch in one world or the other. *Burne,* he began to write.

"When the mages come from Chaumenard," Ambris said, "they'll help Atrix Wolfe, they'll know what to do."

"Mages," Burne said tightly. "Nothing they taught him could save him from this."

"Maybe you're wrong," Ambris argued. "Maybe he'll find a way to save himself."

Burne grunted dubiously. Leaves lifted, swirled over Talis' word. "What can she want?" Burne asked helplessly. "At least she could tell us that." He urged his horse forward abruptly, over what was left of his name. Talis, crouched stubbornly in the horse's path as it rode through him, caught a glimpse through its eyes of leaves and light and a pale, misty shadow on the air that humans could not see.

I ran down a shaft of moonlight, he thought, trembling with the aftermath of horror. *I was taken by the wood. Maybe I'm not dead.* Wonder eased through him, then; he leaned against the oak, looking around him at the bright, golden world. *Maybe I'm in her wood . . .*

"But," he asked the oak, "where is she?"

The oak did not answer. The hunt had passed; he heard its horns in the distance. He searched for some sign, some message, saw only the dreaming oak, the birch with its leaves of green fire.

"I don't," he whispered, "even know your name."

"I am the Queen of the Wood," she said. He whirled and saw her standing where a birch had been. Or had he only imagined the birch? "That is all you need to know. My name is as old as this wood; it is never spoken in your world."

He was mute, gazing at her, wondering, if he touched her hair, would it burn like fire, wondering what her eyes had seen to make them at once so powerful and so troubled. He had bridged worlds; he could not seem to bridge, with a touch, the step between them. He knelt finally, scarcely knowing what he did, gathered cobweb cloth blowing between his hands, and raised it to his lips.

"Tell me," he said, his eyes closed, her silk against his mouth, "what you want."

"And you will do it."

"Yes."

He felt her hands light, like small birds, on his shoulders, and he stood, dazed again by the light in her hair, in her eyes. "You ran from me last night," she reminded him.

He made a helpless gesture, remembering the confusion of hunts. "I know. I was torn. There were too many — "

"Too many hunters," she said softly, her eyes narrowed, glittering dark and amber. "There was my hunt — "

"And there was Burne — "

"Burne?"

"The King of Pelucir."

"Ah. The human hunt. He is still troubling my wood."

"He is searching for me. Last night, I was searching for him, to warn him — I was afraid for him — "

"Afraid?"

"Of the third hunt."

"Yes," she whispered. He saw her hands close, her face close, smooth and pale as ivory. "The third hunt . . . I heard the cry of the Wolf."

He was silent again, gazing at her, his eyes wide. "The White Wolf," he said finally, "of Chaumenard."

"Yes. I called him in his dreams. Where is he?"

"I don't know."

"Find him." She moved closer to him then, her silks flowing on the wind, one hand falling like silk on his bare wrist. "Find him for me. Bring him into this world. He cannot seem to find his way here, though I have called him again and again — "

"Him." His voice was flat. "Atrix Wolfe."

Her face opened slightly at the name. "Yes."

"You couldn't call him here. So you called me."

"To bring him here," she said. "Yes. Because no other human knows both him and me, to bridge the boundary between our worlds."

He opened his mouth, closed it. His eyes closed; his lips caught between his teeth. He tasted blood before he spoke again. "He killed my father."

He heard the faintest of breaths, a butterfly flying out of her mouth. "I need him," she said inexorably, and he opened his eyes to stare at her.

"For what?" he asked in amazement. "You are powerful enough to pull me out of my world. Why do you need a human mage?"

"Because I need him in the human world."

He swallowed, feeling chilled again in the soft spring light. "He is very powerful. I can't find him if he doesn't want to be found. And," he added, precisely, bitterly, "I do not want to find him."

He heard a slightly more substantial sigh, of cobwebs torn, or thousand-year-old tapestry threads breaking apart. "Then," she said as precisely, "you will never return to Pelucir. You will remain here forever, human in an inhuman time and place. No doubt you will forget Pelucir eventually. But Pelucir will never forget you: the prince who vanished in the wood on the hill and never returned."

He drew breath to shout at her. The shout dissolved into fire, burning down his face. He tried to turn away; she seemed everywhere. He closed his eyes; the hot tears ran between his lashes. "The thing that hunts him killed my father." His voice held no sound. "On Hunter's Field. He made the Hunter that hunts him. It was a war between kings, men — Pelucir had no mage. No sorcery to fight his sorcery."

"Who could?" Her voice sounded hollow now; she averted her face, hiding a sudden flick of memory. "He is the greatest living mage."

"He is a lie. He tried to run from what he had made — tried to hide. But it found him."

"And I found him. And I want him, before he and this monstrous thing he made destroy each other."

He opened his eyes finally; she blurred behind the tears caught in his lenses. He made some impatient, despairing sound; she slid them from his face. He felt her fingers brush his skin; a tear clung to one fingertip. Mesmerized, he watched her gaze at it, then touch her own face with it.

"I could never cry," she whispered. "I envy you."

He felt his throat burn again, this time with wonder, with pity. "Why? What have you lost?"

"Love," she said simply. "Sorrow."

He was mute, staring at her. The tear hung like a cut jewel below her eye. He lifted his hand, touched it, and it fell, glittering, to the grass. "No one cries for sorrow."

"I know." She closed her eyes, her face upraised, fierce and desperate, pale as ivory in her autumn hair. He touched her cheek again, his lips parted, not daring to breathe. He touched her mouth. She opened her eyes then, as if waking. Her lips grazed his fingertips. Then she took his hand in her hands, and held it still. "No one cries for her. I cannot cry, and I think that where she is, no one would care to cry for her. That's why I need the mage. And you. I cannot cross into your world to look for her. You can cross boundaries; you can show the mage the way to me. He could break the spell on her, and bring her back to me."

"Who?" Again his voice held no sound.

"My daughter. My Saro. My only child." She paused, searching his face. "You said her name."

He whispered, "I said 'sorrow.' "

"Sorrow," she said. Then: "Saro."

"Saro." He was silent again, watching the shadows and golden lights in her eyes, how expression breathed across her face like wind across water, changing a curve of bone here, a hollow there. He could, he realized slowly, stand there for a season or three and watch her, while leaves the color of her hair drifted down, and the tall birch rose out of snow whiter than the snow. He forced himself to speak. "How did you lose her to the human world?"

Her eyes narrowed; he glimpsed the night in them, the queen who rode without a face through the mage's dream. "She vanished out of this world. Years ago, by mortal reckoning. I have been searching for her that long. I cannot find her here; therefore she must be there. Yet I hear no tales of her from your world; no one dreams of her. She is disguised, hidden in some way. My bright, sweet Saro. I dream of her, trying to speak to me, but I cannot hear what she is saying; her words make no sound. . . ."

"Sometimes — " He stopped, started again. "Sometimes I see a woman in my dreams. With my eyes. I can't hear what she is saying, either."

"Saro is not dead. We change, when we are very old. You see us all around you in the wood. But death is for humans."

"My mother is dead. She died the night my father was killed. The night I was born. They told me . . . it was as if she knew. As if she saw him fall. And so she died." His eyes dropped, hidden from her; he waited, while she considered that argument. But she only said,

"Such matters you must take up with the mage when I am done with him. But first you must find him. You bridge worlds. You saw what he only dreams. If you can find me, you can find him. I want his mage's mind, his mage's eyes, to find my child in your world."

"Have you seen," he asked evenly, "what he made? What came alive and hunted him last night?"

"Yes." There was no pity in her face, no expression at all.

"If he is hiding from that, what makes you think I can find him?"

"I saw him enter my wood, carrying you in his arms. If you don't find him, he will find you."

He slid a hand beneath his lenses, over his eyes. "If I put myself in enough danger, you mean."

"You will find him and persuade him to help me," she said. "It is your only hope of escape from this world. Your only path to Pelucir."

He shifted a little, felt her hold on his hand tighten. His mouth tightened. "He has no reason to care."

"Then," she said softly, "you must find him a reason to care. You have odd powers: You walk between worlds, you see what the White Wolf only dreams. You must remember, though, that if you try to return to your world, you will only wander like a ghost among those you love. Like the shadow I became when I followed you. A reflection. A dream. Until the mage is found, you are hostage in my world."

He caught his breath to protest. Burne, he wanted to say to her. The childless King of Pelucir. "How," he asked reasonably, his voice shaking, "do you expect me to survive what the mage made to destroy us?"

He saw no mercy in her eyes; for a moment she did not, or could not, speak. Her hands were gripping his hand; he waited, feeling her tremble.

"They watched him," she said finally, her face colorless as mist. "From within the wood, when he cast that spell. Saro and my beloved consort. He and she had some human blood; they could see and hear what I could not. Saro seemed open to your world with the intensity of her curiosity. My consort watched with her. And so." Her breath rose and fell. "And so. When the greatest human mage worked his spell on your battlefield, he shattered the weakened boundary between our worlds and pulled my Saro into yours. In what shape, I do not know. I can only guess. By what he did to my consort, who was, himself, among the most powerful in my world. I saw him changed. Warped out of shape and trapped in the mage's terrible spell. I watched him ride away from me onto your battlefield."

Talis felt the blood drain out of his face. Cold shook him; even her hands on his could not warm him. He opened his mouth to speak, could make no sound.

She nodded. "That is what the mage is fighting. His own power. And my consort's enormous power, twisted beyond any recognition."

"Oh," he said without sound. His hands moved, drew at her, slender wrist, elbow, shoulder, until he had gathered all of her into his arms, and held her, feeling sorrow with all its thorns bloom in his heart. He felt her face drop finally against his shoulder.

"So you see — "

"Yes," he whispered, seeing the Hunter in the keep destroying spells, seeing the full moon rising in a tangle of oak, the mage standing under the oak, looking across Hunter's Field, watching his past and his future ride toward him in the dark. "Yes."

Fourteen

～⚜～

The White Wolf prowled the wood in Pelucir.

He followed paths of light until the sun shifted and they faded. He immersed himself in shadow as in water; he found no other land but shadow. He placed his heart into the hearts of trees, listened to their secret murmurings; they told him nothing he did not know. He tried to dream, beneath the oak; the only face he saw in the twilight between waking and sleeping was the face of the black moon rising in a cloud of fire, and then the Hunter's feral, moon-eyed face.

He called Talis in a mage's silent way; he flew with hawks and mourning doves, called him with their voices; he ran with boar and hare and even with Burne's hunting hounds, and used their voices. He slipped into running streams, murmured Talis' name with the voice of water; he called him with the toads among the reeds. He shaped the trumpet's fanfare into Talis' name. He looked out of ravens' eyes, hunting-horses' eyes, deer's eyes, the hunters and the hunted. But the Queen had taken Talis beyond the world, and Atrix could find no sense, no instinct, no eyes, no sorcery, and no dream that could change the wood into another world.

At twilight, he changed himself into a drift of leaves at the edge of the wood, and waited.

The moon rose and set. On Hunter's Field nothing moved.

For three days, he searched the wood for Talis, for three nights he waited for the Hunter. Both had vanished. When he fell, at odd moments, into an exhausted sleep, he dreamed of the wood around him.

The dream had changed, he realized even while dreaming. Three white deer, three white hounds, three white horses, and the Queen of the Wood, with her face made of all the wild beauty in her wood: white birch, owl's eyes, the rich, yellow-gold light of early autumn, the alert, elegant faces of hunting animals. She cried a word; it was the same word, but it meant something else, he felt in his dream. She cried "Sorrow," but it did not mean sorrow . . . She held her bow, but did not shoot.

He dreamed of Talis.

In his dream, the prince was made of air and light. He drifted like old leaves drifted, wandering through the wood. Sometimes he called to Atrix. His callings were complex and surprising. An oak tree opened a mouth in a seam of bark and said, *Atrix Wolfe*. The name formed out of silken rustlings of birch leaves. A pool of light in which the drifting prince had a shadow as pale as cobweb shaped the letters of his name in brighter gold. *Atrix Wolfe*, the air whispered. *Atrix Wolfe*, said the small birds from within the wild roses. Atrix, still hidden in a thick layer of dead leaves that would not crumble underfoot, or move for any wind, knew even in his sleep that while the imagery of the dream might be nebulous, truth lay in it like a nut in a nutshell: Talis had not left the wood, and, with mages' ways, he searched for Atrix Wolfe.

But, waking, Atrix could sense him nowhere; like the woodland queen, Talis called to Atrix in a dream. Atrix, searching for him in the true world, could not hear his voice.

Weary, hungry and bewildered, he rose with the morning sun, and moved with the light across Hunter's Field to talk to the King.

Burne took him into a quiet council chamber. The King looked as if he had slept in his clothes, if he had slept at all. His eyes were bloodshot; he wore blood and dirt on his boots from the hunt. He sat on the council table and watched Atrix pace.

"I know where Talis is," Atrix said, seeing the impossible world as he spoke: the wood where white deer cast shadows of gold, and a queen as ageless as dreams ruled outside of time.

"Where?"

"He is looking for me — I hear him call me. But I only hear him when I sleep, and I can only search for him when I'm awake. He seems to exist only in my dreams."

Burne opened his mouth, closed it. He poured wine instead of speaking, took a hefty swallow. "That's preposterous. How can he live in a dream? He's flesh and blood."

"She existed for me in my dreams, and for Talis in this world. It's like night and day — he is there only when I can't see him. I don't know the path into my own dreams."

Burne stared at his cup. He flung it abruptly across the room; wine stained the far wall in jagged peaks. Atrix, blinking tiredly, thought with longing of the mountains of Chaumenard. "He's all we have." The King's hands clenched. "All I have left. You can't give up."

Atrix shook his head. "Never." He moved again, restlessly, sliding fingers through his hair, scattering bits of leaf behind him. "You can stop hunting, though. Not even your hounds could scent him in her wood."

"Maybe not," Burne said wearily, "but I can't do nothing. If I harry her wood enough, maybe she'll give him back to me."

"I saw her face," Atrix said, "in my dreams." He stopped pacing, dropped into a chair, silent a moment, dreaming of her again. "She is like the wood. Like golden light falling through the golden branches of the oak. The fierce, hot green stillness of midsummer, or the colors blowing everywhere in autumn when the winds are clear and wild as water . . ."

"She is."

"In my dream she is."

"What would she want with Talis, then?" Burne asked perplexedly. "He has our mother's looks, but he isn't extraordinary, and he wears those lenses everywhere. Unless she took him just because she could. Or maybe we did something to offend her. But I would be dreaming of her then, instead of you. It's you she shot her arrows at. It's you Talis is calling, not me. Nobody is sending me any messages."

Atrix stirred a little, frowning. "She shoots at me out of her world. Talis calls to me out of her world . . ."

"It's you she wants," the King said, inspired. "Not Talis at all." He looked at Atrix speculatively, and with relief. "If you go to her, maybe she'll set him free."

"But why take him at all?" Atrix wondered. "If she wants me?"

"A hostage," Burne suggested. "Bait."

"Why didn't she just appear to me in the wood, instead? I was there, when she took Talis. It makes no sense. Why would she use a prince of Pelucir as bait for a mage of Chaumenard? It makes —"

"No sense. You're right. But they're both trying to get your attention. Maybe she needs a mage, and mistook Talis for one."

Atrix was silent, seeing the arrow fly through his dreams again, feeling it strike: That is the message, he thought grimly. The heart of the matter. He rose again, compelled by mysteries, though he wondered how long his weary human shape could bear the confusion and strain of them. A breath of air smelling of pitch and stone and wild strawberry would give him back the mountain's strength, he felt. Pelucir smelled too tamely of slow water and grass and ancient trees . . .

Burne was speaking ". . . wear yourself to the bone. Stay and eat with us. Sleep a little." He paused, asked warily, "Have you seen what Talis made again?"

"No. I've watched for him, these past nights; I've seen nothing."

"Him."

"It. It bore some odd resemblance to its maker. I don't know where it went."

"You destroyed it," Burne suggested. "You sent it back into the pages of the spellbook."

Atrix shook his head wearily. "I won't leave Pelucir until I know exactly what happened to it."

"Thank you," Burne said. Atrix gazed at him, surprised, then lifted a hand to his eyes, blocking the light, trying to think.

"Be careful," he advised the King. "Don't hunt at night. And I want that spellbook out of this castle."

Burne shrugged. "It's in the keep. No one will use it. No one goes up there but Talis."

"I want it out of Pelucir. I'll take it out of the keep for now, hide it somewhere; it may stay put for a while, now that I am here. Perhaps Talis left something in the keep that will help me find him. A hint of a path between worlds."

"Nothing was left whole, they say. Everything broken, torn, all his books in shreds. Yours too, probably."

"It's no ordinary book," Atrix reminded him. "I made it."

He sensed the eccentric power as he walked toward the keep. Its high window jumped from one wall to another to

stare at him. He listened; it was empty except for its memories; the owls had fled, but not the ghosts. His mind trav-
elled up the stairs; the door hung open, sagging on one
hinge. He followed his thoughts.

Standing on the threshold, he studied the room, while
the odd face in the door, askew now, studied him. He sensed
no danger in the restless window, which gave him a view of
the distant wood. Torn pages and paper were scattered
everywhere; some books, heavy, leatherbound tomes, had
been ripped in two. His eyes flicked over them; he lifted the
table, searching, then moved pieces of a bucket, a broken
bowl, scattered firewood, blown torches, feeling, even as he
searched, the emptiness of the room. Disturbed, perhaps by
his own growing unease, the shadows on the walls grew
more profuse, telling him their stories: *Look*, they said. *See.
This happened to me.*

"I know," he breathed between his teeth, haunted. "I
know." His search became desperate; he looked in the ashes
in the grate, into the walls and stones. He stopped himself
finally, chilled. Nothing had ended or resolved itself; he was
still under siege by his past.

The book had moved again, out of a place where no
one came. He stood silently, his mind wandering through
rooms and corridors, looking for that piece of himself, and
sensing himself nowhere. Perhaps it had found its own way
back to Chaumenard, having accomplished its dark and
bewildering purpose in Pelucir. . . .

He found Burne again, beginning breakfast with
guests and hunters in the hall. He had forgotten how to
move unobtrusively among frayed and sleepless humans.
He startled even those who recognized him, shaping out of
air, with his torn tunic and callused feet, and his eyes like
hoarfrost melting over dark water. Cups were overturned,
knives cracked against plate. A chair rattled back across the

stones next to the King; a man with yellow hair and a
scarred face made room for Atrix.

"Did you find it?" Burne asked, as servants poured
pale wine scented with spices into Atrix's cup, filled a plate
with pastries stuffed with nuts and cream, cold salmon, a
swan carved out of melon with its wings full of strawberries.
He cast a glance at Atrix's face and answered his own
question. "No. It was most likely destroyed in that strange
storm. You saw what was left up there."

"It wasn't up there. It has a will of its own."

"It's your book," Burne said, bewildered. "Why did
you write something so dangerous and unpredictable?"

"I didn't intend to." He ate a bite of salmon, some fruit,
while Burne wrestled with the problem of the spellbook. In
the distance, Atrix sensed another storm, vague yet, but
imminent: He tensed, waiting, while Burne argued.

"You saw all those ghosts up there," he said to Atrix.
"You must have."

"Yes."

"They are ghosts of the siege of Hunter's Field. The
place is riddled with memories; everyone knows it's
haunted. My guards hate being up there, even armed, especially those who lived through the siege. I can't believe,
after what happened to Talis, that anyone would set foot up
there now, especially not for a spellbook. Talis is the only
one who knows anything about magic."

"It's more than a book," Atrix said slowly, his mind still
on the roil of thoughts and fears moving through the King's
house. "It's a sign. A message. Something that may tell me
what — " The storm moved down the corridor to the hall; he
stopped, his breath drawn, listening.

"If it's that important," Burne said, "I'll have the castle
searched, dungeon to keep — What?" he asked sharply,
turning, as guards pushed into the hall.

"My lord, there is a messenger back from — from — "
Words dried in the man's throat; he shook his head, unable
to finish. His face looked frozen, haunted; Atrix saw the
ghostly reflection in his eyes.

He stood up; so did the King, his hands coming down
hard on the table. "What?" he demanded again; the guard
swallowed and found his voice.

"A messenger, my lord, that you sent out to Chaumenard."

"I sent a dozen messengers," Burne snapped. Again the
hall was soundless. "They can't have reached the mages so
soon — Where is he?"

"Dead, my lord."

Burne stared at him, He put a hand over his wine cup
but did not throw it. Atrix, his eyes on his morning shadow,
scented the castle for more turmoil, terror; the only storm, it
seemed, was among them. "Dead of what?"

"He came — he came earlier, before dawn. He was
wounded, babbling — no one realized for a while who he
was — no one expected the messengers back — "

"What," Burne barked, "happened?"

"He said — they never reached Chaumenard. They
never got out of Pelucir alive. He was the only one to escape
it. He was old enough to recognize it."

Blood drained out of Burne's face. He lifted his hand
stiffly from his cup, closed it; his thumb had left an indenta-
tion in the gold. "Tell me," he said harshly, "what he recognized."

"The Hunter of Hunter's Field."

The King's face relinquished all expression. "Talis," he
said to Atrix. Atrix dropped his face into one hand, murmuring inarticulately.

"Talis is in the Queen's wood," he answered, lifting his
head again. "Of all of you, he will be safest. Burne — "

"Is this what Talis conjured up in the keep?"

"Yes. No. Yes."

"The Hunter of Hunter's Field? He was in there alone with Talis? What do you mean, yes and no — " He stopped abruptly, reaching out to Atrix, in a sudden plea against his own thoughts. "It was your spellbook — "

"It was my spell," Atrix said. He had to wait a moment for anyone to understand, and then a moment or two longer, for anyone to believe him. Then Burne took a step back from him, and the air everywhere was streaked with silver, catching a blinding fire from the morning light. Even Burne's sword was out, motionless as if it were spellbound, an inch away from Atrix's breastbone.

Atrix bowed his head. "It would be just," he said softly. "And even welcome. I won't fight you. But — "

"Talis," Burne whispered; the sword shook slightly in his grip, then inched forward to stop over Atrix's heart.

"Yes." Atrix looked at the blade, and then at Burne; any spark of sorcery, he knew, would ignite the hall, and leave them fighting ghosts again, in terror and despair. "Kill me later," he suggested to Burne. "You need me now. I will be back. Even in Chaumenard, I live on Hunter's Field."

He waited, motionless, for the weight over his heart to ease, begin to lift, before he disappeared.

Fifteen

~∞~

Saro opened the unnamed book.

It was late; the King's hunt had returned long before; supper and its confusion of plates and pots and tales carried down the stairs, coming in the back door, was long over. For the second day since Talis had disappeared, the hunt had returned without him. The King had retired in fury and despair to his chamber, slamming the door so hard, the boom down the long stone passage sounded, servants said, like one of the prince's explosions. Supper — roast, peppered venison, tiny potatoes roasted crisp, hollowed and filled with cheese and onions and chive, cherries marinated in brandy and folded into beaten cream — sailed over the tray-bearer's head and splashed a lively patchwork across a hundred-year-old tapestry on the wall behind him. Brandy was taken up, and later, another tray, which at least made it through the door. Dirty pots came to an end, fires were banked, the last of the spit-boys wandered in from his night prowls, and settled on the stones. Saro, napping beside the cauldron, was roused by the silence. She pulled the book from its secret place.

Dawn found her face-down between its pages. She shoved it hastily back under the cupboard as the spit-boys, groping, half-asleep, sat up to toss wood on the fires beneath the bread ovens. The head cook entered later to the smell of hot bread, followed by hall-servants and yawning undercooks, and the tray-mistress, red-eyed and grim.

"Hunt," the head cook said tersely. The dogs were barking in the yard. "Again. Take up bread and cheese, smoked fish and cold, sliced venison. Mince the rest of the venison for pie. Also onions, mushrooms, leeks. Take up spiced wine."

Musicians crowded into the kitchen, dressed for the hunt; they chewed blearily on hot black bread, venison, cheese, their instruments tucked under their arms, their faces alert for any impulse of the King's. Saro filled the wash-cauldron. A corner of the book caught her eye; she nudged it farther under the cupboard with her foot.

"We scoured the south wood yesterday," a trumpeter said in answer to the tray-mistress's query. "We sounded fanfares for deer, hare, grouse, quail. But not one for the prince. Wherever he is, he's either hidden or beyond eyesight. But the King will run dogs and horses and hunters into a ghostly hunt before he gives up trying to see what can't be seen."

The tray-mistress closed her eyes and shook her head wordlessly. She opened them a moment later. "Saro," she called, and Saro gathered the loaf pans to wash them.

The end of the day's hunt filled the kitchen with feathers, as grouse and pheasant and wild duck, their cloudy eyes staring at unseen things, were plucked, beheaded, stuffed and spitted. Hare, squirrel and deer were skinned, gutted and left in the cold-meat pantry; tanners took away the pile of skins outside the door, while the yard dogs squabbled over offal.

"It's a war with the wood," the tray-mistress muttered crossly, as the sweeper slowly swept blood and water into the drains. "Shooting everything that moves. Let's hope he misses Prince Talis."

"It's fear," the head cook said, calculating as he spoke, his eyes on the raw meat inside the pantry. "The venison can be smoked, the small game will do for cold pies for the hunters. It's memory of loss and hunger. He'll be saner, when the messengers reach Chaumenard and the mages come."

"Magic," the tray-mistress said tightly. Even the spit-boys glanced up from their fires at the word. "Again in Pelucir. But I suppose there's no help for it." She turned abruptly, clouted a mincer across the head with a wooden spoon. Already sniffing from onions, he only ducked and sniffed harder. "Get to work, brat, or I'll toss you on the offal pile. Something about this has me strung up and simmering. Waiting. And remembering. I keep feeling a shadow inside my bones."

"The mages will come soon," the head cook said absently. "Sauce. Orange and honey for the duck, pear and onion for the pheasant."

Saro's hands slowed; she stared at soap bubbles, trying to fit mages into her vision. Help for the prince, protection against the night-hunter seemed to fit nowhere, not in the kitchen, not among the trees in the wood. "Mages" seemed a dream word, meaningless: The more she looked for them, the more rapidly they vanished, like the airy palaces of bubbles in her cauldron.

"Saro!" a spit-boy cried, and she turned to gather the dripping-pans.

She sat up that night until the fires around her turned into a ring of bright, watching eyes, until the words in the book, always incomprehensible, turned nearly invisible as well. Still she clung to the book, her eyes heavy, unblinking, waiting for the chains of letters, the words skipping across the page like stones across a brook, to speak.

They remained as mute as she.

She touched her lips, and then the words. No one in the kitchen cooked up great platters of words to be eaten,

but somehow an inexhaustible quantity of them came out of
people's mouths. Those in the book had as much to do with
eyes as with lips; they vanished when not looked upon; tears
changed them, and wind, and fire. Her eyes dropped wearily; the watching eyes glowed bright and disappeared. The
book vanished, though she felt it in her hands. It remained
silent. Perhaps she needed to form words in her mouth
before she could form the words on a page. Undercooks
consulted great volumes of recipes, smudged and stained
with oils, sauces, flours. They argued over them, cooked
from them, words made into food, and sent them up to be
eaten. She touched her mouth again, half-dreaming, and
desperate. One hand slid away from the book; the hand
remembered, it seemed, before she did, what it had picked
up in the keep and put in her pocket. Even in the fading
light it gleamed, a single letter, a graceful scrollwork of gold.
She lifted it to her mouth, her eyes closing, raw and gritty
with weariness. Words had to get into her somehow, to get
out again. She yawned, inhaling, and tasted bitterness and
gold, a letter without a sound.

She saw the night-hunter watching her within the fiery
circle of eyes.

She jerked herself awake, her mouth open, trying to
make a sound. Nothing stood in the red, fuming hearth
light. The spit-boys snored, shadowy, fire-limned lumps;
the mincers whimpered in their sleep. Still her heart
pounded its own language of terror, until the vast dark
kitchen, smelling of smoke and rising bread, calmed her
with its insistence of familiar things. At last she moved,
closed the book. As she lay facing it, one hand straying
under the cupboard to touch it, she swallowed again the
unfamiliar taste of gold.

The night-hunter stood over her. She saw his dark,
masked eyes, the dark moon rising in his horns, his face

rippling slightly, as if she saw him reflected in water at the bottom of the cauldron. He said, *Drawkcab.* His black hounds howled at the word. *Drawkcab,* he insisted, through the noises of the hounds, staring down at her. A jewel of blood gleamed at one corner of his mouth. *Drawkcab,* he said a third time, and the baying of the hounds rose, became pure and metallic as the voices of horns.

She woke with a start, hearing horns.

It was a fanfare at the gate, in the early hours before dawn. Spit-boys, sleepily kindling the oven fires, glanced toward the sound.

"Someone wanting in," one breathed, and another answered, lifting his head sharply above his fire,

"Mages, it must be. The mages of Chaumenard."

They learned, at breakfast.

Servants took up silver urns of chocolate, trays of butter pastries, hams glazed with honey and sliced thin as paper, eggs poached in sherry, birds carved out of melons and filled with fruit. They came back white as cream. The tray-mistress listened to their babbling a moment, then sat down slowly, her own cheeks, under the strawberry veins, as colorless as suet.

The head cook said sharply to the head servant, "Sit down. Speak slowly. Who is up there, and why is no one eating?"

"Messengers. Messenger."

"From Chaumenard?"

The servant shook his head. The head cook sat down suddenly on a stool. "Only one came back," the servant whispered. "Of those the King sent out. They were stopped. At night, before they reached the border. The steep, rocky hills, where the pass narrows, and the road overlooks half of Pelucir."

"What happened there?" The undercooks had crowded

around the head cook; no one else moved, except the youngest of the choppers and peelers, who, uneasy, sought safety beneath the tables. The hall servants were clustered together around the head servant. The tray-mistress, rolling her pristine apron in her fists, carried it to her mouth.

"Something — someone stopped them. Something."

"What?" the tray-mistress snapped, like the pitch exploding in the fire, and a spit-boy jumped. The head servant, his face grey, lined, beneath his yellow hair, stared back at her dully.

"A man. A mage. A hunter. His horns like black lightning, a black moon rising in them, hounds and horse shaped out of night, with fire between their teeth. He would not let them pass into Chaumenard."

The tray-mistress made a sound into her apron. The head cook said quickly, "Brandy. Are they dead?"

"The messenger didn't wait. They all turned and ran. He was the only one to return. He was old enough to recognize the Hunter, and that's what's being said up there. That it was the dark making that killed the King's father. The messenger died this morning."

The tray-mistress covered her eyes and rocked a moment. She reappeared, to grip the brandy bottle and drink. Her eyes, usually shiny as beetles' wings, looked sunken and dull. The head cook, wordless in the silence, drew breath audibly.

"After so many years? The sorcery made for that battle still exists?"

"They recognized it," the head servant said softly. "Those who saw it kill on Hunter's Field. The messenger heard the others shouting, as he ran."

He took the bottle from the tray-mistress and drank. The head cook reached for it.

"We must bring a mage here to deal with it."

"We had a mage," the tray-mistress said heavily. "That White Wolf."

"He's been searching for the prince. He'll deal with this too — he told the King that before he vanished. He is the greatest living mage."

There was silence again, in the kitchen. Other servants came down, bearing trays of uneaten food. The head cook gazed at the trays, his face tight. "Cook the eggs until they harden, and roll them in minced sausage. The ham will keep for when the King hunts again. Mash the melon in sweet wine and strain it for cold soup — "

"He can't go hunting," the tray-mistress breathed in horror. "Not with that out there."

"With that and Prince Talis out there together, he'll go," the head cook said tersely. "If that's what drove the mage and the prince out of the keep, then the mage will be around somewhere. He's Atrix Wolfe, not some fly-by-night magician. He knows to guard the heir of Pelucir."

"If he can," the tray-mistress said starkly. "If he's able." She shifted slowly off the stool, her eyes wide. Gradually they focused on the plate-washers, and, for an instant, on Saro, who had turned away from her pots and stood as still as if she understood. "Plates!" the tray-mistress snapped; the plate-washers whirled, bent over the cooling water. "Pots!" But Saro had already vanished headlong into her cauldron, scouring dripping-pans from the hams, and baking trays from the pastries. The head cook, not seeing her face, forgot her listening eyes.

Drawkcab, the water deep in the cauldron said as it weltered against the sides. She felt her lips move, shaping sounds. It was a spell, a message, a riddle, a warning; a terrible, magical word. She could no more say it than she could say "liver sausage." But he had come into her dream and said it to her. Or her dream had spoken to her, out of his image. She scrubbed fiercely at pork grease, the word echoing in her head now instead of in the water. She felt the odd prickling in her eyes again, for it was as meaningless to her as the words in the prince's book.

The King called a council later that morning. Plates of sweetmeats, nuts, tiny seed cakes, were returned to the kitchen untouched; pitchers of cold spiced wine returned empty.

"No one's eating," the tray-mistress said fretfully. "And what is this dent in the bronze tray?"

"The King kicked it," a servant said morosely. "He's boiling and about to froth."

"He's frothing," another servant said, returning with goblets. He wiped a sheen off his face and added starkly, "He's calling the hunt for noon. He thinks something terrible — he says the monster came out of the prince's spellbook, and that Atrix Wolfe wrote the book — so he thinks — he says that Atrix Wolfe made — "

"You're babbling," the head cook snapped. "Nonsense. Cold ham, herb bread, mince pies, red wine. The King may throw it to the dogs. At least it will get eaten."

The hunt returned, to everyone's relief, at twilight. As if preparing for siege, it had cut a deadly swath through the wood, bringing back so much game that the head cook ordered the smokehouse fires lit again, and sent spit-boys out to hang venison and wild duck above the flames. He sent stew and game pies to the supper hall, salads of spinach and radish and bacon, hot black bread, simple, heavy fare that the hunters did not reject. There was more eating than talking, the servants reported. There was no news.

Saro washed pie pans, bread pans, stewpots, frying pans, until, looking around dazedly, she found a world scoured of dirty pots, and very quiet. Sitting in the shadow of her wash cauldron, she waited stolidly for the spit-boys to come in from the night and bank the fires. They settled finally, and began to snore. She drew the book from under the cupboard and set it across her knees.

She did not open it.

There would be, she knew, the same tantalizing drawings of mirrors and mandrake roots, goblets and flying birds. The same clean, precise lines of letters and words that might as well have been spider webs, or splotches of cooking oil, for all they said anything to her. She leaned back against the cupboard, gazed wearily at the hearth fires. She watched little flames spring up now and then out of the darkening embers, like ghosts, like memories of fire, until, half-dreaming, she forgot that fire had a name, and saw only bright random blossoms of color spring up, out of shimmering red and dark, flow gracefully from shape to shape, then burrow down again, hide among the rustling embers, where something restless would snap and fling a sparkling swarm of insects or stars into the air.

Darkness curved across one hearth, hiding half of it: a massive, heavy black that her hands knew as well as her eyes. Sitting still, she felt its rough, familiar swell against her palms as they pushed against it, and its unwieldy weight against her hip as she tilted it, and dirty water slapped the sides and spilled.

She felt its strength in her, its solid, unyielding shape, that resisted any change, unlike the fire that danced to every breath of air and had the power to change whatever it touched. Her mind shifted between them, exploring them: the great bubble of iron that held water, air, dirty pots, visions, in its hard, protective embrace; the fire that ate shadows, and bone, and shone like love in the spit-boys' eyes, and like death in the dead swan's eyes.

They entered her as nameless things: She made herself as strong and unyielding as one, as brilliant and fluid as the other. Her bones were made of iron cauldron, her heart beat with wings of fire. . . .

Saro! she heard someone call, from far away: the tray-mistress, or a spit-boy with a dripping-pan. She built the iron bubble around her. The voice, as light and pure as the horn's voice, crumpled against the iron. Later, she followed the path of fire around the kitchen, saw how it hung moth-like, quivering, in the curve of a copper pot, how it changed the shape of candle wax, making something cold and stiff go warm as tears, and spill, sculpting itself as it cooled. Curious, she let her mind flow into the wax, fall with it, harden again.

Just before it hardened, she felt herself in another place, contemplating another candle, set in a holder of rose-wood and deer horn. The wax warmed, spilled; she slid with it, felt it begin to slow down the sides of the candle, harden . . .

Saro! a voice cried, in the memory, and a word moved in the back of her throat, an answer.

"Saro!"

It was as if the iron cauldron had shouted. Her bones shook, fell into place; her head jerked back. In sudden terror, she gathered the bright moths and blossoms and stars all around her, before she looked across her ring of fire and met the tray-mistress's astonished eyes.

Sixteen

⬥

Talis rode among the hunters of Pelucir.

He had grown accustomed, in the past few days, to being invisible. The horse he rode he had taken from a meadow where horses as beautiful as he had ever seen ran wild. It was the color of butter, with a white-gold mane, and it moved through the human hunt, the horns and dogs and shouts, as if through drifting leaves. Listening at random, Talis heard what had frozen the grim expression on Burne's face, and why there were fewer who ventured into the wood with him, and why they all seemed intent on killing every living thing in the wood, as if preparing for a siege.

Of Atrix Wolfe he found no trace. But if the Hunter still haunted the field, then the mage must still be there, somewhere: in a shadow under a bramble, in a window in the keep, watching Hunter's Field. Talis had searched by day and night. By day the wood, unsettled by the King's hunt, seemed so empty of mages he wondered if they had taken their battle back to Chaumenard. At twilight, the castle across the field sealed itself tightly; no one ventured out. Talis, hidden at the edge of the wood, could see the silent, motionless field until moonrise. Then something blurred the field — mist, or moonlight so bright it concealed what it illumined. When he tried to move into it, he invariably found himself back in the wood, no matter what shape he took.

It was Atrix Wolfe's magic, he had no doubt, and it was meant for him. The hunters saw it also from the castle; they spoke in hushed, shaken voices of battles of mage and Hunter and all the ghosts of Hunter's Field they imagined raging within the mist. Talis spent several nights trying to isolate a single act of magic, trying to see even a moving shadow within the mist. He yielded finally in bewilderment, and let his star-eyed mount find its way back to the meadow, where, hock-deep in wild lilies, it drank from a silver pool that mirrored delicate faces among the lilies. They vanished when Talis looked for them.

Oak receded from the meadow in all directions; he saw nothing else. He found a rock overlooking the pool, and sat down with a sigh, weary, hungry and harrowed with fears. Time seemed arbitrary in the Queen's wood: Night in Pelucir meant perhaps a deeper shade of blue in the tranquil sky, or a dusky, lovely twilight that lingered until the sun rose over Hunter's Field. Once, night had fallen into the Queen's wood as well, for no reason he could find except to cast a powerful urge in him to fall asleep under moonlight. The Queen had walked through all his dreams, in robes of flowing moonlight; he had brought her gifts — a key, a bird's nest, a sparkling stone, a gilded horseshoe, a scarlet mushroom — but she would not tell him her name. When the wood grew light again and he awoke, he found bread and cheese and strawberries wrapped in leaves beside him, as if, he thought wistfully, in her dreams, she had brought him gifts.

She had not come to him, or permitted him to find her again. It was a spur, her absence, a goad to find Atrix Wolfe, so that he could see her face again. He thought of her ceaselessly, adrift and lonely in her realm as he was; his arms remembered circling her, his bones remembered her bones. Light fell through trees, gilding the dead oak leaves, and he saw her hair, fire and amber and gold. The hart raised its head at the sound of a hunting horn, and he saw her beautiful, vulnerable face. He saw wild roses and thought of her; slender white birch, and thought of her; a white dove flying through green leaves, and thought of her. Everything his eyes touched turned into her. Everything his eyes touched had a name, and was not her.

He did not know her name. Nor, he realized, watching tiny fish make endless, interlocking rings in the still pool, did he know her consort's name. Neither did Atrix Wolfe, who was fighting him within the mist on Hunter's Field. Talis stirred restively, deeply disturbed at his own powerlessness. Atrix Wolfe would not let himself be found; neither would the nameless Queen. But unless Atrix could name what he fought, he would never defeat it, for he believed he fought only himself.

A fish touched the surface, made a ring. A face appeared in the ring, so close to the colors of mosses and reflected meadow-grass that Talis did not recognize it until he saw the eyes in the water watching him.

He started, lifting his own eyes to see the rider made of leaves. The rider said, as his dark horse drank from the pool,

"The Queen has lost three birds: a bluebird, a red bird, a bird as yellow as the sun. She asks that, since you have nothing more pressing to do than to sit on a rock watching fish, you might find them for her."

Talis touched his lenses silently, studying the strange, elegant face. "The wood is full of birds," he said finally. "How will I know which are hers?" He felt his heartbeat then, answering his own question: It did not matter, he would catch them all, for the moment in which he gave them to her.

The rider turned his mount indifferently. "You will know," he said.

"Wait!" Talis called impulsively, and the rider halted his horse, glancing back expressionlessly. "What is the name of the Queen's consort?"

He did not see what happened. He found himself in the water suddenly, sitting among the darting fish, his lenses askew and dripping water, his face throbbing oddly, as if he had been struck.

"Humans," the rider snapped, with his back to Talis, and rode away. Talis, amazed, heaved himself out of the pool. A bluebird, he told himself, trying to wipe his lenses with a sodden sleeve. A red bird. A yellow bird. They blame us for the Queen's lost consort and her child. Humans.

He called again, this time silently: *Wait.* The rider, nearly into the wood, drew up under an oak. Among the leaves, he and his mount, dappled with shadow, were nearly invisible.

Talis sensed his surprise across the meadow. He did not answer, but waited while Talis emptied the water out of his boots, then walked barefoot through the grass. Mount and rider gazed at him with the same remote expression as he stood beside them. The layered face reminded him of an unopened bud, an unfurled leaf, something wrapped neatly around itself, protecting an inner mystery.

Talis said, "The mage who cast the spell over the Queen's consort fights him with a human magic. If the mage dies, there will be no hope for the Queen's consort; he will be trapped in that shape as long as he is alive." A leaf-shadow, or the hint of expression, moved across the still face. Talis held up an open hand, continued carefully, "For the mage to unravel the spell, he will need to know what magic he is facing. That's why I asked for the name. I did not ask lightly and I meant no offense. What you did to me beside the pool, I didn't recognize."

A breeze wandered by, shook a leaf from the oak. It

drifted to the ground. A bird called, blue or red or yellow; Talis kept his eyes, with some prudence, on the motionless face. The rider spoke finally. "You don't use your magic here. You made me wait, while you walked across the meadow."

"She didn't take me for my magic." He felt the warm blood rise in his face in spite of himself. "There are many, far better human mages." He paused, heard the unspoken question in the air. "She took me because she knew I would give her my heart. And then whatever else she wants. I walked across the meadow because I don't know the language of magic in this land. I didn't want you to misunderstand me. It's simple to understand a walking man, especially when he is soaking wet and barefoot and carrying his boots."

There was a flicker in the green eyes, almost a glint of light. "It is less easy, I see, to understand the man sitting quietly beside a pool. I will give you nothing for the mage to use against the Queen's consort."

Talis shook his head quickly, swallowing. "I would not want to hurt her more," he said softly. "It's only for the mage to understand what magic he is fighting. If I can find him."

"When."

"When I find him."

The rider dismounted. A dove flew down, settled on his shoulder, beneath his golden hair. He stood very still, holding Talis' eyes; Talis, as still, watched the leaf-mask waver, separate into leaves on a bough, rustling in a gentle wind. An oak formed in his mind, its great dark branches a lovely, complex filigree against the green. A face formed in the leaves; branches pieced themselves together like bones; leaves shaped around the bone. The tree walked away from its roots, turned to look back at itself.

"I am Oak and I speak for the oak. The birds know me,

lightning knows me. You know me now, Talis Pelucir. Take these birds to the Queen of the Wood. Then find me at the boundary between worlds, where wood meets Wood at the edge of Hunter's Field. I have watched there with you. I want to show you what I have seen."

Talis blinked; the face formed again outside of his mind. Birds had landed on his shoulders; he felt feathers brush his cheek, a murmur at his ear. The Oak lord set the dove among them. "Take this, too," he said. "Tell her it's from me." He added, mounting again, hearing the question in Talis' head, "Behind you."

Talis watched him ride into the wood, until leaf and branch and shadow hid him, or he let his mortal shape flow freely back into them. Then Talis let his boots fall, put them on carefully, so as not to disturb the birds on his shoulders. He turned.

A great palace stood in front of him.

It filled the meadow, rose out of it, its lower walls and towers so thickly covered with vines that the palace seemed to be blooming out of something living. Its upper towers seemed made of light, blown glass, rainbow-colored air. Its gate was an arch of green leaves over a long bridge of thick, ancient vines. No one guarded it, except, Talis thought, perhaps the vines themselves. He walked carefully over them; vine-leaves whispered; the dove spoke softly back to them.

He stepped through the oak doors, found a single room as wide as the meadow, with a small silver pool in the middle of it. Lilies made of bronze and glass and wax grew around the pool, some as high as saplings, others lit like candles, scenting the air with honey. The rest of the rooms lay in shadow, a palace waiting to be formed, Talis guessed, at every step.

The figure sitting at the edge of the pool lifted a hand.

The birds took wing off Talis' shoulder, flew, streaks of color, to settle among the frozen lilies. The dove dropped into the Queen's hands.

She smiled across the pool at Talis, and he felt his heart open wings, try to fly.

"I wish," he whispered, "I had brought you every bird in the wood. If I had known you would smile . . ."

"The birds brought you to me," she said. "They were my messengers. But this white one . . . this is a message to me."

"It is from the Oak lord."

"I know. I watched you both within this pool."

Talis flushed. "You saw me sitting with the fish."

"Oak uses the lightning that catches in its boughs. I heard your question. You have not brought the mage to me." She stroked the dove's breast, no longer smiling, her face grave.

"He is hiding from me, I think. He must know I'm searching for him."

"How will you find him?"

"I don't know. Learn from the oak how to attract lightning, perhaps. I must find him quickly, before he leaves Pelucir."

The Queen tossed the dove into the air. "Sit," she said to Talis, and gestured at the shadows. "You are right to want my consort's name. Oak, carrying lightning he has swallowed, can be occasionally testy."

"Is that what hit me?" Talis dropped down, marvelling, beside a cluster of bronze lilies. In the pool, fiery darts of light swarmed like tiny fish. The water was very still. The Queen gestured; servants came out of the shadows, carrying trays of food and wine. Talis ate mushrooms, wild herbs and onions, roast hare steeped in wine and spices, warm bread stuffed with hazelnuts and soft cheese. The Queen drank pale wine while he ate; when he finished, she said,

"Saro looked like my consort. Eyes the color of ripe acorns, hair long and shining, milky-white. She inherited his powers and mine, something from each of us: the wordless, wild wood, and the language of humans. He had taught her many things, young as she was; she knew the languages of birds, of trees, almost before she could speak. My consort also carried a double heritage of power. That is how he became so terrible." She paused; the water in the pool darkened briefly, as if the shadow of the Hunter had passed over it. She whispered, "I do not expect to see him again." She shook her head at Talis' wordless murmur. "Never as he was. Never. After what he became. How could he return from that?"

"If Atrix — when he knows — "

"What could he do? Change the past? My love rode away from me and vanished into the deadly night of humans."

"Atrix will try to save him. Once he knows."

"I am sending you to find him for Saro's sake," she said fiercely. "If a choice must be made, Atrix Wolfe must live. My consort is dead. I know him. He could not live knowing what he had become. Nor — except for Saro's sake — would he permit the mage to live. He will kill Atrix Wolfe if he can, out of fury, out of grief, perhaps in memory of what he once was, once had. Once loved."

"Yes," Talis whispered.

"I have seen him, once or twice, in this pool. And I saw him the night I hunted you. Part of him still remembers my wood. I wonder, if he tries to find his way back here, what might stop him from a wild hunt for his lost memories." She raised her eyes to Talis' bloodless face. "You must not try to save him for my sake. You know how dangerous he is. You must help Atrix Wolfe for Saro's sake." Her voice trembled at the name. She looked down quickly; the water trembled as at a touch across the pool. "He took her from me; he will find her for me. My consort's name was Ilyos."

"And yours?"

She rose. He felt her fingers brush his cheek lightly; he closed his eyes; his hand, rising to touch her hand, closed on air. Swallowing something bittersweet, he listened to her steps until they faded.

The palace vanished behind him when he left it. He made his way back through the wood, to the boundary between wood and field, and saw the sky in the human world bruised blue and purple with twilight. As the twilight deepened, mist rolled across Hunter's Field, hid it and the castle beyond it, all but the single eye high in the ancient keep.

His heart hammering in his throat, Talis walked into the mist.

There was always one moment when the blinding, swirling brightness seemed about to shape itself, become the Hunter or the hunted. And, as Talis walked deeper into it, all the nebulous possibilities would become only leaves, the edge of the wood he had just left. This time, the leaves became an oak, and the oak, as he recognized it and turned, to try again, caught his shoulder in a sinewy, rustling grip and said, "Wait."

Talis stopped, still staring into the mist, baffled and frustrated. "I cannot move beyond the wood," he said tightly. "How can I find the mage if I can't see into this?"

"Close your eyes," the Oak lord suggested. "It blinds you because you're trying to see. Listen."

Talis closed his eyes. A breeze slipped through the trees around him. A bird sang. He concentrated, listening to the field instead of the wood, what sounds the grass might make, what sounds a mage might make, moving silently across it, listening, himself, for the footsteps of the Hunter.

"What do you hear?"

"Nothing." Talis opened his eyes. "Nothing."

"What do you see?"

"Mist. Nothing."

"What do you feel?"

He shook his head, feeling no warnings from the mist, any more than he would have felt a warning from lightning. "Nothing," he said wearily. "It's like a maze with no path, no center — "

"Listen."

"I tried — "

"Listen to yourself."

He paused. *Nothing*, his eyes said, his ears, his listening heart. Nothing. Nothing. "Nothing," he whispered, and heard the word.

He whirled to face the oak, chilled suddenly, as if he still stood in mist. "Atrix Wolfe is gone."

"That's what I felt," the oak said. "Standing here on the edge of an empty field."

"He threw this into my eyes to keep me searching here, while he took his battle someplace else — "

"Where?"

Talis stared into the mist; it began to shape under his eyes, into peaks and crags and luminous clouds. He closed his eyes, finally seeing what the mage had cast across the field. "The Shadow of the Wolf," he said. "Chaumenard."

Seventeen

In the kitchens, Saro stared into a black moon of water. Fire from a torch held by a spit-boy flowed across the water, which stood in the bottom of her wash cauldron and was absolutely still.

An apprentice, sitting beside the cauldron with the mage's book open on his knees, struggled with a word.

"Med-ate — Metation — Anyway, after that comes 'on.'"

"Don't skip words," the spit-boy said tersely, his eyes on Saro. "She has to know."

"Mediation."

The fire unfolded and flowed like silk across the water. Saro, her elbows propped on the rim of the cauldron, watched it thoughtlessly, barely hearing words. They sorted words and implements, whoever could read, whoever had a hand free. They pushed things under her nose and read words at her. She understood the fire better, whispering on the torch, flooding the dark iron with its light, trying to see something in the motionless water.

"Meditation, you cheese curd," another apprentice said, passing with his arms full of onions.

"Well, how am I to know? It's not a cooking word."

"You mind what you're doing," the tray-mistress said tartly, "or you'll have her turning us into beetles."

"Well, what is meditation," the apprentice on the floor asked aggrievedly, "when it's not in a sauce?"

"Contemplation," an undercook said.

"What?"

"Thinking!" the grey-eyed boner said, and whacked a fowl in two with her cleaver. "Now get on with it! She's doing it already, anyway. Look at her. Like she was born knowing how."

"Then what am I doing sitting here reading?"

"Shut up and read," the spit-boy said.

"Meditation on the desired object. I guess that would be Prince Talis."

"Right," the tray-mistress said approvingly, sorting napkins for the morning. "She looks into fire and water and thinks of him."

"The object — or subject — will be seen in the mingling of elmenents. Elements. That's all." He shoved the book away and rose to his knees, to look over the side of the cauldron. The spit-boy loosed his stiff, attentive stance to bend forward an inch. The tray-mistress peered, saw her reflection mingling with the curious faces.

"Out of there," she snapped. "How can she see anything with your great cloudy faces floating around?" She patted Saro's shoulder gently. "That's it, then, girl. Think of Prince Talis." She raised her voice. "Pots! No, not you," she said hastily as Saro started. "You're not pots anymore. You're — I don't know what you are. But not pots."

Saro drifted back into the fire. She heard dripping-pans scrape along the floor, and her bones, used to jumping at an unwashed pot, settled down. Talis, she thought, as if she heard his name for the first time. She saw his face, grave, thoughtful, his eyes hidden under circles of light. Then his head turned slightly; she saw his eyes clearly, dark blue, beginning to smile.

She saw him walk into a mist. A white owl flew out of the mist toward the castle. An eye in the keep watched it, shifting as the owl passed it, above the heads of guards on the walls watching the bright cloud that had dropped out of the clear night sky to cover the field. The owl left the castle behind. Its swift, smooth flight faltered then; it began to change shape in midair. The bird caught itself, spun down a little, caught itself again, wings laboring. It dropped finally among some trees. Touching the ground, it became Talis. He leaned wearily against a tree, catching his breath, looking back at the stars of fire in the dark rise of stone he had left behind. He turned his back to it finally and began to walk.

"What?" Saro heard all around her, as the prince walked through fire and water and disappeared. "She saw something. She did. Look at her eyes. Round as owl's eyes. What did you see? Saro, what did you see?"

They surrounded her, all the waiting eyes. The spit-boy holding the torch broke the silence. "How can she say? She can't talk."

Later, after the hall servants had carried back the bones and cold broken fragments of salmon wrapped in pie crust, roast venison seared over flames and simmered in wine, garlic and rosemary, carrots and onions fried in butter and ale, baked apples stuffed with cabbage and cream, baskets of fruit woven out of egg white and drizzled with chocolate flavored with brandy, the undercooks pored over the spellbook, looking for a recipe that would make Saro talk. The mincers, boners, pluckers, spit-boys and peelers fell on the leftovers like mice, then scattered again under tables, to the hearths, out of the way of the bakers and washers and the disgusted plucker who had to do pots, and who left trails of ash and grease behind her as she hauled dirty pots across the kitchen. They had taken a cauldron from the tallow-makers for her to wash in; Saro had refused to leave her cauldron.

"It's what she knows best," the tray-mistress decided.

But they gave her a sheepskin to sleep on, and moved the cauldron to a warm place beside the ovens.

The kitchen quieted, but for the rhythmic shaking of bakers' tables as they kneaded butter into rich dough for the morning pastries. The plate-washers dried the last plates, put them gently away. Then, with the smoky-eyed boner, they came to look at Saro as she sat in the shadow of the cauldron.

"She's fey," the boner said, twirling a strand of dark hair around a bitten forefinger. "Some witch was her mother, not a milker at all."

"No, a mage," the washer said. Her eyes caught Saro's, pale brown, like nuts. Saro stared at them a moment, then looked away, wrapping her arms nervously around her knees. The boner touched her.

"We won't hurt you, girl. Look." She unwrapped a slice of crusted salmon from her apron, untouched but for a bite at one corner. She put it on Saro's knees. "Eat it. You need your strength."

Saro unwound herself after a moment, took a bite. On stools above her, the undercooks turned the pages of the spellbook, entranced.

"Look at this one. To Leave a Message in Water. And this: To Sound a Bell at a Distance. To Open a Latched Door . . . Wasn't that the one—"

"Wasn't the prince trying to open a door that day—"

"When he made lightning and nearly killed the King."

They glanced doubtfully at Saro, eating cold salmon with her fingers. "She wouldn't have accidents, would she? She's born with it, the prince wasn't."

"Anyway, you have to speak with this spell. So she couldn't do it, anyway. Must be something in here can help her talk."

"Some are just born mute."

"Mages aren't."

"Saro," said the boner, when Saro had swallowed the last of the salmon. She put her hand on Saro's clasped, tense hands. "Listen to me. We want to teach you to talk. Say words. You need it, to do magic."

"She hasn't so far," the blue-eyed washer murmured.

"Well, we need her to talk. Listen. Saro. Can you say your name? Like this. First a hiss. Then open wide. Say *ah.* Then *ro.* Do this with your lips. Like a growl. Then *O.* It's easy. Try it. *Saro.*" She opened one of Saro's hands, laid it against her throat. "Can you feel my voice?" Saro, feeling wings under her hand, water moving, stirred with surprise. She felt her own throat with her other hand: Nothing moved.

"Maybe she hasn't got a voice."

"Should have a spit-boy scare her," the nut-eyed washer mused. "See if she screams."

"She never has. She has never made a sound."

They gazed at her, baffled. "Just try," the boner coaxed. "Just move your lips. *Sa. Ro.*"

"We should tell the King," the tray-mistress said to the head cook as he stood for a rare, idle moment beside the cluster of undercooks, looking over their shoulders at the spellbook. "There's a mage in his kitchen who has seen Prince Talis."

The head cook snorted. "Or that there is a mute pot-scrubber whom we asked to look for the prince in the bottom of a wash-cauldron."

"Well, if you put it that way —"

"No matter how it is put, that's what the King will see."

"But he's desperate for any word of Prince Talis!"

"I know. So are we all. Leave her to it. She must find her way to tell him — he'd never listen to us. He'd just start throwing."

"Maybe," the tray-mistress said dubiously. "She did look as surprised as any of us by what she did to the fire. I don't think she knows what she is. How could she, and still be happy scrubbing pots all those years? I think she's feeling her way to something. She doesn't go by that book. She doesn't know if the words are on their heads or on their heels. She's just doing. And even she doesn't know what she'll do next."

"But she knew enough to find the spellbook. She knows something."

"Yes," the tray-mistress agreed. "So we should tell the King."

Saro touched her mouth, felt her lips move, as she watched the boner's mouth. *Sa. Ro.* The wings in her throat refused to fly. Words could not get out that way. Yet that's what they all wanted from her: words. She had to say what she had seen, make a picture into words. She dropped her face against her knees abruptly, blinding herself to hear the sounds around her.

"She's tired," the tray-mistress said. "She's confused, poor thing."

The wings must fly in her throat, fly out of her mouth, carrying words with them. Her lips moved again, shaping her name. *Sa. Ro.* She lifted her head abruptly, stared at the boner, feeling that she had been given something of her own, something she would never lose.

Saro, her lips said, with no sound, no wings. But the boner smiled suddenly.

"Good. That's a place to begin, anyway. Your name."

In the next few days, Saro watched Prince Talis fly through fire and water as a hawk, an owl, a wild goose, each time staying a little longer in the air before his magic began to wear away and he reached for earth again. She watched him walk dark roads and rocky fields; she watched him run with wild horses through craggy hills. She watched him drift among humans in small, crowded, smoky rooms, listening to them. They never looked at him, or spoke to him;

he might have been a pot-scrubber, the way their eyes passed over him without seeing. Yet she saw him, in her magic cauldron, and she felt an odd tumult in her, as if she had swallowed a thundercloud, its rumbles and flashes of illumination like words trying to form.

She did things without thinking, as she watched him. She sparked the spit-boy's dwindling torch with a touch when the cauldron grew dark. She lifted her hand, and an apple fell into it, or a heel of bread, and she ate absently, not moving her eyes from Talis. Once, as she studied him, trying to envision what had made him invisible to humans, she heard a commotion around her, cries and hail of dropped utensils. She looked around and found all their eyes searching in bewilderment for her, passing over her as eyes passed over Talis. Then, in the next moment, their eyes found her again, knew her; she had gone and come back.

"We must tell the King," the tray-mistress said adamantly. "She's watching the prince. She knows where he is. He sent for mages who could not come; well, here's the mage who can find him."

"He won't listen," the head cook warned.

"He must listen."

The head cook flung up his hands, nearly clipping a mincer with a saucepan lid. "Who's to tell him Prince Talis is in the bottom of a cauldron of water?"

"You."

The King still hunted the wood each day for Talis, and each night, doors and gates and windows were locked tight against the strange magic that misted over the field. But the wood was empty of Talis. He had set his path toward a distant blue mist that slowly changed, the closer he came to it, revealing lines, shadows, vast sweeps of green and upthrusts of grey that disappeared into cloud. Saro watched, clinging to the edges of the cauldron as if she might slip headlong into such bewildering land, that towered into the sky instead of lying flat, like the fields Talis had left behind.

She heard the apprentices whispering late one night, as she half-dreamed beside the cauldron. They huddled under a spit-boy's torch; he watched them narrowly, as if they might somehow take light away from Saro. They turned pages slowly, discussed and discarded spells like recipes for tomorrow's supper.

"Here's one. What about this? To Make Small Objects Fall."

"Too noisy."

"How to See in the Dark."

"We'd have to put the fires out. Stock's simmering, bread rising in the ovens — Anyway, Saro has to see. Here. How to Levitate an Object."

"We could levitate something quiet."

"A mincer."

"They get noisy if they're dropped."

"An onion."

"Boring."

"This book, then! We'll levitate the spellbook."

"Saro," someone said; their faces, pale under the torch-fire, turned toward her briefly. She felt their eyes.

"She's busy. Besides, she won't care; she never looks at it. Besides — "

"It's just one spell."

"Just a small one."

"First: Place the object to be levitated in a place where its upward momentum will be unimpeded." There was a small silence. "Upward momentum . . . unimpeded. What's that? Herbs or something?"

"Must be a special language — mage words. Upward. All right. We know that means up. But what if it doesn't have a momentum? Most books don't, do they?"

"The head cook's do, when he throws them. It means, you wattle-brains, where it won't bump into something on the way up. Go on."

"It'll hit the torch. Shove it to one side. Move your elbow. There. Now go on."

Their voices slid away from Saro, mingled with the kitchen noises: the crackling pitch in the fires, the slow, patient bubbling of stock in iron pots, the spit-boys' sleepy, open-mouthed breathing, small invisible pluckers, telling stories under a table, the sweeper, a crooked bundle of bones, snoring beside his broom. Talis was flying toward the jagged end of the world: a massive crown of stone washed by moonlight, that snagged clouds as they sailed by, changed their shapes, then loosed them again. The hard wind tore the bird's shape away from Talis now and then, caused him to drop wildly, catching at his balance with a wing and an arm for a moment, until he tucked himself away again behind the feathers. There was magic in that wind, Saro sensed; light shimmered in it, odd shapes and shadows spun through it like leaves, disappeared. The bird flew high above a great, dark forest that climbed so far up, and then stopped, leaving bare stone rising upward against the stars. Wind fought the bird as it neared the stones, forced it to drop finally, spin down into the trees. The bird changed as it touched ground. The prince, sagging against one of the trees, rocked with it in the wind as he slid slowly down among its roots. Saro saw his face, white and hollowed with shadows, his eyes half-closed, watching the winds ride like wild hunters through the trees, watching for something within the winds.

After a while, he changed shape again.

"It's hopeless," an apprentice cook groaned behind her. "We might as well try to levitate a mountain."

The book shut with a bang. A white wolf moved through the trees toward the barren peak where the winds began.

Eighteen

On the highest peak of the mountains of Chaumenard, Atrix, an illusion of granite among broken slabs and boulders of granite, contemplated his creation. The Hunter, roaming the ledges below, would find him: He seemed linked, Atrix thought wearily, closer than a shadow to his maker. Moonlight cascaded down the peaks and slopes to flood the valley below; the dark hounds moved through it silently, little more than shadows themselves, sliding over the crags. The Hunter's inexhaustible power astonished the mage.

Drawkcab, he heard when he had a moment to sleep; the Hunter, quiet by day, prowled through the mage's dreams. *Xirta Eflow*: the backward face of Atrix's sorcery, himself transposed into that terrible reflection of power. But even a shadow resembled the one who cast it, in gesture, movement; it could be controlled. This shadow seemed to have no familiar shape, no predictable limits, no gestures that blurred into Atrix's gestures of power. The Hunter was isolated and stark as the moon. Atrix, seeking himself in the Hunter's mind, only fanned an endless rage.

You are mine, he reminded himself and the Hunter. *You are me. I made you. I am in you. You have hidden my face, the other side of that dark moon, but I am in you. I am you.*

Granite exploded next to him, as if the Hunter had heard his musings. Atrix became a shard in the explosion, flying down the face of the cliff toward the Hunter. He aimed himself at the Hunter's heart. The Hunter, deflecting stones with a sweep of his hand, found the one that did not veer, or drop, but sped even more quickly toward him, changing, as it neared the Hunter, into a wordless question.

What are you?

He caught the Hunter by surprise, slid beneath his defenses and, for a moment, looked into the Hunter's eyes.

He saw a field of fire and night, on which darkness shaped itself constantly into ravens, hounds, black moons, the hollow in the skull's eye. He felt the Hunter try to break free, block the mage from his mind; for another moment Atrix clung to him, stared into the darkness within the skull's eye, trying to see the power that insisted on such darkness, trying to find his own face within the bone.

He saw the green wood of his dreams.

Then fire swept through the wood and he heard himself cry out. He spun toward the fire, caught himself and withdrew from the Hunter's mind. He found himself splayed against the face of a cliff, wind seeking out his hidden shape, relentlessly drawing him into the moonlit world.

He melted deep into the rock, stayed there, hearing the Hunter's hounds howling in fury, and feeling the wild wind shake the face of the mountain as it searched for him.

I left a dream in the Hunter's mind, he thought, amazed, remembering the fury out of which he had worked his spell on that grim battlefield. Then he felt a terrible mingling of exhaustion and despair well up in him: He had finally seen himself in his shadow. *I am the raven, I am the hounds, I am the black moon rising in the flames, I am the Hunter's dream . . . And before I can destroy the Hunter, I must become the Hunter.*

Or he must become me.

But which, he wondered, *is which? And why, if I am the maker, and he is what I have made, is he so powerful?*

Beyond the solid stone, the wind was exhausting its fury. He gathered himself to face the Hunter again, before the moon turned its bloody face toward Pelucir.

At sunrise, he trapped the Hunter deep in the mountain within a great column of limestone; his hounds were frozen around him. The mage felt light touch the cold crags, high above him, and drew himself gratefully toward the warmth. He fell asleep among the scattered shards of granite on the top of the mountain.

In his dream, he watched a white wolf emerge from the edge of the shadowy forest, move along the bare, wind-whipped face of the mountain. He watched the wolf for a long time before it changed, in the way of dreams, into a young man standing on the stones, looking up, his lenses flashing with light, trying to see something that was only a word, a legend in his world. The young man touched his eyes; his lenses dropped suddenly into the rubble at his feet.

The White Wolf watched him from the top of the mountain. There was something disturbing in the young man's presence, though he had done nothing more than climb and stop and lose his lenses. He still looked up, his face bare, his eyes searching, though the stones must be only a blur against the sky. The mage sparked light in the lenses; the young man ignored them. He moved again; his next step shattered the lenses underfoot. Still he climbed, changing again into the white wolf, leaving the world behind to reach the top of the mountain.

Atrix felt the icy flash of fear snap out of him even before he woke.

"Talis," he heard himself say, pulling himself out of the stones to stand blinking at the light, groggy with exhaustion. On the face of the mountain, nothing moved. But he was there, the prince of Pelucir, still searching for the mage. He had seen the mist on Hunter's Field for what it was, and had followed Atrix into Chaumenard.

He dared not pull Talis into that world, even if he could: What he could see, so could the Hunter. He dared not let Talis stay on the mountain, in any world: What he knew, the Hunter would know, and Atrix could not guess what he might do. There was only one thing to do, and he had no idea how to do it. He sat down in the shadow of a boulder, and closed his eyes, trying to see into the dream again. "Talis," he whispered helplessly. "Where are you? I can't see you. Tell me how to reach you . . ."

The shadow of the stone he leaned against lay like stone across his eyes. He struggled against it a moment, lying vulnerable, exposed to wind and light and any passing life in his human shape. Then he felt himself fall a long way into blackness.

He stood in the green wood, where the small birds sang and invisible roses scented the air. The Queen walked toward him through her trees. They swayed, bowing as she passed; their leaves trailed through her hair, touched her face. She wore green the color of the leaves; it drifted around her, behind her, like cloud, mingling with her fiery hair, so that she seemed always a little blurred, as if she were just stepping out of wind.

"Atrix Wolfe." Her voice was as he remembered, low, sweet, touched with passion and sorrow. "Where are you?"

"I am here," he said, standing in her wood. "In Chaumenard."

"You must come to me."

"I am here."

"You are not here. I need you. Talis is searching for you."

"I know," he said helplessly. "He looks for me in my dreams; awake, I look for him. We cannot find each other that way. You must help me."

"How can I? I know nothing of your ways, or your world."

"But you know my name," he said perplexedly, and watched her eyes grow dark, luminous with secret pain.

"I know you," she said. Leaves whirled around her suddenly, a great storm of green, as if they had been torn away by a season out of time. Through them he glimpsed her face, her hair, her hand. When the leaves finally fell, the trees were bare around her, and above them the sky was black.

He tasted snow, smelled burning wood. The blowing leaves were raven-black; they cried in hoarse ragged voices as they spun away. He could not see the Queen's face; it was a black, empty oval.

"Talis will bring you to me," she said. "He has found you for me. I will give him back to you."

"Not here —" he said, terrified again. "Not now —"

"You wanted him," she reminded him. "You could not find him in my wood. Now find him in Chaumenard."

"No!" he shouted, and woke himself.

The sun had shifted; he lay in light, sprawled across the stones. He moved stiffly, drawing back into shadow, and scanned the mountainside with a hawk's eye. Nothing moved. He let his thoughts drift among the trees, found their webbed, windblown boughs busy with life. No white wolves prowled among their shadows. None waited hidden among the crags around him. It was only a dream, he thought. Still, dread clung to him, formed a vision in his mind: the prince of Pelucir caught on that strange battle-field between the Hunter and the Wolf.

The sun still hung above the mountain; it was late afternoon. Hungry, he changed shape and hunted the lower meadows, forgetting, for a brief hour, everything except what the wind told him, or the earth underfoot, or the small movements among the wildflowers. He took his own shape again and stepped through memory and time, back up to the mountaintop.

The white wolf moved out of the shadows to meet him.

Atrix stopped; the fear flared through him again, coloring his shadow. The wolf changed shape. Talis stood on the high, barren peak, trembling a little, wind-shaken, as if he had been pulled too abruptly out of a dream. He said, confused, "Atrix Wolfe. Can you see me?"

"I can see you," Atrix said grimly. "Far too clearly."

"How did I — Did you —"

"She sent you here. The Queen of the Wood."

The prince's lenses flashed, catching light. He slid them straight, silently, and cast a glance around them, and then down the slope, still searching, it seemed, for a vanished world. "Talis," Atrix said, and touched him lightly, trying to wake him. The prince looked at him again, still stunned. "She should never have done this. He'll kill you. You must go — I'll take you down —"

"No."

"Talis — Listen —"

"You listen." Talis reached out suddenly, caught the worn cloth over Atrix's breast in both hands, shook him. Color streaked the prince's face; he was not seeing Atrix, the mage realized, or the mountain; his eyes were filled with trees, light, the hushed secret green of the wood. "I told her yes. To whatever she wanted. If this is what she wants, then this is where I stay, on this mountain with you until the moon rises and turns black and falls out of the sky. You made your choice on Hunter's Field the night I was born. I have made mine. She wants you. She needs me to bring you to her, and between the two of us, we will find a way, or blood of Pelucir will be shed on a mountain in Chaumenard, and that will be on your head, too." He loosed Atrix, stepped back, breathing quickly. He added, "You lied to the mages of Chaumenard. You lied to Pelucir and to Kardeth. You lied in your writings. Why should you expect me to listen to you?"

For a moment, Atrix could not answer. Then a long finger of light cut between them, the last, dazzling light of day, and he found an answer in it. "I watched your father die on Hunter's Field," he said. "I will not watch you die here, not for the sake of any woodland queen. I promised your brother I would bring you back to him, wherever you were. And then I promised him he could kill me. You will leave this place before the sun sets. This is not your battle, and you are not powerful enough to argue the point with me."

"You promised Burne—" A sudden evening wind rocked Talis a step; he caught his balance, staring at Atrix. "Burne can't—" He reached out to Atrix again, more gently. "Listen to me. You can't—"

"I can't what? What can't I do? Tell me that: where the limits are to what I can do."

"You can't bring my father back to life by letting Burne kill you. You can't leave your ghost to haunt Pelucir."

"Argue with Burne—Argue with me, later, but not here, and not now. I'll take you to the school. Stay there. Tell them, there, what is happening here, under the Shadow of the Wolf—warn them to stay away—"

"Atrix, listen." Talis' voice held a sharp, urgent note that snagged Atrix's attention an instant before he moved. "The Hunter has a name."

"What?"

"You never knew that. She sent me here to tell you that."

"She—" Atrix turned, his hands locking on Talis' arms. "He is my making—he has no other name but mine!"

"Listen. Think back. What did you make the Hunter out of?"

"Night." Atrix's voice shook. "Blood. Fire. Fury. Despair. All the terrors and nightmares I found on that field—What could she know of him?"

"What else?"

He no longer saw the prince's face; he saw snow-streaked winds, a field of fire and snow, trees as bare as bone crowning a hill buried in winter, a wood through which desperate, weary animals fled the desperate hunters stalking them. "Starving deer. Hunter. Ravens. Warriors. Hunters."

"You took humans—"

"No. Only their skills. Their desires. The memory of them, in animals' minds, from the wood."

"And what else?"

"The new moon."

"And what else?" The prince held him again, tightly, his voice as implacable as stone hammering stone.

And what else? Atrix demanded of his memories. *And what else? Snow, night, wind, fire, the wood on the hill.* His breath caught. A green mist flushed across the trees, across the barren field. He entered, again, the wood of his dreams. "Did I take something of hers," he whispered, "when I worked that spell?" He paused again, remembering the glimpse of the green wood he had caught in the Hunter's eye. "Someone?"

Light faded between them, left the prince's face without expression. "His name," Talis said, "is Ilyos."

He came to them as if summoned. His horse's hooves sparked fire from the granite they barely touched, his hounds howled beside him. The new moon smoldered through his horns. His eyes held Talis; his hounds swarmed toward the prince, who, transfixed by the sight, seemed incapable of moving. The Hunter lifted a hand, pulled the moon from between his horns and threw it at Talis.

"Drawkcab," he said. The black moon streaked through the twilight, as if it had fallen out of the sky. Talis, spellbound, raised his hands to catch it.

Atrix shattered it into a shower of burning tears. "Ilyos!" he cried, and the Hunter's face swung toward him. Atrix felt the shock of his memories, and then of his sudden, overwhelming rage. Atrix caught Talis' wrist, hid them both within a dream of the green wood, trees rising still and endless around them, spilling light between their leaves.

The Hunter rode through the wood. Every oak branch blazed with fire; a dark moon hung from every oak. The ground shook beneath his horse's hooves; lightning snapped from his hounds' teeth. "Xirta Eflow," he said. "Atrix Wolfe."

Atrix felt Talis slip from his grip. "Atrix," Talis called, from very far away, it seemed, from the other side of night. "Talis!" he shouted, and saw a black streak split the burning wood, a dark road leading to the black moon rising above the wood.

Talis ran down the road. "Atrix," he called, and, as burning oak began to fall across the road between them, he called again, "Drawkcab."

Fire began to streak down the path behind Talis. Atrix, his heart burning, melted through the fire after the prince, and found himself moving down the pale, cold, glittering path of the rising moon.

Silver turned gold; all around him, in their secret ways, the oak watched. He turned, bewildered; moon and sun spun together above him in the sky.

The Queen of the Wood rode the path of gold through the oak to meet him.

Her following rode with her. He saw faces of layered leaf and pale birch, and woven willow among more human faces which, ageless and secret, held little human expression. As in his dream, the Queen carried a bow. He scarcely noticed it, for as in his dream, her face was like nothing he had ever seen; it seemed to belong in the places he loved most, among the elegant, wild faces of wolf and hawk and snow leopard, the faces in mountains, in amber, in blue running water so cold it burned. She raised the bow; he watched light through the windblown leaves above her pick out a strand of fire in her hair, and then a strand of gold.

He felt Talis beside him then, heard his quick, startled breathing. Then the wind in the oak trees around them roared through leaf and branch. A rider behind the Queen with a face of smooth leaves opened nut-green eyes to stare at Atrix. Lightning leaped out of nowhere, struck the ground at Atrix's feet.

He melted instinctively into the sudden, violent whip of air and light. Then he heard Talis' voice and reappeared, in time to feel the next bolt, or perhaps an arrow from the Queen's upraised bow, bore into his heart.

He heard Talis' voice again, somewhere above him. He felt oak leaves under his face, his hands; within his heart something burned past bearing. He felt Talis' hands gripping him, heard words form in the wild, chaotic winds.

"I didn't bring him to you for this!"

"It doesn't matter," he whispered to the leaves, but Talis heard him.

"It matters," he said sharply. "We need you." His voice angled away. "Please. You need him, too. You want him to find Saro for you."

I have found sorrow for her, Atrix told him silently; the prince read his mind.

"It's her daughter. Saro. You did something to her that night. She vanished out of the wood into the world. That's why the Queen sent you dreams. To summon you. But you couldn't come to her, so she called me instead, because I can see her, in the world, and you never could. She used me to bring you here."

Atrix opened his eyes. Talis knelt over him, shielding him for some reason that Atrix could not fathom. He said blankly, "Saro." Then he lifted his head, raised himself on one arm to see the Queen's face. He saw her poised arrow first, and then her fierce and troubled eye. He said incredulously, "I took your daughter, too?"

"Saro," she said, in the voice out of her dreams, and then grew very still, the bowstring pulled taut, her eye and the arrow's blind eye fixed on Atrix's fate. He waited, his own breath stopped. Then she loosed the bow and arrow, let them slide from her hands, drop to the ground. Talis' hands loosened; he still knelt, supplicant, in the oak leaves, his face as pale as moonlight, until she spoke again.

"No. I did not bring him here for this." The Queen dismounted. Atrix groped for Talis' shoulder, pulled himself painfully to his feet, keeping a hand on the prince as Talis stood.

"Tell me," he said heavily to the Queen, whose eyes, like his, were shadowed with his past. "Tell me what I have done. To Ilyos. To Saro."

"Ilyos was my consort," she said, "Saro our daughter. You took them both from me that night; I have never seen them since." He stared at her, and felt the fading fire in his heart leap through him, burn dryly behind his eyes.

"Sorrow," he said, shaken by the word. "When you spoke in my dreams, that was always what I heard."

"Now you know why."

"Now I know," he whispered. Her face was colorless, expressionless, within the fall of her hair; she gave him, for the moment, nothing but words.

"I do not expect to see Ilyos again. Not alive, not after what your power forced him to do. But I want Saro. She is in your world. Find her. I don't know what you care about, except Talis. I will free him now because he did what I asked: He brought you to me. But I will take him and keep him until Pelucir is only a memory in mortals' minds, if you fail to find Saro. If you ever love again, I will take what you love, if you fail to find Saro. I will take whatever peace you find waking, and there will be no peace, ever, in your dreams, if you fail to find Saro."

"I will find Saro," he said softly. "There is no need to threaten me."

Her face changed then, its icy stiffness trembling a little. Color touched it. "You have so much power," she said, "and so little regard for your life, you would have let me kill you. I don't know what you care about enough to threaten you with."

"I am still alive," he reminded her. "I seem to care about that. And you have already threatened me with Talis' life. It seems I care about that, too."

She was silent, then, studying him, her brows knit, as if he spoke a language she did not expect. She said slowly, "I spoke to you in your dreams. I rode through them. I sent you portents, images. But I never saw your face. I thought you would be different."

"You thought," he suggested painfully, "I would resemble what I had made."

"I thought," she said, "you would be less human. Arrogant, thoughtless, dangerous with power. Or perhaps I should say more human."

"I have been all of those things."

Talis stirred under his hand, turned to look at him. "There are rules," he reminded Atrix tightly, "governing the choices of powerful and dangerous mages."

"I know," Atrix said painfully. "Such rules are made by powerful and dangerous mages, who are also more or less human. You will forgive me for that night on Hunter's Field long before I will ever forgive myself."

Talis' lenses flashed away from him. "Perhaps," he breathed to the ground, then looked at the mage again, still aloof, but curious. "How will you find Saro?"

"I don't know. First I must deal with what I have made. Tell me," he said to the Queen, "something about your consort. Anything."

She was silent again, her hands locked on her arms, her face mist-pale as she gazed into the winter-mists of memory. "He has the power of the wood," she said finally. "Of oak, and the red deer and the running stream. Time means little to him. He —" She stopped, then stopped Atrix as he began to speak. "He will not die as humans die." She stopped him again, her hand upraised, her eyes dark. "One thing more. He loved Saro. He must not find you with her. They heard you speaking that night. A wolf, Saro said. Later, when I could think, I had that small piece to wonder about. Names drift into my world, dreams, enchantments. Saro gave me a name before she vanished. So I began to listen for it, Atrix Wolfe."

He bowed his head. "And you gave me a word. How will I find you if I need you?"

"Talis will guide you here." Her face softened then, at the name. She turned to the prince, took his hands in hers. "You have been very faithful, and very brave." She touched his cheek with her fingers, then kissed him. "Thank you. Now I will send you back."

"Where?" he asked, bewildered, as if he had only dreamed Pelucir.

"To your world." His hands shifted, locked around her hands as if he were sliding into deep water. "I have kept you long enough."

"Not long." His voice shook. "Not long at all. Will I see you again?"

She did not answer. She stepped back from them both, began to fade. Atrix caught Talis moving blindly in her wake. The prince twisted away from him, but found no place to go in the empty, moonlit wood, except to the castle rising across the silent field.

Nineteen

⊸≫

Talis walked into a hall full of weary, bedraggled hunters. Moving with a mage's ways, out of habit, he had avoided the gate and the guards; it must have seemed, he realized, that he had formed out of shadow and torch fire, for the pale faces and bloodshot eyes around him were as immobile as if he had cast a spell over them. He said to the statue that was Burne,

"I'm back."

Burne stood up; his chair fell over. Behind him, a mound of fish skeletons carried by a startled servant tilted on the tray and slid like leaves to the floor. Other servants leaped to life, righted the King's chair, settled Talis into the empty chair beside the King, poured wine. Burne, staring at Talis, sat down again slowly.

"You're all right?"

Talis nodded, staring into his cup. Fingers glided like silk across his cheek; the corner of his mouth still burned. He felt her kiss again, brief and sweet, her lips the secret, closed petals of a rose. Fire shivered across the dark wine; he picked up the cup and drank. "I'm all right," he said to Burne. Servants laid things on his plate; he gazed at them without interest. Around him, people came to life again, murmuring, but softly, so they could listen.

"Well, where were you?" Burne demanded.

"In the wood. In her wood."

"We hunted for you, we searched everywhere, every day. The mage — " He stopped, his face tightening. "That mage said you were in a dream."

"It was him she wanted." He lifted the cup again. "She needed me to find him. That was all."

"So you found him."

"Yes."

"So he's with her now."

"Yes." He put the cup down again without drinking. "No. She needs him to find her child. I don't know where he is. In Chaumenard, I think."

"Do you know that Atrix Wolfe — "

"Yes." His hands locked around the cup; he sat silently, trying to be patient with the cold grey stones, the unshaven, untidy hunters, the flickering candles, the tapestries that, if lifted, would only reveal more stone. If he did not look at the walls, he could see the green wood, leaves trembling around him as if a hand had just brushed them. If he did not look, she would be among them. . . .

"Talis."

He looked up, saw massive grey squares of stone, unkempt faces, jewelled hands that moved among fire and gold without grace. Burne's face, haggard and furrowed with sleeplessness, looked oddly unfamiliar. "What?"

"What is wrong with you? You've been gone for days, trapped in another world; you've found the mage responsible for the death of our father and the horror on Hunter's Field; we've ridden ourselves into wraiths looking for you, and now you're back and you can't seem to speak in words longer than one syllable — Are you under some spell?"

"Yes." He was on his feet before he thought, cup in his hands, wanting to throw it for no good reason except that stones were not leaves, and shadow was not light. "Yes," he said again. "I am under some spell." Around him, faces had turned immobile again. "No. I'm not under some spell. I wish I were. I would give anything to be spellbound."

Burne set his own cup down slowly. If he said one word, Talis knew, it would be the wrong word, and any word would be too many. He waited, tense, unable to leave for there was no place to go, unable to stay and keep looking at Burne's tired, human face.

"We need you, too," Burne said, and then he was sitting again, his heart battered and rent, but somehow still alive. He drank more wine, ate something, unable to speak, aware of Burne's silence, his unusual patience.

Talis said finally, wearily, when some of the faces had turned away from him, and random conversations disguised the attention on him, "What do you want me to do?"

"Be here," Burne pleaded, "for a start. You're the only one here who knows anything at all about sorcery, and you must know by now what rose with the moon to ride again on Hunter's Field."

"Atrix Wolfe is still fighting it. Him." He ate another tasteless bite, and heard her voice again: *His name is Ilyos.* He swallowed, forced himself to speak. "In Chaumenard. Atrix drove him there."

"Will it stay there?"

"I don't know."

"Maybe they'll kill each other," Burne said without hope. "Another thing: We can't find that book."

"What book?"

"Atrix Wolfe's book. He said we had to get it out of the castle: It is connected to the Hunter, somehow. I don't understand, but the mage thought it was important."

"It's in the keep."

"It's not in the keep. I looked."

"You went up there?" Talis said sharply.

"I didn't trust anyone else to look. There are bindings

and pages scattered everywhere; nothing is left whole. He said it would be unharmed. Either he was wrong, or it wasn't there. He." He sat silently, his brows knit, brooding over the mage. "Atrix Wolfe," he said softly, to the candle-light; Talis could not read the expression in his eyes.

Talis said, hunched over his cup, scattering words so that he didn't have to think: "The book is a lie, words in it are untrue, the spells go awry. He was writing one spell and thinking always of another. That's why the book is so dangerous. He wrote down 'mirror,' but thought 'Hunter.' He wrote 'water' and thought 'Hunter.' The words twisted in his thoughts, in his writing of them. Because he is so powerful, each act must be unambiguous. And he hasn't had a thought without the Hunter in it since that night."

"Why?" Burne asked the candle as if it were the mage. The flame stilled, reflected in his eyes. Talis shook his head silently, seeing the wood on the hill, the winter wood the mage saw, the green, timeless wood he had torn into. A mistake, an accident, a thoughtless impulse — there seemed no word for it.

"Ask him," he said finally. "He was there. I wasn't. You don't want an answer from me."

He stayed away from the keep until morning. In his dreams, he wandered through a leafless wood searching for something: for green, for a white deer, a tree full of autumn leaves. The only deer he saw were brown, thin in the bitter cold. *Go home*, they said. *It is always winter now*. When he woke, he rose and went to a window. He felt his heart leap toward that secret cloud of green on the hill. He could go there, he could wait among the trees, asking nothing but a little water, a nut now and then, simply wait among her trees, hoping she might notice him, lay a hand of light upon his cheek, a rose against his mouth.

He went into the keep instead.

He searched awhile among the torn, damp pages. He recognized them all, and none of them were Atrix's. Perplexed and uneasy, he found the guards who had been with him in the keep when the Hunter had returned. They had taken nothing, they had seen no one, for there was no one in the castle who would venture up there after that, except the King, who had looked also and found nothing.

He stayed away from the wood until noon. Then he rode without thought and without hope through the trees, heard them whisper around him, the birds sing a language she understood. She seemed to stand just beyond eyesight in every fall of light; her reflection had just vanished out of every stream he crossed. He returned to the castle at sunset. Trumpeters at the gate told of his return; he was told three times, before he even set foot on the ground, that the King wanted him.

He found Burne pacing on the parapet walk overlooking Hunter's Field. "What is it?" Talis asked. "What happened?"

Burne stopped pacing and looked at him. "Nothing, apparently," he said tersely. "But how am I to know that when you vanish?"

"Oh." He leaned into a crenellation, losing whatever fleeting interest he had in Burne's worries. He watched the fiery green of the wood at sunset fade into a cool, shadowed green as the light drained out of it. *Saro*, he thought without hope. *If I could find Saro before Atrix Wolfe does, perhaps she would love me, then* . . . Burne had said something, he realized, and turned reluctantly from the wood.

"Book?"

"Atrix Wolfe's book."

"Oh. No. I went up and looked this morning." He felt wind at his cheek and closed his eyes. "I didn't find it."

"Talis."

"What?"

"She knows where to find you, if she wanted you."

He opened his eyes, touched his lenses straight with a trembling hand. "I know," he breathed. "Of course I know. Why do you think that makes any difference?"

"I suppose it wouldn't. What was it like, there? What do you see, when you ride in the wood? Is it so different, there?"

Talis shook his head, unable to say, having no words for the taste of light, for the intensity in the air where she might appear. "She doesn't want me," he said at last, his face turned to the wood again. "She won't take me, like she did before. You don't have to fear that."

Burne's hand fell heavily onto his shoulder, closed. "Is she that cruel?" he asked incredulously. "To leave you like this?"

"Cruel things were done to her." He watched the wood a moment longer, a still, twilight world growing opaque with shadow, his own face haunted, drained of light. Then he sighed, and looked at Burne.

"You warned me," he said. "But how did you know?"

Burne shrugged. "I don't know. How does anyone learn these things." He was, Talis realized with a touch of interest, avoiding Talis' eyes. "Let's go in. We're still under siege, at night, until the mage tells us otherwise. I don't understand how even he can be in danger from his own spell. It makes no sense to me."

"That is the other reason the Queen wanted Atrix Wolfe."

He told Burne the tale during supper, made him see the winter night again, the cold wind blowing between worlds, snow falling in the green wood, into the burning horns of the Queen's consort, the snow-streaked wind hiding the Queen's daughter, carrying her away into a world of chaos, death and dark enchantments. Burne, grim and astonished, pushed the venison on his plate away, as if it might have had magical origins. "What a nightmare," he said. "A single night's work. Where will he even begin to look for the child?"

"Here, I suppose. In Pelucir. And then wherever he goes for the rest of his life." He paused, watching Burne's face, his eyes still, unreadable behind his lenses. "Atrix Wolfe cast the spell," he said. "But we gave him the words for it."

For an instant, Burne saw what he saw. Then the King's face closed, and he said harshly, "War is war. It's as old as breathing, and he made himself part of it. He forged the best weapon and he took the field. If he was too innocent to know what he was doing, that's his fault. And he's paying for it."

Talis drank. "He is paying for our father's death," he said somberly. "Let's hope he doesn't pay with his life, or we'll be under siege for the rest of ours."

He rode out to the wood again the next day, and the next. The wood in his dreams was empty, barren; the wood of his waking hours was hardly less empty, except for the hunters in it, for none of the guests wanted to risk the fate of Burne's messengers, and they needed to be fed. He rode with them a time or two, hoping to be struck from his horse by Oak, and hobble out of water to see the Queen of the Wood. The noise, the arrows slicing randomly into trees, birds, deer, the excited, triumphant fanfares for death, only made him impatient and despondent. He wandered back up into the keep, one morning, and began to clean up the litter of ripped parchment and broken wood. He was, he told Burne, searching for the mage's book: Since it could be nowhere else, it must be there. But he knew it was no longer in the keep. It had opened itself, its grim power had escaped, and looking for it seemed pointless. A book that could find its way out of solid granite into a mop closet, and then into Pelucir to summon a mage and his making, would not reveal itself at some human whim. He himself, wary of sorcery, summoned a broom and a hammer to the keep; he swept up glass and nailed the table back together, burned the broken buckets and the fragments of spells. The ghosts on the walls seemed to pause sometimes, to watch him; they turned away from his eyes, but he felt theirs, as if they saw into him, knowing that the light that fell into the keep was not the light that filled his eyes, knowing that the memory he looked for on the walls had nothing to do with theirs.

Burne, suspicious, came up to see him. "You're not," he said succinctly, "beginning that again."

"The book is gone," Talis sighed. "Nothing else I can do is dangerous. And I promise: no sorcery in here until the Hunter is dead."

"You're not staying up here!" Burne shouted. "You nearly lost your life here! I want you down where I can see you, surrounded by the living instead of by ghosts. If you're not in the wood hunting a dream, you're up here courting disaster — Can't you take an interest in anything human?"

Talis, startled by his vehemence, heard his own voice, unexpectedly raised, almost unfamiliar. "How?" he demanded. "When I have been surrounded all my life by ghosts? I grew up knowing how these ghosts died! This war has never ended — Atrix kept it alive, and you, and everyone in this house, blaming sorcery, blaming Kardeth — Can you blame me for taking what peace I can in the only place where I recognize the word?"

"You might as well be pining after a ghost," Burne snapped. "You're in love with your own memories. Nothing else. She'll give you nothing now but pain. And there will be little more of you up here than what haunts these walls."

Talis stared at him, tight-lipped. He flung down the hammer in his hand, walked to the window. His vision cleared after a moment. The window gave him a view of his thoughts: Hunter's Field, the Queen's wood. He turned his face after a moment, pushed it against the stones.

"I can't help her," he whispered. "And Atrix Wolfe can. She doesn't need me. She needs him. There's nothing left for me to do for her. I can't even help you. All I can do is wait, and for what? For the emptiness in that wood, in my dreams, to wear away at my heart, until I can no longer feel. And then I can live among the living again. Is that what you want?"

"Atrix Wolfe," Burne said tightly. "Atrix Wolfe. Why is his name always underfoot?" His voice rose again. "Can you be reasonable! He killed her consort! Or as good as killed him! What makes you think you must be jealous of him?"

Talis lifted his face from the stones, stared at them. Then he turned, to stare at Burne again. "I have to hate him." Light fell between them; for once it held no imminence of memory. "Otherwise, I might forgive him. And I was raised with too many ghosts to do that."

"No one," Burne said, shouting again, "said you had to forgive him! We weren't arguing about him! How did she turn into him?"

"I don't know." His voice shook. "It's a tangled piece of magic to unravel, what happened on Hunter's Field. I have to understand what happened to him that night, or it will haunt me and any sorcery I ever do again. How will I ever trust anything I ever do, if his magic could twist itself into such terrible shapes, wear such a terrible face? I have to understand him."

"I wish," Burne said between his teeth, "I could understand you." He turned abruptly, nearly colliding, in the doorway, with the mute ghost of a girl who came up with Talis' tray. She flinched; he glanced at the tray and fumed again. "Take that back to the kitchen! You can at least eat among the living instead of the dead." He added, as she pulled herself and her tray aside so he could pass, her eyes wide, unfocused with alarm, "And find that spellbook. If he says it's dangerous, it's dangerous; he should know. It will give you something to do besides haunt the keep and the wood."

"It's not — All right," Talis said wearily, to Burne's back. He moved to retrieve the tray pulled into the King's wake. But it seemed, in the unpredictable shadows, to have magicked itself away. Catching up with Burne at the bottom of the steps, he glimpsed nothing either of the tray or of its bearer.

"Maybe she's a ghost," he mused. Burne caught his arm, but gently.

"I'm trying to be patient," he said. "I'm trying to understand."

"I know."

"Who's a ghost?"

"That girl."

"What girl?"

He ate with the King, made soothing, meaningless noises to the anxious guests, and went back to the keep afterward, to shut up the room for the sake of some peace with Burne.

He found the spellbook lying on the table.

He did not touch it. He sat down on the window ledge and gazed at it, his eyes wide, still, as he thought. No one comes up here, the guards had said. No one ever comes . . .

A face appeared in his mind's eye: pale, silent, utterly insignificant. He watched her walk into the room, carrying his tray, watched her look here, there, and then at him, with her face that kept changing, eyes he could never remember. She had come once at night, he recalled suddenly, to tell him something, but she could not speak. She had come up, alone, in the dark, to tell him something.

No one ever comes here.

"You come here," he whispered. *Nothing that exists is insignificant*, Atrix Wolfe had written in the book that had returned to him. He left it there and went to find her.

Twenty

Saro watched him.

She leaned over the edge of the cauldron. The prince moved through the dark water, down through the keep, his face visible as light from the narrow windows flashed over him, then obscured by the sudden, dense shadows. He did not carry the spellbook. She watched him thoughtlessly, out of habit, not knowing at what moment he might turn his head and see what she had seen. In the past, she had watched him ride through a wood that seemed a reflection of the wood the cauldron dreamed: Like him, she searched for things in it she could not find, for faces emerging out of leaves, out of light. She had watched him burn torn pages in the keep, feeding broken spells, one by one, to the hungry flame. She had watched him lean against the moving shadows on the wall, take off his lenses and weep.

"Saro," the tray-mistress had said earlier. Saro saw the heavy silver tray in her hands: onion soup with a melting crust of cheese over it, a loaf of dark bread, a flagon of wine, a tart of oranges sliced into thin bright circles glistening under a glaze that smelled of ginger. "Nobody will go up there but you."

So she left her cauldron to take the tray to the prince in the keep.

Nobody questioned her when the tray came back down intact, nor when, still wide-eyed, she shut the book under the spit-boys' watching eyes, and hurried out with it. "He wants his book back," the tray-mistress guessed. One of the under-cooks muttered, "Never worked, anyway."

Now the prince walked out of the keep into the yard. Light floated across the water, angles of cloudy blue above harsh angles of stone. He did not enter the house again; he came along the outer wall, as she had gone, the narrow neglected stretch where the wildflowers grew between the house and the wall. Guards and pages, hurrying past, looked astonished at the sight of him. The strip of ground widened at the corner of the house, into the kitchen garden, with its long, tidy rows of herbs and vegetables, its vast woodpile, its moldering midden. Wood-boys splitting logs snagged their upraised axes on air, staring at the prince. He rounded the woodpile; ahead of him, the garden rows ended in a high stone wall that hid its unseemly sprawling squash vines and lettuces from the formal gardens beyond it. He turned onto the worn path that ended at the open kitchen door.

Saro lifted her head, blinking. Noises and movement in the kitchen behind her stopped dead. She turned, saw everyone, cooks, mincers, spit-boys, frozen over pots, knives, fires, staring at the kitchen door. She shifted, saw the shadow falling through the doorway, and blinked again, feeling some word trying to come alive in her throat. She stood up slowly, and met the prince's eyes.

The tray-mistress, raising her apron to her mouth, made a muffled exclamation into it. The prince's eyes moved to her.

"I don't know her name," he said.

The tray-mistress moved her apron and wobbled a curtsy. "Saro, my lord," she said.

For a moment, staring at Saro, he seemed as frozen as everyone staring at him. Then he lifted a hand, touched his lenses. A word tried to come out of him and failed, Saro saw with wonder. His eyes went back to the tray-mistress.

"She doesn't speak?"

"She never has, my lord," the tray-mistress said faintly. She rallied herself, apron to her heart, and added, "Never since she was found."

"Where?"

"Out there beside the woodpile."

"When?"

The tray-mistress shook her head, speechless again. "Years ago, my lord," she said finally. "Just after the winter siege, we found her, just a scrap of a child, barely alive in the cold, and mute as a mop. My lord."

He touched his lenses again; they turned back to Saro. "Then how," he asked huskily, "did you know her name?"

"She was someone's sorrow," the tray-mistress said simply. "So we called her that."

She saw her name in his face, then, in his eyes, glittering suddenly behind the lenses. He pulled them off, brushed the back of his sleeve across his face. A spit-boy made a soft noise, then went frozen again, staring. Everyone else seemed to unfreeze, as if the prince's tears had broken some spell. The head cook asked, amazed,

"Who is she, my lord? Can you tell us? She's been down here scrubbing pots all of your life. And then she got your book somehow. She's something magical —"

"Yes." He looked at the head cook. "No one thought to tell the King?"

"We were thinking, yes," the tray-mistress said hastily. "But you weren't here to tell, then, and she —"

"We knew she watched you," the head cook interrupted, "in that cauldron. We found the spell in your book, and we asked her to find you. We could see her watching you, see the magic in her eyes. But none of us could see you, and she couldn't speak, and all the King would have seen was a pot of water and a mute pot-scrubber and a kitchen full of mad fools."

"Still we've been thinking of how to tell him," the tray-mistress said, "but he's been so — so fraught. Scalding, you might say, if you'll forgive me, my lord. When he wasn't boiling over."

The prince stepped into the kitchen, gazing at Saro again. She watched him out of habit, relieved that he was out of the cauldron and under her eyes, but uneasy, too, since what would come seemed oddly imminent, and she was as far as ever from being able to warn him.

He stood silently, looking at her for a long time, without moving or speaking; the kitchen hushed again around him. Nothing about him spoke, not even his eyes, which seemed dark and secret, suddenly, like her cauldron when the dreams in it were about to well up from the bottom and glide across the water. Then he moved, murmuring something, and slid one hand under his lenses to rub his eyes.

"She's under a very powerful spell," he said, and enchanted the entire kitchen. The tray-mistress sat down on a stool, waving her apron at her face. Boner and plate-washer nudged each other and whispered. Mincers and pluckers emerged from under the tables to see what he did. The spit-boys grinned, their fiery eyes clinging to him. Cooks and undercooks forgot their bubbling sauces. The head cook forgot supper.

"But who is she?" he asked again. "If you can tell us, my lord?"

The prince did not answer. He took Saro's hand. Unused to being touched, she started to pull away, not knowing what he wanted. He kept his hand out, open; her fingers, sliding away from it, edged back slowly across hollows and lines and skin that was not her own. She heard a sigh from a plate-washer. The prince smiled a little, his face opening again, briefly, before the thoughts slid back across it. "I wonder . . ." he whispered, gazing at her without seeing her, as everyone had all her life. "I wonder . . ." Now they saw her, she realized with surprise. As if she had enchanted herself into being, with her own magic. He was seeing her again, and then not, thoughts coming and going in his eyes, expressions changing. "No," he decided finally, aloud, "I can't tell Burne." He looked at the head cook. "You tell him."

"Tell the King what, my lord?" the head cook asked, bewildered.

"Where I've gone."

"And that would be — ?"

"Back into the wood."

"The wood." The head cook rubbed a lifted eyebrow with his thumbnail and added without hope, "Hunting, my lord?"

"Not that wood," Talis said evenly.

The head cook closed his eyes briefly. "My lord Talis," he breathed, "show some mercy to him — you just came back. He'll throw a table at me and have me cook it for his supper, nails and all."

"I know." Talis' voice was soft, but inflexible. "But magic has laid siege to this house again, and I can't fight it locked inside."

"Atrix Wolfe," the head cook said, then stopped abruptly, his face a pale, hard mask of itself. "What has the wood got to do with what Atrix Wolfe made? Or with Saro?"

"It's all his magic," the prince said. Saro looked at him, hearing things in his voice, like something searing too long in a pan, or a sauce boiling too quickly instead of simmering.

Her fingers tightened on his hand. He looked at her, surprised, as if she had spoken. His voice cleared. "You don't have to tell him that. Or about Saro. Just tell him I have gone back to the Queen's wood. He'll believe I'm safe, there."

"But, my lord," the head cook exclaimed. "If you're not, then you must not —"

"Tell him I'll return as soon as I can."

"But, my lord —"

"What queen?" the tray-mistress asked quickly, gazing at Talis, the apron bunched between her clasped hands. All around him, mouths were open again, eyes round, some watching him, some Saro. Talis' face changed, as if torchlight or a hand had brushed it.

"The Queen of the Wood." He paused, then added very gently, "This is her Saro."

As he led her out, she stopped in the kitchen doorway, to cast a glance back at her cauldron, wanting it to come with her, as if its hard plain shell in which she had washed every pot in the world, and all its wordless inner mysteries, were a part of her she dared not leave behind. But she had no way to say "cauldron" to the prince. She tried to lift it with her thoughts, but, perversely, it refused to budge. Talis seemed to feel her loss; he looked back quickly, and then at her.

"What is it?" he asked. "Show me."

She looked at him. His eyes narrowed slightly, surprised, perhaps, at what they saw in his mind. Then she felt the cauldron's iron, strong, heavy, solid, just beneath her skin, within her bones, and knew she carried its strange visions with her; its dark eye was her eye, seeing. But like her, it was silent, and she needed to make words for Talis, who waited patiently, catching stray arrows of sunlight in his lenses.

She felt something simmering in her froth suddenly and begin to rise, wanting to spill over its confines, pour into the fire. She let it pour. Talis pulled away from her suddenly, catching his breath. The kitchen, stunned as he was, by the flash between them, bubbled wildly, crowding to the door.

"Easy, girl," the tray-mistress called anxiously. "The prince wants only to help. Go with him quietly. No one will hurt you."

Talis held out his hand again. Pale under the warm light, he had grown very still, all his thoughts indrawn except one: She saw herself everywhere in his eyes. She felt the wild stirring in her again; she wanted to see out of his eyes, see what he saw of her, what Saro meant. This time she drew the implacable, cold iron around the wildness, subduing it, and put her hand again into his.

He led her with him into a dream. Faces turned toward him everywhere he moved, always with the same mute question, as if they saw the prince out of one eye and the pot-scrubber out of the other, and could not tell what they were really looking at. A horse was brought to him. He mounted, and held out his hand to Saro, who took it as she was told, and then was in his arms, amazed and troubled again with visions: The horse had not been this horse, the arms around her, holding her steady, had not been his. The gates opened slowly; green flowed everywhere beyond them, blue flowed to meet it, farther than anyone could go.

They rode toward the wood on the hill.

She almost recognized it: These were the pale trees within the cauldron, still and streaked with light; these were only a reflection of the true dream. This water flowed, silver and sweet as honey among ancient roots, but somewhere else the same stream flowed as silver as the moon, and the deer lifting its head at the sound of hooves, water glittering from its mouth, was white instead of brown. She felt words,

like leaves, falling endlessly, silently through her. Talis
spoke now and then; listening for the voices of trees, she
scarcely heard him. Perhaps he spoke to the trees, perhaps
they answered him. Their boughs seemed to bend over to
listen, and the light pouring from leaf to leaf onto her face
seemed to blind her with its brightness.

A woman moved within the light, walked out of it to
meet them. For a breath the prince was motionless behind
Saro. Then his hands spoke to her, coaxed her down, where
she stood at his stirrup, trying to see clearly through the
light. The woman's face rippled and blurred, as if Saro saw
her through the gently moving water in the cauldron.

"Saro!" the woman cried finally, but her voice, startling birds in the trees, seemed to come from very far away,
and the word itself, reaching Saro, meant nothing to her in
that wood.

Twenty-one

Atrix dreamed.

The Queen of the Wood and her following pursued a young deer through the wood. The deer was white as milk, with eyes the color of hazelnuts. As fast as the hunters rode, it ran faster, flowing with an impossible grace over fallen trees, through streams, across thickets and patches of wild rose and brambles. The Queen cried one word again and again; sometimes it meant one thing, sometimes another. The deer never faltered, though it did turn its head to look back at the sound of the Queen's voice. The hunters did not shoot at it, for they carried no bows, and they did not catch it; it was still running when Atrix woke.

The sun was beginning to set, silvery behind the mist in which Atrix had shrouded the mountain peak. The mist clung day and night to the mountain. The strongest wind could not tear it away. Thunder rolled from it by night, sudden fires snapped through it, turning it gold, purple, blood-red, vivid colors visible even at midnight, Atrix knew, to those living on the mountain, and within the school. It was a warning: the Shadow of the Wolf. The mages would recognize it; he could only hope the students, tales of the Hunter and the Wolf igniting in their imaginations, would not think it worth their lives to penetrate the mist.

He had been fighting for years, it seemed, for centuries. At times he felt he fought time, or death itself, the granite heart of the mountain, the unchanging heart of the moon, something he would never vanquish, but never cease to battle as long as it existed. At other times he felt that he simply fought his shadow, for it matched his every thought and movement. The glimpse he had caught of the Queen's consort had been the glimpse of a ghost, a fragment of memory, for the Hunter gave Atrix nothing more of a past than the stark faces on Hunter's Field. Nor did he speak.

Night fell beyond the mist. Atrix drew himself within stone, and waited.

He has the power of the wood, the Queen had said. *He will not die as humans die.*

The power of oak and the red deer and the running stream . . . the power of the Queen's wood, which Atrix had barely known existed. He thought, while he waited for the Hunter's hounds to scent him, for the fire in the Hunter's horns to draw his shadow out of stone. He knew the shapes of oak and deer and water in the human world. But oak in the Queen's world was rooted to a different power; it turned a different face to time and memory. The hunter in the Queen's following, whose face was shaped of oak leaves, had turned his face to Atrix, and Atrix had caught lightning in his heart. He could fashion light out of thought, but he could not snag lightning out of the sky, let it cleave through him, branch and bole and root, and capture it within him, let it sing silently like sap until he needed it.

Ilyos could, but where, within the Hunter, was he, to use his powers, or to be summoned? The Queen's consort had been swallowed by the dark moon, it seemed; the fiery horns were his bones. The Hunter had killed all memory of him but his name and a moment of light within the wood.

Ilyos, Atrix thought, and the rock he hid in shattered.

He searched when he could find a crack in time, a chink in the Hunter's mind, for memories of the Queen's wood. A tangle of oak bough, a flash of green, were all he saw, before the Hunter, furious, flung him into the wind, or halfway down the mountain. Tumbling, shapeless, on a fierce wind, he took the raven's shape and, turning, saw the Hunter out of an eye black as the moon among his horns. The Hunter watched him. *I know you*, his silence said. *I am you. The raven and the dark moon. I am you.* A flock of ravens swarmed up from where he stood, with eyes like white moons and claws of finger bone. Atrix dropped among them like a black flame, into the Hunter's mind as he shaped his ravens and let them fly.

Massed, rustling feathers in the dark filled his mind, the vague shape beneath them motionless, but not quite dead. Nothing more: no oak, no green so translucent that leaves seemed made of light. Only ravens in the dark, silent but never still, and the heart's shadow slowly seeping into the snow. Atrix recognized the memory; he had woven it, this single thread, into his spell. A raven lifted its head, looked at him, as it had on the field.

This, its glittering eye said. *This is all.*

Sickened, despairing, he felt the Hunter's sudden attention. The ravens scattered, swept away on a furious winter wind. Atrix flew with them, withdrawing his mind from the Hunter's thoughts, shaping a hair-fine strand of light along the wind's path. The Hunter's fire illumined him, a thin streak of gold in the mist. Flame billowed toward him; he dropped into moon-shadows among the broken pillars of stone at the top of the peak, became a shadow among them. A hound leaped out of nowhere, its claws tearing the shadows away, shredding scraps of dark into the wind. Atrix faded into stone; the hound smelled the human, or the magic, within granite, and bayed. Its baying, vast and too deep to be heard by humans, shook the pillars and boulders until they broke, fell together and began a thundering slide down the face of the mountain. Atrix, falling with them, fearing for the school, wove a net of thought in their path, and caught the wild current of stone, crazily wheeling pillars colliding and cracking against massive boulders brought abruptly to a halt. He shattered them like glass. A thin flood of shards and pebbles slid down toward the edge of the mist and stopped.

Thoughtless a moment, exhausted, he shaped more of himself than he realized, lying among the debris of the slide. A dark cloud swarmed over him; he breathed feathers, saw feathers, felt them everywhere, for a split-second, while he heard the thin, wailing winter winds of Hunter's Field.

This is all, the ravens said, and a talon of darkness stabbed at one eye and then at his heart.

He drew himself into a pebble, and then slid down between the broken stones until he felt the earth, and eased down into that like water, deep into it, until he found a secret mountain stream, and dropped into that, flowed with it through the blackness until he smelled pitch and pine and dark, thirsty roots. Then he followed rootwork up into night, and separated himself from the tree at the edge of the forest.

He found the Hunter waiting for him.

The massive, dark figure, crowned with horn and fire, the dark, smoldering moon above his head, the dark hounds circling him restively, seemed suddenly to Atrix something ancient and indomitable, something he had not made so much as wakened out of himself, or out of a place beyond day and time and night. He gazed back at the Hunter, shaking, battered, uncomprehending, asking, because he did not know what else to ask,

"What are you? Are you only what I made that night on Hunter's Field? What I made out of the wood, and out of that bloody field? Or are you something that was never made and never dies?" The Hunter did not move, did not answer, but waited, his eyes as mute and alien as the moon, as if for a different question. Atrix added, gambling without hope, "I can't let you kill me. I promised the Queen of the Wood that I would find Saro."

The world seemed to explode around him. He fled back beneath the mist. As fast as he moved, the wild, baying hounds moved, and no matter what shape he took, the dark moon saw him, until the true moon finally hid itself behind the mountain, and the Shadow of the Wolf around the broken peak turned colorless and silent.

He dreamed again: the fleet white deer, the unarmed hunters, the Queen calling a word that constantly changed, yet always sounded the same. The deer leaped across a stream and someone touched him.

He vanished as he woke. From somewhere in the air, he saw Talis, kneeling on the stones where Atrix had been, looking around him perplexedly. The prince started at the sudden flash of fear and anger that streaked the air just before Atrix reappeared.

"Talis!" He gripped the prince, drew him to his feet. "What are you doing back here? I left you safe in Pelucir."

"I came through the Queen's wood," Talis said. "Atrix, she needs you —"

"What are you doing there? Even she sent you back home. Can't you stay with Burne at least until I'm finished here?"

"Atrix, I found Saro." The words made no sense to Atrix for a moment: Saro was a dream, a mystery, a problem for the future, if he had one. Talis said again, "I found Saro. And your spellbook. She's been in the kitchen all these years, cleaning pots, until one day she took your book out of the keep and began learning magic. I don't know why, or how she knew it was there — she can't talk.

She needs your help. She barely remembers the wood, she doesn't seem to understand the Queen, she's under a spell. Your spell. Your magic changed her, somehow, that night on Hunter's Field."

Atrix loosed him, sat down slowly on a stone. For once the winds brought him neither strength nor comfort; he hunched his frayed human shape against them, shivering. "She found my book?" he said, amazed. "First you, then she —"

"She had it hidden in the kitchen." The prince paused, studying Atrix. "You look terrible," he said shortly, and slid a pack from his shoulder. "The Queen thought you might be hungry."

Atrix shook his head, too weary to eat. Talis opened the pack, drew out bread and meat and wine. The wine, when he uncorked it, smelled like spring air, full of pitch and strawberry. Atrix reached for it wordlessly, drank. He glanced at the sun; it was mid-afternoon.

"I can't leave," he said. Talis wrapped bread around roast boar and handed it to him. He waited, until Atrix had eaten half of it, before he spoke.

"If you die here," he said, not entirely dispassionately, "no one will be able to help Saro. You must come now, she says. You can return here before moonrise."

Atrix ate another bite. There seemed no argument besides the angle of the sun, and that was high enough yet for him to abandon the peak for a while. He nodded, chewing. Talis, his eyes caught by unexpected emptiness around him, said slowly,

"I thought — I remembered more crags up here."

"They broke." Atrix reached for the wine again, found Talis staring at him, his face shocked, stripped of color. He handed Atrix the rest of the bread and meat. "Atrix. Are you going to die here?"

"I don't know." Atrix was silent a moment, staring at nothing, then asked, "What does she look like? Saro?"

"Like someone who has scrubbed pots in a kitchen for twenty years." Talis smiled a little, tightly. "You don't see her. No one ever noticed her. But that was part of your magic, I think — that you could look straight at her and not see the color of her eyes. And her face changes constantly, as if winds are always reshaping it. She has never spoken. But her eyes are beginning to speak. She can put her thoughts into my head. When I led her out of the kitchen, she let me take her hand. And then — for some reason, perhaps I frightened her — she let a flash of power flow between us that nearly set the woodpile on fire." He paused, and got around to Atrix's question. "Her hair is the color of wax. I think. Underneath the wood smoke. Her eyes — I still can't remember." He paused again, flicked a pebble into nowhere. "She barely comes up to my shoulder. I thought that knowing about Ilyos would make the battle simpler."

Atrix shook his head, gazing through his mist at the trees flowing down the mountain. High on the edge, he could see a thumbprint of crumpled trunks, like a bruise, where he had said Saro's name. "He — what there is of him — is furious with me, too. But there's something else . . ."

"What?" the prince asked warily.

"I don't know."

"Try. Try to tell me." He added, his eyes opaque behind his lenses, "Who else have you got to listen to you up here?"

"Why do you want to listen to me?"

"Because I don't want to make your mistake."

Atrix flinched. He felt the winds again, hard, bright, painfully cold. "No," he said hollowly. "That's what Hedrix said to me, the night he told me that you had my book. That what I should have written was the truth of Hunter's Field, so that other mages could learn from it. Instead, as you saw, I lied."

Talis was silent. He rose suddenly, took his cloak off, and settled it, fighting the wind, onto Atrix's shoulders. "It's frightening," he said finally, so softly that Atrix strained to hear, "knowing that someone as powerful and experienced and wise as you, could make such a mockery of everything we were taught."

"Drawkcab," Atrix whispered. "The other face of power. And yet, that's not all . . . If that were all . . ."

"All what?"

"All I'm fighting. There seems to be a force beyond the war and the wood, that I awoke . . . I don't know what it is. Something ancient, immutable, that I do not recognize and cannot name. . . ."

Talis swallowed dryly, touching his lenses. "Death."

"No."

"Then it is not death."

"No," Atrix said again.

"Drawkcab," Talis said. His voice shook; his hands fell suddenly on Atrix's shoulders; Atrix felt him trembling. "It's your spell. Your word. If it is not death, then it is life. Maybe that's what you are fighting, Atrix Wolfe. Life."

Atrix rose. He was shaking again, not with cold but with a sudden, haunting vision: the figure hidden beneath the ravens' wings, blind, motionless, but still alive. What lay beneath the ravens' wings? An unknown warrior on Hunter's Field?

Or himself?

He said softly, not seeing Talis, or the mountain, or anything in Chaumenard, but only night on a field in Pelucir, where the merciless winter winds blew out of memory to shake him now, "I cannot see past or future, beyond that night. Time stopped, that night. The White Wolf ceased to exist, that night. I cannot see beyond the Hunter's face. He is the shape of my power; I cannot change that."

"Why," Talis whispered, "did you make him?"

"I was trying to end the siege. Trying to make Riven of Kardeth retreat. To keep Pelucir and Chaumenard safe. That's all. And I did all of those things. But I turned myself into something even more terrible than the army of Kardeth. And that's what I fight now, and what I cannot seem to change." He paused, looking at Talis, wondering how much he understood. "I took the shapes of what I saw on Hunter's Field. I don't know how to change the shape of death."

Talis drew breath; Atrix could not read the expression behind his lenses. "You must find a way," the prince said. His voice shook. "Atrix Wolfe. You can't die here and leave us with the Hunter. You can't die at Burne's hands in Pelucir. Kings of Pelucir don't kill great mages of Chaumenard. Your shadow would fall across Pelucir as long as the name exists. Your death would haunt Burne all his life. You must find another way." Talis' eyes glittered behind his lenses, struck by the cold edge of wind, or by an edge of sorrow. He reached out, touched Atrix gently. "You must find a way to live."

Atrix followed Talis through his own mist, though he could not see what the prince saw that led him unfalteringly through Atrix's blank enchantment to the place where mist frayed into memory and the green wood rose about them. Perhaps, he thought, the enchantment lay in Talis; his heart's need found the wood when the Queen's need summoned him.

The Queen waited for them. Her daughter stood beside her. Atrix swallowed sound when he saw her, appalled, for no spell he might have imagined could have been so thorough or so cruel.

She was slight, as Talis had said, and very thin, barefoot, and dressed in something shapeless, colorless. Her eyes narrowed on his face, as if she saw him dimly through a harsh, snow-flecked wind. They did not lack color, but it was nothing that the eye retained long enough to name. Nothing about her held the attention long, for as soon as attention focused, her face would alter, slide away, begin to disappear.

But she had her father's power. He said to her, "Saro. My name is Atrix Wolfe." He felt the sudden riveting response to his name, the inner eye of power. He looked at the Queen then. Her hands were linked hard around Saro's hand; her face, unlike her daughter's, was unforgettable, and, at the moment, as unchangeable as stone.

She said, "She does not know me."

"She will," Atrix said softly. "She remembers me." He added, with care, "She has a very strong power which may become uncontrolled when she remembers that night. It will be focused at me. You may be hurt, if you hold her."

The Queen's mouth thinned; her eyes were cold as winter stars. "I will not part from her again. Do what you came to do."

He bowed his head. Then he put his hands very gently on Saro's shoulders, to channel the flow of her wild power, and found her eyes. They saw and did not see; color seemed always to recede. Her lips moved, soundlessly; they shaped her name.

"Yes," he said. "Saro —"

And then the mountain winds of Chaumenard seemed to pour through the wood, stripping leaves from the trees, tearing away limbs. Birds beat against the winds, calling; the Queen cried out, and pulled Saro close to her, staring at what had ridden down the winds into her wood.

"Saro," said the Hunter, and around him the ancient oak trees kindled lightning in their boughs.

Twenty-two

❧

Saro slipped free of the Queen and ran into the Hunter's path.

For an instant, facing him, she stood in snow. Winds snarled like wolves around them, the flame in his horns streamed wildly behind him, the black moon rose above the fire, hung in a mist of white. A word filled her mouth; it meant him, she knew, but she could not find it to say it, and she could not find him, in that masked, feral face crowned with fire and horn. Voices cried at her beyond the snow-streaked winds as he rode toward her; they were the cries of startled, fleeing birds.

Saro.

Found, she thought, transfixed in the Hunter's eye. *Found*. And as the snows of memory melted away and light fell over them both, she felt bewildered and impatient with both their mute faces, as if neither belonged in that falling light, in that wood.

Saro, a bird cried. And then again, in the prince's voice, "Saro!"

She whirled. Talis stood beneath one of the fuming oak trees. Light ran like a live thing behind him, through every branch, every leaf; even its roots, beneath the ground, sent up an eerie web of light. His lenses were flashing in that brilliance, at Saro, at the Hunter; at Atrix, who vanished suddenly under a whip of light; at the Queen, who stood spellbound, her eyes on the Hunter, tears like hard cut jewels glittering down her face.

"Saro!" Talis called desperately, as the dark hounds flowed toward her and she felt their hot breath on her skin. His lenses flashed again, and she caught her breath in horror.

The hounds reached her, milling through the soft air like thunderbolts, silent yet, dangerous, about to explode after the lightning struck. But she had no time for their coal eyes. Talis moved, with a strange, underwater slowness, snagged a strand of light from the oak between his fingers. His eyes went to the Hunter; his hand began to rise.

Something flashed through Saro, as if she were oak, struck and burning with power. Her throat moved; sounds and shapes tangled together, fighting to get out. Something struggled free, dropped out of her mouth, but it was only a hard jewel of light. Talis' hand arched high, stopped. Light wove through his fingers. A small, dark bird pushed its way out of Saro's mouth, and flew, panicked, crying her word in its own language. Tears dropped, cold and diamond-hard, from her eyes. The light flared in Talis' hand. Then an arrow of white fire streaked from the Hunter toward Talis, and Saro felt something that was not bird or jewel, but torn out of her breath and blood and heart, shaping the one word she knew.

"Saro!" she cried, and Talis' face swung toward her. The Hunter's fire struck the edge of his lens and shattered it.

The power flung him back against the oak. He slid limply; its light wove a gleaming web around him. Its roots lifted long, swollen fingers to grip him as he fell, hold him fast to earth. He shuddered once, his face turning blindly toward the Hunter, and then lay still.

Atrix appeared beside him suddenly, kneeling, one hand on Talis, the other uplifted toward the Hunter, whose hounds flowed in a dark circle around the oak. The Hunter, his eyes fixed on the fallen prince, rode inexorably as night, his hand rising again, his horse's hooves beating an un-swerving path toward mage and prince as if what stood before him were of no more substance than air or light. Another word struggled out of heart and need, and the memory of a harsh winter night; Saro screamed, "Father!"

The horse reared above her; she saw a confusion of hooves and sky and glowing trees. Then hooves thudded down like stone beside her, and the horse stood still as stone. She watched her father's face emerge beneath the Hunter's face, as it emerged in her memory. His eyes changed color, black fading to the light, dusty gold of ripe acorns. She felt her own face change then, lost expressions and memories surfacing, reshaping her as he found her among his own memories. His eyes loosed her finally, to find the Queen standing among her trees, the tears melting now, burning down her face.

"Saro," she said. "Ilyos."

He made a sound that might have come out of the split heart of an oak. His gaze swept across the trees; the shimmering webs of lightning withdrew into them. He lifted his hand: Mist the colors of leaf and light gathered around them, so that they stood together in the private wood of memory.

He bent carefully under the weight of the burning horns. His trembling hand touched Saro's face.

He breathed her name. She closed her eyes, felt his touch, in memory, on an endless summer day. "I can say them now," she whispered. "All the words you taught me before I learned sorrow."

He made another sound, a word with no shape that spoke of sorrow. His hand slid away from her to the Queen, who had come to stand beside Saro. He caught her tears in his fingers.

"You are crying." His voice shook. "You could never cry before."

She caught his hand in hers, held it to her eyes, her mouth. "I learned," she said into his palm. Still gripping him, she reached out to Saro, held her tightly, wiping her tears in Saro's hair. Saro twisted her hands into her father's cloak, clung to it, her eyes moving from face to face, as she saw her strange past unfold from green wood to stone kitchen, to wood again, from their child to no one's child, and now the Hunter's child.

"I saw you," she told him, feeling the tears on her own face. "In my cauldron. In my dreams. *Drawkcab*, you said to me. Your eyes found me."

He shook his head wordlessly. "Some part of me found you," he said at last. "Some part of me must always have been trying to return." He was silent again, struggling with his own past; she saw the shadows of it in his eyes, the Hunter's face lying in wait beneath his face. He whispered, "I did not even see you. You were nothing to me. If you were something I did not hate, then you were nothing. And then you spoke, and summoned out of me what you had loved."

"You changed, then." The Queen's hand loosed Saro, stroked her hair, then held her again. Saro gazed into her eyes, remembering the gold and dark, remembering her voice, her touch, and how she thought she would have those things forever. "One moment you could not speak; you were a small, pale, shadowy wraith; you could not remember me — Then you spoke and broke the mage's spell yourself."

Saro turned suddenly in her hold, looked back; her father's mist his past and future. Sorrow burned, she learned then, like dry kindling, like scalding water. "I had to," she said to him. The words ached in her throat. "I saw you kill Prince Talis, long ago, in my wash-cauldron. I tried to learn to speak, to warn him. But I saw what I saw. There were only words for that."

"Prince Talis."

"He was kind to me." She swallowed pain again, which seemed to come with language. "His eyes saw me. 'Death' was the last word you taught me."

His face twisted away from her. "It is the only word I know now."

"Ilyos," the Queen said urgently, and he looked down again, a terrible darkness fading from his eyes. "Ilyos. Stay with us. You have found my wood again. You have found us. Stay."

"This is a dream," he said wearily. "This is only a dream. I am Atrix Wolfe's making. If I could stay — if somehow I could unweave myself from his spell and stay — I would burn these woods again with memory. I was born that night. These Hunter's hands are my hands, these hounds and burning horns are mine. I died that night. There is nothing left of Ilyos but memory." His voice faded; he gazed at her, remembering. Her face grew still then, tearless. Saro sensed something waking in her, a word growing, secret and very powerful.

"Stay," the Queen said softly. "If you are nothing but memory, then stay. Here among my memories."

He started to speak, stopped. Words passed between them, without shape, without sound. He began to tremble; the Queen's hold tightened on his hand.

"Stay," she said again. But Saro heard other things, the secret language beneath words. The Queen clung to them both, her eyes moving back and forth between their faces, gathering memories like flowers. Her face blurred suddenly, the fire and ivory of it melting in the fire in Saro's eyes.

"How could I have forgotten you?" Saro whispered. "How could I have looked at you and not known you?"

"I never forgot you," the Queen said fiercely. "Not for a breath. Not for a dream." She looked at her consort again, crowned with fire, trapped in night. "She broke the mage's

spell over herself. And over you. It is your power she
inherited."

He drew breath soundlessly. "This is what you want."

"Yes." A tear fell, glittered in the light between them.
"Yes," she said again. "I want this. I want you here in my
thoughts. In my wood. You fought your way past the mage's
spell to find us here. You still have that much power. Free
yourself. For my sake. And for yours."

His face grew quiet, then. He was still, looking at the
Queen, and she at him, until the green wood and the golden
light seemed to become the world in Saro's memory, that
held all time and no time within it. He loosed the Queen's
hand finally, touched her lips with his fingers.

Then he looked at Saro. "I thought I knew what sorrow is," he said. "Now I must leave you, and now I know."

The rich, still light around them turned silver with the
smoke of smoldering trees. Atrix knelt among the oak roots,
his eyes closed, his hands moving futilely over the thick,
living bindings that held Talis to the earth. The prince's body
seemed to be disappearing in a weave of root; the ground
crumbled slowly beneath him, opening into darkness under
the tree. A word leaped out of Saro; the mage's face, strained
and desperate, lifted sharply. For an instant, the unmasked
face of the Hunter, the Queen's pale-haired consort, stunned
him. Then he rose swiftly, as the Hunter, his hounds swarming out of shadow and leaf, rode as if to run down the mage,
and the prince behind him, and the oak itself.

Atrix flung up a hand before the dark wave of hounds
broke against him. "Ilyos," he cried. "Wait — " The Queen's
consort gave him no more time. The mage turned to fire, a
burning circle around the oak, shielding Talis within it. Saro,
racing the hounds, plunged into what stopped them: There
seemed no great difference between the mage and what
burned beneath a simmering pot. Her mind flowed into fire;

she heard its voice, its secret, feathery language. The oak roots under her bare feet moved away from her, as if she, too, burned. She shook fire out of her hair as she knelt beside Talis. A root shifted; he slid a little, deeper into the earth.

A sound jerked out of him, as if he felt himself falling, and Saro froze. She stared down at him, hearing the hard, startled pound of her heart. "Talis," she said, but he did not answer. She gripped the roots over him desperately, and heard the oak's ancient, dreaming voice.

. . . Trouble in the wood . . . bone into tree, hold deep, hold fast, bone into wood, breath into fire, deep, bone into root, bone into wood, human into dreams . . . hold bone and dream deep in the root . . .

"No," she said to it. Beyond the fire she heard a hound yelp sharply; the ground shook. "I want this human. You have no use for him."

I must bury him, deep, where no human eyes will ever look.

A root tightened across Talis' chest. He flinched, gasping for air too heavy to breathe. Sweat rolled down his face. She touched his cheek gently, and he moved again. One eye was crusted with blood behind the shattered lens; his other eye fluttered open, stared at her senselessly. She turned back to the oak, keeping her voice and hands calm despite her terror, patting Oak as if it were a weeping mincer, or a kitchen dog.

"I am Saro, daughter of the Queen of the Wood, and I want this human back. What can I give you in return?" The fire billowed too close; she pushed it away as if it were a windblown tapestry, and it settled back. The oak was silent; the wood was not, nor was the color of the fire always familiar. She tried again. "Tell me what I can promise you. You are very old, and he is too young to bury. All his dreams will be too young."

He was given to me . . .

"I will ask the Queen to come and sit among your roots

and comb her hair and sing . . ." The words came out of a
song, she remembered; as she spoke, she heard the Queen
singing to her. The oak roots shifted slightly.

The Queen.

"She will come, if I ask."

The Queen of the Wood.

"She will come with her crown of gold and her golden
comb, and she will sing to you and braid your leaves into
her hair."

The Queen of the Wood . . .

The roots around Talis eased, began to pull away from
him, bury themselves again in the earth. He struggled,
murmuring incoherently, trying to sit and straighten his
lenses at the same time. The lenses slid out of his shaking
hand, dropped. Blood pooled in his eye, ran down his
cheek. He wiped it with his sleeve and winced, then blinked
Saro clear through blood and hot, shimmering air.

"Saro?" he said tentatively, as if the ring of fire, blazing
with mages' lights, worked such changes on her face that he
no longer recognized her. But his hand knew her; his fingers
found her wrist, circled it tightly. "Saro?"

"Yes," she said. He groped for his lenses, to see her
more clearly, then stared down at them. The shattered lens
of her dark vision struck her mute; there seemed suddenly
too much to say, and again no words with which to say it.
She put her hand to her mouth. "I thought he killed you."

"Nearly."

"In my cauldron, I thought you died."

He slid the lenses on, looked at her. A word moved in
his throat; he spoke it after a moment. "You saw this?"

"In my cauldron. I saw the — I saw my father. I saw
this happen. But I could not speak — I went to you but I
could not speak — " She felt the tears, hotter than the fire,

burn in her eyes; she felt herself trembling. He stared at her, still gripping her wrist. "I had to say this. But I could only say my name —"

"I heard you." His voice shook. He put his arm around her, drew her close, so close she felt his heartbeat, his unsteady breathing against her hair. "You were down in the kitchen learning magic because of me?"

"You were kind to me," she said. He made a sound, of wonder or pain; his hold tightened.

"I did nothing —"

"Your eyes saw me." She paused, gazing back into those strange, bleak years. "No one ever saw me," she whispered. "They saw a dirty pot, or a clean pot. I saw myself like that. I did not remember where words came from. I never needed them until I saw the Hunter — I saw death —" She pulled away from him suddenly, remembering. "And I saw someone else in the cauldron, crying out to warn you. But I never knew — I never knew who it was or what word she cried until now."

He made the little, inarticulate sound again. "She cried sorrow," he said. He took her hands, bending over them; she saw the blood in his hair, where he had struck the oak. She felt his lips on her fingers, and then his cheek. The fire roared over them suddenly, color melting through it; he lifted his head, swallowing. "Atrix. How can he still be fighting? How can he have the strength?" He rose with an effort, catching his balance against the oak.

"Atrix is the fire. It's my father fighting him. Fighting against the spell. My mother wants my father to stay in the wood with her."

"I don't understand." He leaned dizzily against the tree, staring at her out of one good eye. "Why must he fight Atrix Wolfe for that? Atrix would not stop him. Does he just want Atrix dead? Or is there something more to that spell than just Atrix and your father — ?" He reached out to her, as she began to fray into flame. "Saro — "

"My father knows me now." She touched him still. "Wait."

But, reappearing on the other side of fire, she almost did not know her father.

The Hunter's horse and hounds had disappeared. Her father stood among the trees. Instead of horns, he wore a flaming crown of oak branches. His hands were webbed with twigs and leaves; his feet were rooted to the ground. His skin had hardened, darkened; his acorn eyes reflected the fire that was Atrix Wolfe. The mage did not fight; as fire, he engulfed every flare of power that Ilyos threw at him. Her father's battle never stopped, except for the moment when Saro appeared, freeing herself from the mage's fire, and they stared at one another.

Saro saw her mother watching from the green shade. Her face held the still, intent expression; she no longer wept. Her face changed color with every flash from her consort's hands and burning crown. She did not take her eyes from Ilyos, but as Saro came to her, she reached out, pulled Saro close to her.

"What is he doing?" Saro breathed. "Why is he still fighting the mage?" Her mother did not answer, only watched as each gesture her father made drew another leaf among the lightning weaving through his hair, another ring of bark around his skin. The boughs crowning him seemed to arch closer and closer to the mage's fire, as if to drink from it; as fire streaked from the branches, leaves formed in its wake, hard and bright as jewels at first, then slowly flushing with life. His arms were growing stiff, rising, arch-ing, bending more and more slowly, his fingers long and slender, branching with new twigs.

He stopped moving finally, both hands upraised. His face was still visible, planes and hollowed contours of bark, his open eyes, his mouth.

He said, "Atrix Wolfe."

The fire drew together, slowly shaped the mage. Talis stood behind him, clinging to the oak. The mage, his face waxen in the sunlight, did not take his eyes from Ilyos. He stumbled against a root, swaying with weariness, and almost lost his balance. He spoke finally, heavily,

"Is there no other way?"

"None," said the Queen's consort. Atrix looked away from him then, to the Queen. She met his eyes, her own face white within the wild fall of her hair.

"None," she whispered, her voice as dry and brittle as falling leaves. Atrix looked back at Ilyos.

"Sorrow," he said, his voice shaking, and lifted his hand.

Bark ringed Ilyos' eyes and mouth, smoothed his body until there was only a suggestion of what had been human in the knots where branches lifted away from the trunk, and in a vague profile that seemed, in the dreaming light, at last to have grown peaceful.

Saro moved. Her bones seemed heavy as wood, her steps as unwieldy as a sapling pulling up its roots and walking, but she reached the tree finally, put her arms around it. She heard the Queen say wearily,

"Go now. No. Do not speak again in my wood. Just go."

Saro, still clinging to the tree, turned her face, saw Talis' white, frozen face turn to her, as he stumbled away from the oak. He could not speak. He tried, and then his eyes closed. Atrix caught him as he fell. Saro said nothing, though she felt words gather in her, secretly. She watched, as sunlight burned around her, the wood growing so bright and strangely beautiful that the mage with the prince in his arms, having no place in it, finally faded away.

Twenty-three

~~~

Atrix stood on Hunter's Field.

The Queen's vanishing wood had left him there, the green mist of leaves and the lovely light fading around him, then showing him a startling reflection of them: the wide green field across which his shadow stretched endlessly, and the dazzling late-afternoon light which drew the shadow of the King's castle across half the field. He looked around a little dazedly, expecting the crags and harsh winds of Chaumenard. Then he settled Talis more securely in his arms, to take one last step into the castle, where he could finally see how much damage his twisted making had done to Pelucir's heir.

He could barely see to take the step. Sun streaked across his eyes, burned painfully; his heart, too, seemed scored with fire. He wanted to turn to stone where he stood, a dark monument to the dead on Hunter's Field. He wanted to return to the Queen's wood, bury himself in the ground over which the Queen walked, and never speak or think again. But he could not turn to stone with the prince of Pelucir unconscious in his arms, and he had to seek, not the Queen of the Wood, but Burne Pelucir. The burden in his arms was a shadow's weight; it was his heart, carrying all the memories of the field, the sorrows of the wood, that made any movement he might make futile, any direction wrong.

He blinked his vision clear of tears or weariness or light, whatever blinded him, and saw the Hunter.

The Hunter stood in the light as if he had just been made, forged out of night and fire and the raven's eye, his horns holding not only the dark moon, but reaching out to swallow the setting sun in the sky. He seemed, in daylight, an impossible spell for Atrix to have cast, or for any mage; he belonged to no one, and all of Atrix's battles meant no more to him than the upraised swords of warriors he had left splintered in the grass around them. He did not even look at Atrix. His dark gaze and the eyes of all his hounds were on the prince in Atrix's arms.

Atrix felt all the fierce and icy winds of Chaumenard sweep through him at once. His shout, so loud it was at first soundless and then shattered windows in the castle, drew faces to the walls and turrets. He heard answering shouts, as guards saw what stood in daylight on Hunter's Field: the Hunter and his maker and the heir of Pelucir, motionless in the mage's arms. Atrix turned away from the sun, hid Talis within his shadow on the grass. Then he pulled apart his making.

He drew the fire out of the horns and scattered it across the field. He sent the dark moon spinning into the sky, where it hung like a dark eye, watching, expressionless. He felt the ghosts of Hunter's Field rousing around him then, and loosed the hounds among them. Pulling at an arm or dragging down a horse and rider, they snapped at memory, at air. He drew ravens out of the Hunter's mind and sent them swirling around the Hunter, so that when Atrix grasped his horns, there was only a mass of feathers beneath them, jabbing heads and dark wings beginning to fleck with blood. He held the Hunter's horns and shaped a starving deer beneath them: They dwindled to carry time and famine instead of the hidden moon.

He swept away the ravens and looked into the Hunter's eyes.

The Hunter stood again in light, carrying the new moon and the ancient fires in his horns, his hounds at his knees, his horse as black as night beside him. All of Atrix's power had troubled him little more than dead leaves blowing against him. Atrix, staring at him, trembling, asked helplessly, "Who are you? Out of what battlefield of the heart did I summon you?"

"Xirta Eflow."

The battle trumpets of Pelucir sounded from the castle. The gates swung wide; Burne Pelucir led an army of household guards and guests and scarred, seasoned warriors onto Hunter's Field. They flowed into a single line spanning the field behind the King. Atrix heard their secret fury and dread clamor across the silence. The Hunter, scenting it, turned and mounted his dark horse. He paused, his dead moon-eyes holding Atrix's eyes. "Drawkcab," he said. "I am what you see when you see Atrix Wolfe."

His hounds streaking like shadows across the windblown grass, he rode to meet the King.

Atrix, stunned for a breath, felt his own name shock through him, in a heartbeat so powerful and painful, he thought his heart had broken.

Then he reached into his dreams to shape a making that would stop the Hunter on Hunter's Field.

He made it out of leaves and light, and warm, scented air so still that time seemed to end within it. He made it of the golden shadows of white deer, and the gold in their eyes, and in the leaves lying in a pool of sunlit gold around the oak. He took the paths of sun and moon, wound them together, ivory and gold, and braided into them the dreaming noonday shadows, the misty shadows of the moon. He took the fierce beauty in the owl's eye, the flight of white doves soaring into light, the leap of hare beneath the moon, the lightning tangled in the golden oak.

He reached backward into memory, beyond the endless winter night, and found, buried behind the Hunter's eyes, all he had loved in Chaumenard.

Barren crags and ancient forests, winds scented with honey, wolf, wildflowers, swift water so pure it tasted like the wind, deep snow lying tranquilly beneath moonlight, summer light cascading down warm stone under sky so bright it held no color: These he put into his making. Tranquil nights he spent within stone, listening to parchment pages rustle around him while the stars turned overhead, the magic in young mages' eyes, quick and lucent as flame, he spun out of memory into magic. He took the Healer's powerless past and turned it into power: the newborn animals in his hands, trembling with their first breaths; the faces of children who roamed with him, their eyes alive to every color, every shadowy movement in the underbrush, their voices, calling him Healer; his healing hands. Shapes he had taken in his long life mingled together as swiftly as his body remembered them: the white owl in winter, the golden hawk, ferret and weasel and mink, stone, wind, the tree smelling of sun-soaked pitch, water thundering over stone, endlessly falling, the stag that drank the water, the White Wolf. He remembered faces he had loved, of friend and lover, teacher and ruler, their eyes speaking his name, Atrix Wolfe, beginning to smile; he worked that name in their eyes into his making. He fashioned with what came to him, what had freed itself out of his heart, so quickly he did not know what he shaped. He only knew that something grew out of him, blazed brighter and brighter in his eyes, until, trying to see his making, to set it free on Hunter's Field, he could see only light.

He turned blindly, standing, it seemed, in the eye of the

sun. Then he heard the odd silence on the field, as if, around him, no one moved, no one even thought. The light faded at his sudden fear; he began to see again, a rippling corner of Talis' cloak, his hand lying in the grass. Color returned to the world: green, the black of his shadow, the prince's face staring up at him out of one unbroken lens, and one lens splintered and flecked with blood.

Talis swallowed, but he could not seem to speak. Then he smiled, and Atrix saw the magic, quick and lucent as flame in his face, and the name his eyes gave back to the mage.

Burne's army, still lining the field, was spellbound, it seemed; they stared at him, unharmed but unable to move or speak. Then Burne Pelucir broke free of the spell, rode across the field alone. Atrix glanced swiftly around: The only shadows he found were human, stretched long by the setting sun across the blazing grass.

He said to Talis, "Where is the Hunter?"

"Where shadows go," the prince said elliptically. He pushed himself up slowly, clung dizzily to the ground, trying to steady it under his hands as he sat. Burne reached them. Like Talis, he seemed stunned by something; staring at Atrix, he could not speak. Then he looked at Talis, and found words.

"Where's your other eye?"

"It saw too much in the wood."

"Did you leave it there?"

He touched it, and winced. "No."

"I can heal him," Atrix promised. Burne dismounted, knelt next to Talis. The mage drew their eyes; in their silence, again he heard the stillness that had fallen over the field. He searched it with his thoughts, wary, perplexed. "Where is my making?"

"Gone," Burne said. "When we could see again, there were a few shadows on the ground. Horse, a hunter, hounds. Then they became shadows of deer and ravens and a tree. And then they burned away."

"But I made something else — the making that destroyed the Hunter. Where is it?"

They looked at him, wordless again. Burne spoke at last. "There was nothing else," he said. "There was only you."

Talis dreamed.

He was in the keep, opening a spellbook that had no maker's name on it. The spells were simple, precise, written for beginning mages. On each page was a single word, the name of an object for contemplation. *Wood*, he said, and became wood. He turned a page. *Stone*, he said, and became stone. *Fire*, he said, and became fire. He turned pages, spoke words, each clear and unambiguous: *water, light, leaf*, and became water, light, leaf. He felt the morning sun on his hands between words. The door to the room stood open, unguarded; no ghosts moved along the walls. He felt each word in his mouth, listened to it as he spoke, melted into it easily, and then became himself again. He turned a page. *Saro*, he said, the first ambiguous word, and woke.

He opened his eyes, saw noon light sliding down the silken hangings at his chamber windows. Then he saw the mage, seated beside the window, his head in his arms on the casement, asleep. He wore a long, loose robe that Burne had given him, a shade paler than the warm light falling over him. Talis lay still, watching him, seeing the mage in the field shaping himself into all the magic in the world at once, each shape strange and wild, and more beautiful, more haunting, than the last, until there was no room anywhere, on the field or in memory, for the Hunter or the ghosts of Hunter's Field.

Talis stirred finally, groped on the table beside the bed where he kept his lenses.

The broken lens was whole again. He put them on, remembering Atrix's hands lightly touching his bloody eye, the back of his head, drawing pain out of him, spinning memory into a dream, and dream into sleep. His healing, apparently, had extended itself to Talis' lenses. He stood up too quickly, grabbed for the table and clung to it until the dark receded. Then he walked carefully to the window.

"Atrix?" He touched Atrix's shoulder. The mage woke slowly, pulling himself out of some bottomless well of sleep. Straightening, he blurred a little into stone and light, as if his human body were an arbitrary shape, and too stiff, now, for comfort.

"I fell asleep," he said, surprised.

"There's no need for you to sleep on stone."

"I got used to it."

"I had a dream about your spellbook," Talis said, and Atrix looked at him silently, his eyes streaking silver in the light. "That the words in it simply meant what they said, nothing more. That it was no longer dangerous."

"It's not," Atrix said. He rose, dropped his hand gently on Talis' shoulder. "I was looking through it just before I came in here to see you. You were dreaming of the mage in the keep, as I dreamed about you once, using that book."

"Strange," Talis breathed. "It seems so simple, for something so powerful. . . ."

"There are no simple words. I don't know why I thought I could hide anything behind language." He turned Talis' face toward the light with his fingers and studied his work. "You came within one word of losing that eye," he said grimly. "If not your life."

"Saro," Talis said softly, thinking of her within the ring of fire. "I woke up and found a tree trying to bury me, and Saro talking, making bargains for my life with an oak root. Even now, it seems like some very peculiar nightmare."

"It was just that," Atrix said with feeling. "I couldn't free you. The oak refused to give you to me — I was the enemy within the wood." He stopped abruptly; Talis saw the memories well into his eyes, stark and terrible, before he turned away, looked out over Hunter's Field.

The bone beside his eye began to ache, the first touch of pain. Talis rested his brow against the cool stones, watching the wood above the field. "I wonder . . ."

"What?" Atrix said after a moment.

"About Saro. There are so many things I wish I could ask her. But I don't think the Queen will permit anyone human into her wood again, and Saro would never come back here."

"I will never see that wood," Atrix said softly, "except in dreams. But you found the Queen's child for her, and you found me, and your heart found its way into her wood."

Talis was silent, feeling the dry lick of fire again behind his eye. "Not always," he said. He turned away from the wood, touching his lenses straight. "Thank you for fixing these."

"I was curious," Atrix said, "why you wore them, how much you could see . . ." His face, no longer haunted, looked gentler, but something of all the shapes he had taken, of hawk and wolf and wind, seemed very close to the surface. Talis, looking at him, caught a dizzying glimpse of power and freedom that he would never find in Pelucir.

"Where will you go?" he asked, not wanting to hear, filled with a sudden, hopeless longing to follow the mage into all his wild magic. "Back to the wolves?"

"I'll return to Chaumenard eventually. But not to the wolves." He touched Talis again, lightly, as if he had heard, beneath the question, all that Talis did not say. "I find I like to heal. It's what I've done, in some fashion, for twenty years. But first I promised Burne something."

"The last time you promised him something it was your life."

"I know," Atrix said. "I reminded him." He seemed to sense the sudden, jarring tangle of Talis' thoughts; he added dispassionately, "I did not want to run from anything again."

"Yes, but —"

"Burne said that the mage who cast that spell on Hunter's Field twenty years ago vanished with the Hunter." His head bowed slightly, turned away from the light to meet Talis' gaze. "Burne is wrong. But he is far more interested in my life. He told me that he had never imagined what could be done with magic, since all he had ever seen were your uncontrollable spells and my deadly sorcery. He asked me to stay and teach you."

"He did." Talis gripped stone as they floated suddenly and settled again. The bone beside his eye was pounding. "You're staying."

"Yes."

"Thank you." He loosed stone to grip the mage. "Thank you."

"It might lay a few ghosts to rest . . . Those in the keep are gone," he added. "The walls were quiet around me when I worked."

"You left no room for shadows."

"Except in the heart." Atrix's eyes strayed again to the green field. "Burne asked me why I didn't do that twenty years ago. He said even Riven of Kardeth would have been stunned into submission. If I could have done it, I would have. I wonder when in the past twenty years I learned . . ."

"You used the words we gave you on that battlefield."

"I should have used a different language." He drew Talis away from the light, took off his lenses. Fires receded under his gaze; his calm face grew slowly distant, a memory, an ancient stone, the face of the wind, the Wolf. "Sleep now."

Talis dreamed, this time, of a still wood, oak trees standing in the rich light, remembering, and dropping their memories one by one, a leaf here, there, to the ground. He woke again at evening, and remembered the Hunter, the sharp edge of night, the bone-white scythe of the moon.

But when he went to the window, the field lay peacefully in his blurred vision, and the moon was full. A square of light from a high tower fell onto the grass. The keep window, he realized: Atrix was up there, for no one else would go there.

No one ever goes there . . .

There was a tap on his door; supper, he assumed, and called, but no one came. He rose, blind in the darkened room, and opened the door.

His heart saw before he did: the pale, shining hair, long and wild, like her mother's, the skin as pale as birch, the long, elegant bones of her face, that seemed to belong to something that ran free in secret places and spoke a different language.

She carried his supper on a tray. He took it from her wordlessly. When she met his eyes, he wondered how he could have ever forgotten that dusty gold, the color of ripe acorns.

She said simply, "No one in my mother's wood knew if you were still alive. So I came here, to the kitchen, to ask. They knew. They always know."

He still stared at her, holding the tray between them. "You came here. I didn't think you would ever come back here."

"I'm used to this world," she said.

"Come in. Please. Stay and talk to me." He glanced into the darkness; the fire he coaxed from a candle sputtered blue and died. She looked at it as she entered; flame bloomed, under her eyes, in candle after candle, all around the room, until again they were circled in fire. Entranced, he turned slowly, feeling as if she had enclosed his heart within her magic.

"In the kitchen, there was always a fire awake, watching with me. I learned how it speaks before I remembered words." She sat down on the rumpled silk at the foot of the bed; still wordless, he stood watching the candlelight brush an opal's fire into her hair. Then he remembered the tray, and set it between them on the bed. She looked around the room curiously. "Things in this world don't change unless you change them."

"Do they in yours?"

"Colors change. Things appear, then become something else. You know. You were there."

"Not long enough. To know that, I mean."

She looked at him, her eyes as clear and golden as wine in a cup. "Long enough," she said, "to know other things."

He drew a deep breath. "Yes. It was not easy to return here. You helped, giving me a mystery."

Her brows crooked a little; he wondered if, in either world, she had learned what, in both worlds, she had been. "I gave you something?"

"Something to think about. The missing spellbook."

"Oh." She nodded, remembering. "The King was shouting at you. I never used it, so I brought it back."

"You never —"

"I couldn't remember how to read. The undercooks read it to each other like a cookbook. But it didn't work for them."

He stared at her. "Then how did you learn all that magic down there?"

She was silent; he saw a memory shiver through her.

"My father. I had visions of him, the Hunter with his burning horns and his dead eyes. He woke the magic in me, that I had learned so long before. I didn't remember him — I was so frightened of him — I only knew the kitchen."

Her voice shook; too many memories were crowding into her eyes. He reached out quickly, took her hand, held it against his lips, and then against his heart. "You saved my life. Even Atrix Wolfe said that. I wanted so much to see you again, to talk to you."

"I hoped you would talk to me," she said, and he saw the long shadow cast across twenty years, of loneliness in her eyes. "So many of the words I know belong in this world, not my mother's. So many things I know, she would not understand. But I thought you might. No one else knows both worlds."

"Yes." He held her hand more tightly, in both of his. "Yes. No one else but you. Though you know more kitchen words than I do."

"Pastry," she said, her face quieting again. "Scrub brush. Mince. Pluck. Spit-boy."

"What?"

"They turn the spits over the fires, and feed the fires, and sleep next to them. Their eyes become fire, and their hearts."

He gazed at her, entranced again. "There are so many things I don't know."

"How you found me in the kitchen," she said.

"How you found the spellbook in the keep."

"How you found your way into my mother's wood."

"How much you saw, in that cauldron of yours. And how you lived, through all the days and years down there. Will you tell me that?"

"And what happened that night, in the human world,

when the mage stole my father out of our world. Will you tell me that?"

"I will. Or he will. And why, after all that happened to you and to her, the Queen let you return here."

Her hand slid gently from his hold. "My mother did not want me to come," she said slowly. "But she did not stop me. She said that she heard your heart calling out to her sometimes and she began to understand how she gave you something to love, and then took it away again." He looked away from her then; his empty hands wandered over the tray, toyed with bread, broke it. He tried to speak; there seemed no words for what his heart had glimpsed, and no real world to say them in. "She said that if I could find a way to you, I could come." She paused, watching him. "Eyes speak," she said softly. "Hands, pulling swans apart, speak. In all those years I could not speak, I learned so many languages."

His eyes rose again, caught hers, wide, questioning. "How did you find your way here?"

"I needed to," she said simply. "Do you want me to come again?"

He opened his mouth to answer. Then he answered her without words.

She took the tray back down to the kitchen later, knowing that the tray-mistress would be counting scratches, and the plate-washers would still be at the sinks, and the head cook debating tomorrow's meals, and everyone picking at leftovers. She walked down the stairs and watched their faces turn toward her, grow wondering, mute, as if they were all under some enchantment and only she could break the spell.

She said, "Tell me all your names."